THE CRITICS PRAISE *Shoshone Mike*

"A terrific novel . . . The story is based on actual events, but its historical accuracy is less important than the fact that it feels true; no cardboard cut-out heroes and villains here."
— *The Seattle Times*

"Bergon tells the sad tale that lies just beneath our cherished dime-novel, Hollywood-polished American West. . . . *Shoshone Mike* eloquently excavates dark truths about America's past, truths even darker now because they are still with us." — *Voice Literary Supplement*

"A highly detailed and authentic report that captures not only a terrific story but also a period of time . . . an account of real importance" — *Milwaukee Journal*

"The point of this novel is the detailing and dignifying of so-called minor lives and heroism as they are spun around an event which is in so many ways emblematic of our public troubles with the disenfranchised today."
— *The New York Times Book Review*

"Bergon weaves back and forth in time, with much variation in point of view, to produce the antithesis of a blood-and-guts Western; he is as much concerned with perceptions as events." — *The Kirkus Reviews*

"A wonderfully written novel of great historical significance. Frank Bergon has captured a tragic moment in this nation's past with intelligence and power. *Shoshone Mike* will move you." — James Welch, author of *Fool's Crow*

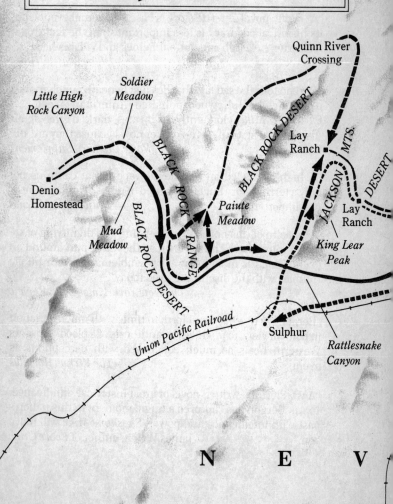

Pursuit of Shoshone Mike and His Family
by Donnelley's Posse and Sheriff Lamb

→ Shoshone Mike

- - → Donnelley's Posse

··· → Sheriff Lamb

Quinn River Crossing

Little High Rock Canyon

Soldier Meadow

BLACK ROCK

BLACK ROCK DESERT

Lay Ranch

JACKSON MTS.

DESERT

Denio Homestead

Paiute Meadow

Lay Ranch

BLACK ROCK DESERT

Mud Meadow

BLACK ROCK RANGE

King Lear Peak

Union Pacific Railroad

Sulphur

Rattlesnake Canyon

N   E   V

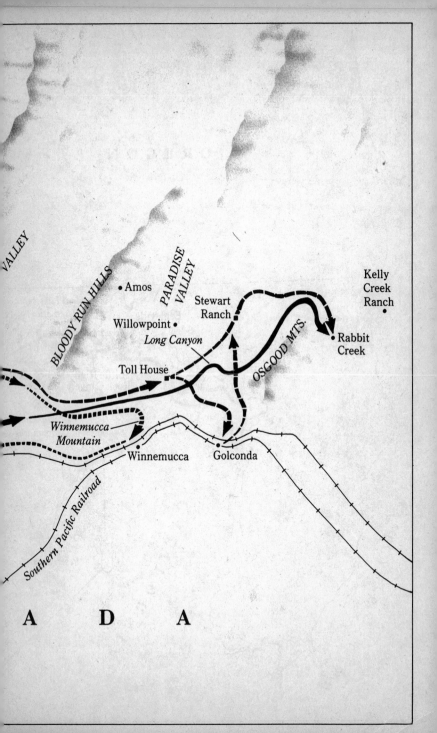

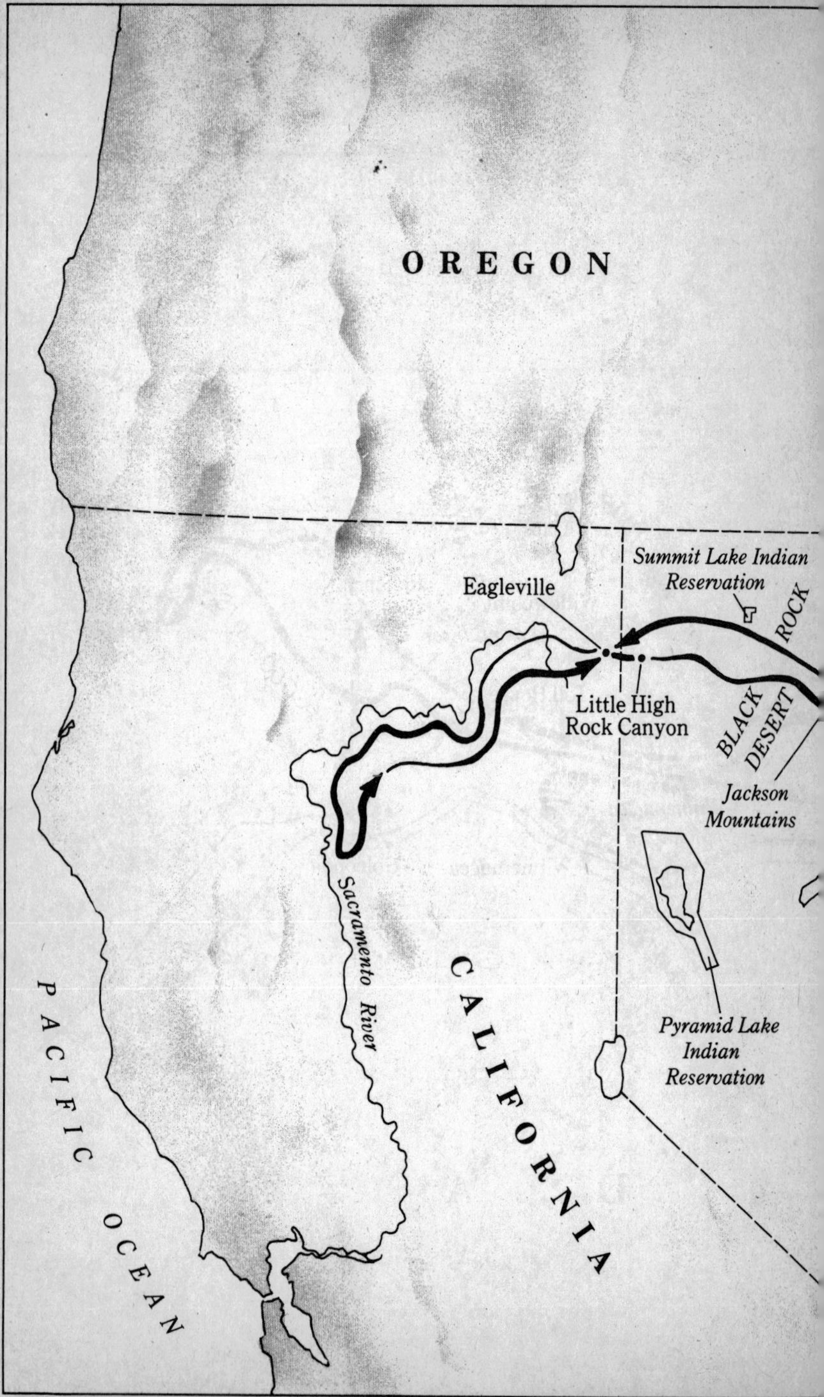
OREGON
Summit Lake Indian Reservation
Eagleville
ROCK
Little High Rock Canyon
BLACK
DESERT
Jackson Mountains
Sacramento River
CALIFORNIA
Pyramid Lake Indian Reservation
PACIFIC OCEAN

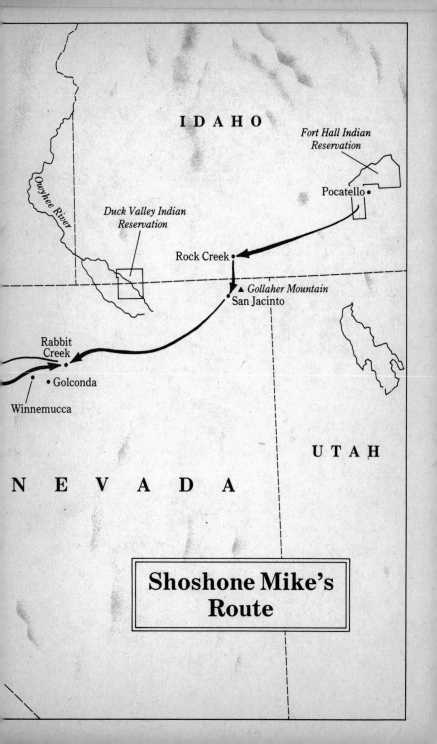

Shoshone Mike's Route

PENGUIN BOOKS

SHOSHONE MIKE

Frank Bergon was born in Ely, Nevada. His books include *Stephen Crane's Artistry*, *The Wilderness Reader*, and *Looking Far West: The Search for the American West in History, Myth, and Literature*. He teaches at Vassar College. *Shoshone Mike* is his first novel.

SHOSHONE MIKE

FRANK BERGON

PENGUIN BOOKS

PENGUIN BOOKS
Published by the Penguin Group
Viking Penguin, a division of Penguin Books USA Inc.
40 West 23rd Street, New York, New York 10010, U.S.A.
Penguin Books Ltd, 27 Wrights Lane,
London W8 5TZ, England
Penguin Books Australia Ltd, Ringwood,
Victoria, Australia
Penguin Books Canada Ltd, 2801 John Street,
Markham, Ontario, Canada L3R 1B4
Penguin Books (N.Z.) Ltd, 182–190 Wairau Road,
Auckland 10, New Zealand

Penguin Books Ltd, Registered Offices:
Harmondsworth, Middlesex, England

First published in the United States of America by Viking Penguin,
a division of Penguin Books USA Inc. 1987
Published in Penguin Books 1989

1 3 5 7 9 10 8 6 4 2

LIBRARY OF CONGRESS CATALOGING IN PUBLICATION DATA
Bergon, Frank.
Shoshone Mike / Frank Bergon.
p. cm.
ISBN 0 14 00.9876 3
1. Shoshonean Indians—Fiction. I. Title.
[PS3552.E71935S5 1989]
813′.54—dc19   89–3743

Printed in the United States of America
Set in Primer
Designed by Camilla Filancia

To Holly

I
SHERIFF LAMB
1911

1

Alone in his office, Lamb watched the clock. On his desk, among newspapers and cables, lay a telegram from his wife Nellie saying she would arrive in Winnemucca on the Southern Pacific that afternoon, if the weather held out. Next to the telegram was an older letter, dated January 20, 1911, telling him about the aviator show she'd seen with her sister in San Bruno. The sky on that day, Nellie wrote, looked like glass in a blue bottle. Airplanes flew in relay races, endurance tests, and altitude flights. Out of the sky rolled an aviator named Mad Jack, who made his airplane do spins, stall-outs, belly rolls, and a touch-and-go. A brass band played march music, and people ate popcorn and pink cotton candy. Streamers blew in the wind. Airplanes dropped bombs on an open field. Aviators engaged in rifle practice from airplanes swooping low to the ground. Nellie could smell the sea.

Her letter made Lamb think of the sea and the bay where he'd worked for the San Francisco Fire Department before moving to Nevada. He thought of the cable cars on Powell Street and the crowds on Market Street. On Sacramento Street, the waiters at Jack's Restaurant wore tuxedos and silk shirts. It was easy to imagine Nellie there, eating buttery sand-dabs that flaked apart on her tongue, to see her strong fingers cracking open scarlet crab claws, freeing moist white meat as broken shells clattered to her plate. One spring, after his first election as sheriff, he'd shared a rack of lamb with her at Jack's. The meat was pink and silky. That was years ago, before the fire. Nellie said that now there were almost no signs of the fire and earthquake left in the city. It was all so new, he wouldn't recognize the place. On the steps of St. James Cathedral, she had her picture taken with her sister. The sky behind them was white. They were surrounded by pigeons.

Almost a month had passed since Nellie had left Winnemucca to visit her sister. Lamb originally had planned to go with her to Reno. After the fall elections he'd looked forward to a diversion to share with her since she was bored with the usual Sunday drives, whist parties, theater parties, and occasional movies in Winnemucca. She wanted to go to San Francisco. He offered to send her. She wanted both of them to go to San Francisco. His job wouldn't let him, and with that admission, although they'd been married twelve years and had two children, he knew again with a dull ache that their time as lovers was over, and if they were to stay married, they had to learn, as a lot of people did, to become friends again.

No sooner had Nellie left alone on the Southern Pacific in mid-January than winter rains washed out the tracks west of town. Playas grew dark and slick as grease. Ducks swam in what was once open desert. A week later, Lamb, who slept uneasily after Nellie had left, awoke one night to see all the bunchgrass and sagebrush silver with beads of ice stretching out across the moonlit desert. The next day, three feet of snow fell on the northwest plains, and storms closed the passes and roads over the Sierra Nevada. Nellie, who was to return to Winnemucca at that time, remained with her sister in San Francisco. Then the storms stopped and the temperature dropped. The snow froze into high hard mounds against the sides of houses. Broken electric and telephone lines remained unrepaired. A letter from Nellie finally came through, and in response to her concern about Lamb and the boys, Lamb wrote back, "Your fingers get a little cold when you're out, but you get used to it. Mrs. Gonzales is doing a good job taking care of the boys."

It was thirteen below zero that night, and Lamb put the envelope on the table until mail service to California started up again. The temperature stayed below zero for days. Outside, while nailing makeshift shutters to the windows of the boys' room, Lamb dropped the hammer and it clanged against the frozen snow like iron.

In early February trains again moved sluggishly across the Nevada desert, and Lamb hoped that the line over Donner Pass would stay open long enough for Nellie to make her way home. Instead, a three-week-old letter arrived telling him about her ferry trip across the bay to Oakland and Berkeley. The cities were out of a fairy tale, Nellie wrote, full of flowers. She fed the ducks at Lake Merritt in Oakland and walked under the blue eucalyptus trees dripping with rain water and smelling like sweet gum. She heard a woman with honey-colored curls talk about ways to lead a good and successful life. The woman said that Biblical guides and principles could now be rendered with the same accuracy as those of any other science. Nellie said the woman's talk took the Bible out of the dark ages for her.

She visited the University of California and was told that the wild Indian who recently had come out of the northern California mountains was now living in the university's anthropology museum across the bay. The Indian's name was Ishi, but Nellie did not see him. She ate ice cream with blueberries at a sidewalk restaurant where a red, white, and blue umbrella protected the table. There seemed to be a lot of activity because President Taft was in town for a Republican fund-raising dinner. The Berkeley hills in the distance were green with new grass. Life in these cities could be orderly, Nellie said, and beautiful. She went to the public library. At night, back at her sister's apartment, she had been reading, by the fire, a book about Paris.

Lamb was looking out the window in the direction of the northwest desert. Somewhere out there the posse was starting to pursue the perpetrators of what the newspapers called the most brutal murder in the history of Nevada. On his desk was a telegram from Reno saying a band of Indians had done the killing. Lamb thought that some riffraff and thieves like Frank Tranmer were the more likely killers. In a desperate situation, a man like Frank Tranmer, who was now sitting in the county jail, seemed capable of such murders. But under the telegram on Lamb's desk, a newspaper reported that it was now definitely settled that the deaths and mutilations of the four stockmen were the work of a large band of Indians. The newspaper added that with these reports came the fear that unless the pursuing force was greatly augmented their members also might fall victims to massacre. Captain Donnelley of the Nevada State Police reported the Indian massacre to Governor Oddie, and the governor sent a telegram to Senator Nixon in Washington, D.C.

Lamb remained incredulous. This was 1911. There hadn't even been rumors of any roving bands of outlaw Indians in Nevada for decades. The Indians he knew in Nevada were the Paiutes and Shoshones who lived on reservations or colonies near towns and who sometimes worked on ranches. Like the harmless Shoshones recently reported killed up in Idaho, some of the itinerant Indians moved from ranch to ranch, where they set up their wickiups in designated places. They always looked the same, the women in their shapeless dresses and kerchiefs and shawls, the men in working clothes and broad-brimmed hats, moving like gypsies through the country, stopping to camp along river bottoms and streams. In the fall, ranches filled with Indians harvesting wild hay, gathering it into windrows with buck rakes, or stacking it with pitchforks. Some also helped out with the fall gathering of stock while the women worked as cleaning ladies or kitchen help. A year ago a half-breed Paiute named Queho went berserk near Las Vegas and killed some people. But he was alone and known to be hiding in the southern El Dorado canyons; the state police were still on his trail. Two years earlier, on the outskirts of San Bernardino, another loner, a Paiute farm-hand named Willie Boy, killed his girlfriend's father and then ran off across the Mojave desert with his girl. When a posse cornered him, Willie Boy killed his girlfriend and himself. These were isolated berserk individuals, under-standable incidents. The massacre in Little High Rock Can-yon seemed entirely different. Who were these Indians? people asked. Where did they come from? Lamb didn't know.

That morning Herb Baker, the editor of the *Humboldt Star,* had come to the courthouse office to ask Lamb what he was going to do about the Indians. Lamb puffed on his cigar and said nothing. His deputy, Charlie Muller, a slight, fastidious man, neatly dressed in a dark three-piece suit with gold watch chains crossing his vest, watched him. Next to his small dapper deputy, Lamb looked like a large, rumpled bear with his thick eyebrows and bushy mustache. A loosely knotted blue tie hung around his neck as he con-tinued to smoke his cigar.

Lamb's deputies and constables were accustomed to the waiting and silence until after perhaps five or ten min-utes, or maybe even twenty minutes, he would lean forward in his chair and slowly ask, stopping between each word, "What. Do. You. Think?" Any attempts to hurry him were futile. Over the course of a term as constable of Golconda and four consecutive two-year terms as Humboldt County sheriff, he'd moved only when he was good and ready to move. When a piece of information came in about a crime, a phone call from Battle Mountain or a new lead from Ely, Lamb would say, "We'll wait and see." The phrase became a joke to the officers. Someone might say, "Charlie, your house is on fire, and your mother is over at the church potluck having a heart attack. What do you want to do?" To which the proper response was, "We'll wait and see." The officers thought it would be appropriate for Lamb, if he ever decided to leave office and start a ranch, as his wife wanted him to do, to adopt for his brand a design composed of a scale weight and the letter C, so that the Weight & C Ranch could be clearly identified.

Lamb had learned the value of patience during his first summer as sheriff. Shortly after his election he'd infuriated several local citizens when he refused to form a posse after a robbery in Golconda, the small town just east of Winnemucca. Everyone knew that a man named Sevener and his gang had committed the robbery, but Lamb remained in his office and did nothing. For over two years the Sevener gang had operated along the stretch of Southern Pacific Railroad from Truckee in the west to Salt Lake City in the east. They were wanted for murder and robbery but they had managed to elude law officers from California to Utah. They always seemed to be aboard a train heading in the opposite direction from the police. It wasn't until Lamb got word that some goods from the robbery had turned up in Reno that he boarded a train alone out of Winnemucca. In Reno he learned of a robbery on an eastbound train. On his way back into central Nevada, he got word of a murder on a westbound train. Lamb stayed on the train heading east. He'd picked up a clue one evening that Sevener and some of his men hung out in Lovelock, a small town between Reno and Winnemucca. Getting off the eastbound train at midnight, he joined the town constable and walked down the street into Lovelock where he found Sevener himself and three of his ringleaders lounging in front of a saloon. Rumpled from the train ride, without a gun in sight—he always kept his pistol holster tucked into the waistband of his pants and covered with his coat—Lamb caused no suspicion until he was face to face with Sevener and took the four men into custody. All four were tried for murder and hanged.

No one could believe that Lamb had captured Sevener without firing a shot. By the end of the year he'd arrested seven more members of the gang, and all of them were either jailed or hanged. People afterward let Lamb do things pretty much the way he wished. He sometimes said if he had the Sevener incident to do over again he'd wait even longer before leaving his office. It might have saved him a trip to Reno. On some level, the state police, ready to meet force with force, seemed to operate on the assumption that something always had to be done right away because there was no way to understand what was going on until things were forcefully brought to a standstill. Sevener was always one step ahead of them in that game. Lamb's view was that once you knew what was going on you could do something about it.

Now he was starting his fifth consecutive term as sheriff after a landslide victory in the fall and he'd fired a gun at only one man during his ten years as a law officer. It had happened during his third term in office and the man was Jim Taylor, a buckaroo and miner who'd shot a rancher in the face with a pistol. The court issued a warrant for attempted murder. The stock association hired a gunman to track Taylor down and the state police sent out three men to arrest him. Lamb stayed in Winnemucca and did nothing until he got word that Taylor was back in the county planning to sell some horses at a desert camp northeast of town. That night Lamb left alone on horseback and rode to the Kelly Creek ranch in Clover Valley where he met three state policemen. Lamb said he wanted only one of them to go with him. For a day and night Lamb and a state policeman, Sergeant Donnelley, lay hidden in a small tent at the camp where Taylor was to sell his horses. Lamb could see the policeman's shadowy face covered with perspiration as flickering light danced over the canvas walls of the tent. When he heard the beat of horse hooves and Taylor's voice, Lamb turned to face the dark entrance of the tent with a sawed-off shotgun across his knees. He could hear the state policeman's nervous breathing behind him. Taylor sat at a rough-hewn table when Lamb stepped out of the tent behind him and told him to throw up his hands. Taylor jumped from the table, started to turn, his right hand level with his right hip pocket as the blast of number two shot shattered the back of his skull, just at the base of the brain.

It was an election year and several of Lamb's enemies used the shooting against him. They pointed out that if Lamb could arrest a murderer like Sevener without even drawing a gun, why couldn't he have done the same with Jim Taylor, who was just an ordinary miner and buckaroo. In November, Lamb lost the election in several mining camps and outlying districts, but his victory in Winnemucca was large enough to give him the county vote. It was as close as he ever came to losing an election.

Several times Lamb woke from a dream where he was waiting in a small tent with a sawed-off twelve-gauge shotgun. Sometimes in his dream the gun would go off, sometimes it wouldn't. He told only his wife Nellie about the dream.

"Next time let the state police do the shooting," Nellie said.

"I would if they knew when to shoot," Lamb said.

In his dream Lamb saw Taylor reach for the pistol they later found under his coat. Sometimes he dreamed that he himself was shot but he usually always woke before he died. In the moments after waking, the memory that he murdered a man seemed less real than a dream.

The police sergeant who'd waited with him in the tent was now the leader of the posse pursuing the murderers of the stockmen in Little High Rock Canyon. He was now Captain Donnelley of the Nevada State Police. He'd been promoted after the Taylor incident, then again after busting up the strike in the Ely copper mines. He was the one ready to bust up any future strikes in the southern mines of the state. Lamb did not like the way Donnelley worked. He was a company man who put order above everything else. He'd done nothing to bring in the men who'd shot and killed the striking miners. Lamb no longer felt that force was the way to handle such things. Despite what some people in Winnemucca thought, Lamb felt his job was to let different people live in different ways without killing each other.

Lamb looked up as Deputy Muller came into the office with more mail and telegrams. "We got some more news," he told Lamb. "It looks like that posse will be in our county by nightfall. I'll go try and find Skinny in case you want to hook up with them." He meant Skinny Pascal, the Paiute trailer Lamb always used when he needed a tracker in the desert.

"That might be a good idea," Lamb said. "We'll just wait and see."

Captain Donnelley and his posse would soon enter a cold, bleak country of box canyons and lava beds. As soon as they left Little High Rock Canyon, they would cross the border into Humboldt County, Lamb's territory. Ahead of them lay snow and the white alkali wastes of the Black Rock Desert. The Indians, whoever they were, had left Little High Rock Canyon almost a month earlier. They might be a hundred miles ahead of the posse. Their trail would be covered with drifting snow and difficult to follow. If they were still ahead of the posse, people said, they had to be coming toward Winnemucca. In that case Lamb knew the job ahead of him was to keep people alive, even if they happened to be Indians.

Lamb looked at the clock. He stood up and straightened the knot on his blue tie. He reached for his hat on the wall. It was time to go to the station to meet the train. Nellie was coming home.

2

When Jean Erramouspe left the National mining camp, he knew only that his father, his uncle, and two others were missing in the desert and he was wanted at home. Word had come from Sheriff Lamb and he felt he had no choice except to leave. In Winnemucca the sheriff told him that a search party had left Eagleville to look for the missing men but he had no other news.

"It's not the first time my father's been gone this long," Jean told Lamb.

"All I know is that people in Eagleville are concerned," Lamb told him, "and your family wants you home."

"I'll probably just get there and have to turn around again," Jean said.

"Let's hope so," Lamb said.

Jean boarded the Western Pacific for Gerlach. From there he could make his way to Eagleville. The train departed into the cold white expanse of the frozen desert. He cleared a square of moisture from the window and pressed his cheek against the wet glass, rocking and swaying with the slow-moving train. The interior of the Pullman was dim, suffused with the same cold winter light as the vague landscape passing outside. Rolling hills and vast flats of snow in the distance lingered and shifted with agonizing slowness.

The view continually repeated itself. It seemed a man could walk as fast as the train moved.

He now realized he was actually going home, and he saw himself suspended between Winnemucca and Eagleville like a man without a place in either town. He felt as if he were waking from a drunk, when in the gray light of morning actions that seemed acceptable while he was drunk suddenly made him ashamed of his life. He saw his time in Winnemucca as a waste, a senseless repetition in one town of what he'd tried to escape in another. There was nothing for him in Winnemucca, and at home there was even less. It seemed he'd done little with his life except make himself and others unhappy.

At the National mines he'd first worked as a roustabout above ground, doing odd jobs, surrounded by racket. The noise at the mines shocked him. After herding sheep and digging ditches, he found the incessant beating on his nerves hard to take. Metal gondolas loaded with rocks rolled on rails out of tunnels, feeding ore into the jaw crushers of stamp mills. Steam hissed from hoists, spraying the air with rainbow tints. The ground trembled, making his legs shake, followed by dull, muffled thuds of dynamite exploding deep in shafts. Later he joined the gopher gang as a mucker, shoveling out debris after a blast so miners could lay track deeper into the tunnel and drill holes for another round of blasting. It was the hardest job at the mines. The first time he entered the mines after the explosions of dynamite, the air was so bad he thought he was going to pass out. "You just have to eat it," an older man named Porky told Jean. Porky had been in the mines in Peru and Colombia and the Yukon. He'd been in South Africa. He'd been in Tonopah during the bloom of the boom, as it was called, when milk sold for eight cents a gallon but water was so scarce it cost fifteen dollars a barrel. Porky said the sight of a green blade of grass could drive a man to his knees in Tonopah.

Porky was the dirtiest man Jean had ever seen. He seemed never to change his clothes, and his neck was the color of dry cracking mud. He taught Jean to cut off the back pockets of his pants and the front pockets of his shirt—worthless he said, except for losing things out of— and to wear khaki pants instead of the Levis which had left Jean's legs stained blue at the end of his first day in the dank tunnel. Porky was working at National to earn enough to help grubstake him in his search for a lost mine near Jarbridge. He had a map.

When he was younger, Porky had been a jacker, and claimed he could single-jack a foot hole into the hardest rock in fifteen minutes. Now, like Jean, he was a mucker. Together they would enter a tunnel while dust and smoke still billowed around them after a blast. Jean grew accustomed to the odors, oily smells of powder gas and damp earth, the stench—the men claimed—of the wet bowels of the devil. Once, their carbide lamps went out, but thinking they'd hit only a temporary pocket of nitroglycerine gas, they decided to eat it. Soon they knew they had no air. Jean began running the hundred feet toward the mouth of the tunnel and shouting in the hope that someone might hear. When he came to, outside the tunnel, he and Porky had shit their pants. The same thing had happened to both Stall brothers, who owned the mines, when a round of blasts between shifts at three in the afternoon had caused the tunnel they were inspecting to cave in. Jean had helped to dig the men out. It was raining, and he began to wonder what he was doing in the mines. There was only one other Basque at National, and at first Jean saw the two of them as free from work most Bascos were bound to. Later, it seemed to him to make little difference whether he wasted his life looking sheep in the face or breathing quartz dust and powder gas. Stupefied miners at the National camp plodding into the mess hall sounded little different from the herders plodding from their rooms to the tables at the Basque Hotel. He thought of that old herder, dying in the hotel, who'd spent his whole life raising other men's sheep. Jean had grown depressed at the prospect of raising sheep just so they could be killed to feed people who raised more sheep. He grew equally depressed to learn that gold and silver dug out of the ground at one end of the country were shipped to the other end to be stored in underground vaults. He saw himself as a ludicrous gopher. Soon he would be like Porky, dreaming of a lost mine and coughing up specks of blood from the quartz in his lungs.

All for what? Work for the sake of work was what these men believed in. At the end of a shift, they bragged about how hard they'd worked, and Jean, too, felt himself accepted into their company only after he heard one of them say, "That kid's a worker." Wages seemed to matter more in principle than in actuality. He once watched five men each bet a day's wages on the proclivities of a mosquito buzzing in one of the tent-covered bunkhouses. The men sat motionless until the mosquito landed on Jean and drew blood, causing the stakes to be divided between the two men who had bet Jean would be the one chosen for the mosquito's meal. Wages also went for booze and flings with the sporting girls in Golconda or Winnemucca. With the same tones as when talking of feats of strength, they boasted of a former miner who could lay nine silver dollars end to end on his dick. Jean knew that work alone was not enough to let him move in the company of men.

The first time he went with four miners to Golconda, he had begged Porky to come along, but the older miner lay back on his bunk and drawled, "Gawd, no, Jean, why don't you stay home and go to bed?" He felt he had to go. The five of them danced with girls who seemed only able to giggle. Before he knew exactly what was happening the four men disappeared down the hall and he was left with the least attractive girl of the bunch, a small, sad-eyed girl with a sharp nose and short hair who began to cough as soon as they went back to the rooms and continued coughing as she undressed until Jean, feeling sober and bored, told her to forget it. "Just another dumb black Basco," the girl said as he was leaving, "afraid to make it in the rooms." Jean had an impulse to sock her, but she began to cough and he left to wait for the other men outside. To be a Basque, he felt, was to get other men's rejects.

It was later in Winnemucca during the fall carnival, when he and some of the other miners were drunk at a dance, that Jean found himself face to face with one of the girls who was a candidate for Queen of the Eagles Fall Festival. He'd been watching her for two days. She had curly brown hair and bright blue eyes. When he asked her to dance, she said, "All right," and his stomach softly caved in. At the end of the dance, happy and less nervous, he told the girl he would like to see her again. He'd pressed against her while dancing and she hadn't resisted. He wondered if she would like to go with him to Dreamland, the roller-skating rink in the mercantile warehouse on Bridge Street. He had no idea where else he might take her for a date, although he'd never been on roller skates in his life. "I can't," she said, and as a way of explanation, she looked down at the floor, and Jean knew he was expected to know his place. Bold from alcohol he urged her to defy whoever or whatever kept her from saying yes, until her childlike gaze hardened and her eyes grew dull as she snapped, "No, leave me alone. I don't want to see *you*."

That same night, among a group of miners who moved together from club to club, Jean was the one who somehow left the Silver Dollar Club with the singer. The miners had grown drunker in the early morning hours and the short-skirted singer with the deep whispering voice seemed a vision to all of them. Jean could not believe what was happening to him through his drunkenness when he realized it was this singer of sweet promises, Cherry or Cynthia, whatever her name was, who stood with him on a porch. He remembered kissing her and the surprise of her tongue exploring his mouth like the inside of an ice cream cone. In a room he felt her tugging at his belt and his pants sliding down his legs. There was the warm shock of Cynthia washing him and the further surprise of the wet cloth running between his legs as her mouth and tongue sucked and licked him while she rubbed the wet cloth over his stomach. Jean had fallen backward on the bed and her face came up close to his and spoke to him, saying, "No more samples, cowboy. You'll ride when you pay."

"Huh?" Jean said.

It was later at the mines when the other men's amused reminiscence forced moments of the night to fall into place. He recalled the roll of bills he'd held in his hand while the men had talked to Cynthia in the club. Was it worth it? they asked Jean later. Was it worth all that scratch? He couldn't remember. He only remembered paying the girl Cynthia and leaving the hotel in a rage, looking for another drink, and later waking behind the Masonic Hall, dirty and thirsty, his head feeling as though a steel bar had pierced his skull. He wandered into an all-night saloon for a drink but had no money. The first signs of white appeared on the horizon and he wandered into another saloon and ordered a drink but he still had no money. He awoke later with the sun hot against his neck, stiff, lying on the dirt, still enraged, tasting the bile gathered after his night's drinking.

Afterward, he never went to town. He stayed at the camp and during his off-shifts he lay on his bunk and slept or read magazines. When a law prohibiting gambling threatened to go into effect, the men seemed to gamble with greater fervor than before, seeking out clandestine clubs, but Jean would not go with them.

"Leave him alone," Porky told the men. "God knows it's enough to be a mucker."

"It's that hundred-dollar gold piece," they said. "She did it to him. Made him a monk in one night."

Jean learned not to listen. As he lay on his bunk, his future seemed to extend no further than the next day or night when he would again be mucking in the mines. With his future gone, faces from his past became vivid and accusatory. It was his mother, he then realized, her stories about Reno, her own unspoken regret as she sang with talent but no audience, her insistence that Jean learn English—all leading Jean to think that anywhere else was better than where he was. Once, as a child, while walking with his parents through Eagleville, he'd asked his father when they were going to California. His father said, "We are in California." It made no sense to Jean, who looked out across the white flats of Surprise Valley to the bruised Nevada hills where his father ran sheep. Although he later learned that they already lived just inside the border of California, the land to him was still Nevada. California really lay on the other side of the pine-and-oak-covered Warner Range to the west, mountains where he ran sheep in the summer but never crossed until he was sixteen and made his first trip to Alturas. He was nineteen before he visited Reno and saw the hotel where his mother had been a cleaning lady when she met his father.

The girl he began seeing in Eagleville made him forget about leaving. He was working with his father, learning all he'd need to know about sheep, and thinking that soon he'd marry Jennie and be building his own life. The need to be married, or at least to promise marriage, became more urgent as his desire for the girl grew with lengthening kisses and a fuller sense of the woman pressing against him beneath layers of clothes. One night she let his hand slide into her blouse and the nakedness of her breast and the stiffness of her nipple so surprised him with the intimacy of her offering that when he saw the traces of fright in her eyes, he withdrew his hand. That night, at her door, she kissed him again and her face was so relaxed and happy that he had no doubt about what he wanted to do with his life. She said, "Thank you for making it nice, Jean."

He returned from the sheep camp two months later to learn that Jennie had been seen at a church potluck with a storeowner's son who'd returned from a year of college in San Francisco.

"What is this?" Jean asked her that night outside her house.

"I want you to understand, Jean," she told him. "I love you as a friend, Jean. To tell you that hurts me as much as you. But I can't love you any other way. I'm going to marry Marty."

Jean grabbed her shoulders. She screamed and when he let her go she slapped him and he slapped her. Her uncle opened the screen door, and before Jean turned away, he saw her holding her cheek. "You filthy pig." Her voice clawed at his back. Then for all to hear, she screamed, "He hit me."

The next day his father, not saying what he'd heard or who had told him, simply said, "What are you, an animal?" That was all he said, and Jennie's brothers, cousins, aunts, uncles, and parents treated him with the same silence. Soon Jean's shame grew less than his anger. Sensing the injustice of the situation, he packed his duffel. "Go to the sheep camp," his father told him. "Be a man and forget it. If you run away, it will only be worse."

"Worse for who?" Jean said. "Worse for you because I won't be following your shitty life?"

He was sorry now for all he'd said and done. But what could he do? He remembered the looks of his mother, his sisters, and his younger brother when he left. He knew they wanted him to stay. Even his father, from the distance, making no gesture to stop him, looked at him with concern.

Now his father was missing on the desert. Jean really wasn't worried. Three weeks on the desert, even in the worst of storms, was not an unusual length of time for him to be gone. Just last winter, after a blizzard, his father had left alone to check sheep near the Smoke Creek Desert and was gone for almost three weeks. His father had found over a thousand sheep dead in the snow and spent the rest of the time with a herder driving scattered bands into protected hollows where they could forage for bunch grass. This time his father hadn't left alone. Jean's uncle, John Laxague,

was with him, and one of their camptenders, Bertrand Indiano, as well as a cattleman, Harry Cambron. All of them
knew how to take care of themselves on the desert.

Jean took off his shoes and tried to warm his feet, covered with wool socks, on the hissing steam pipes running
along the side of the car. People had taped newspapers over
the cold rattling windows and curled under blankets in the
faded velvet seats. There seemed to be little difference between the inside of the car and the cold outside when the
train pulled into Gerlach.

The next morning, he rode north into the gray light on a
horse left at the livery by his uncle's camptender from Soldier Meadow. Nothing but snow spread before him, and
clumps of sagebrush stretched to the horizon, spotting the
whiteness like a mange. His nose and ears grew numb,
then his fingers in his leather gloves. He felt a new sadness
that he could only identify in some way with the sound of
the horse's hooves breaking through frozen snow. Everything else was quiet.

He'd first made this trip between Gerlach and Eagleville when he was seven, with his father, in warmer
weather. It was the same year, during lambing season, that
his father had taught him what to do when it was necessary
to help a ewe deliver a lamb. That spring, in imitation of his
father, Jean had greased his hands and arms with olive oil
and carefully entered the wet softness of the ewe, held
firmly by his father, and felt inside the womb for the lamb.
It was harder than he imagined to find the legs and head
and to turn the lamb, but his father kept talking to him
calmly, telling him he could do it. Jean knew that if he
failed, his father might have to cut the ewe's throat and slit
open her belly to free the lamb. Better one life than none.
Jean had the lamb's two front legs, and his father, still
speaking softly, told him to pull in rhythm with the contrac-
tions. Through a stinging blur of sweat and tears, Jean saw
the sudden opening of flesh and the appearance of the
lamb's pink face, sticky with slime, eyes shut. Jean's gid-

diness lasted only a moment, until he saw the ewe try to bolt away from the newborn lamb. His father held the ewe against his legs until the lamb nursed. Some ewes, he told Jean, did not want their lambs at first. Most did, but a few didn't, and sometimes it took a while before those mothers accepted their offspring.

That was the year Jean went with his father to the bands every day. Each day seemed to offer something that made Jean realize how strange the world was. There were rams that would not mount ewes but only tried to mount other rams, and there were ewes who could not be mounted because they were half-male themselves. Jean learned that sheep had faces as distinctive as human beings, and it no longer surprised him when a herder could distinguish individual sheep from among hundreds. His father taught him how to move bands without startling them, how to work the dogs, and how to look out for sick lambs. He heard the absolute silence that would pass over a band of bleating sheep when they were frightened. He learned how to castrate lambs, making a knife slit in the sack and protecting the lambs from infection by pulling the balls free with his teeth. Those were the early days when his mother sometimes went with them to cook, and he remembered his parents sitting together in the evenings, like sheep themselves, watching their own children play. He remembered his father nudging his mother and pointing to Jean's younger brother and sister playing in the grass with a sheep hook, and his father and mother seemed delighted, laughing together at their children.

Both his parents came from the mountain village of Banca in the Pyrenees. Sometimes when they were on the desert his father talked about the green, wet mountains, the whitewashed stone house with the red tiled roof where he was born. Heat from the cows and pigs living on the first floor rose up into the house to keep his family warm. When he came to America as a boy, Jean's father knew nothing about herding sheep, but his first boss assumed he did—

after all, he was a Basco—and he ended up on the range with a band of sheep and no dogs. He said nothing because he could speak no English. The first day was all right because it took a full day for the sheep to realize there were no dogs, no *txakurrak*, to keep them in line. Then they started wandering. "I didn't know what I was supposed to do," his father said. "I ran around like a crazy man but as soon as I got one bunch together, another bunch was already climbing over a hill. I knew other *artzainak* whistled at their sheep, so I tried whistling. I tried talking to them, the way you're supposed to do, but that didn't do any good. For two days I ran through sagebrush pleading with two thousand sheep to stay together, but the more I pleaded, the more they scattered. I was a young man, you see, and at night I just cried. Those sheep were nearly driving me out of my mind. For two more days I tried to manage them but then they were scattered all over the desert and I just told them good-bye and walked to town and jumped the train to Reno."

His father was the strongest man Jean knew. At picnics he would arm-wrestle with men, and once after some joking from the herders, he stripped to the waist to take on a new *vizcaíno* herder who was as big as his father but younger. Jean was frightened. His father's face grew twisted and red, squeezed in a headlock against the herder's body, until, grabbing the herder around the waist with one arm and through the crotch with the other, his father lifted the man up and fell over backward, hitting the ground with such force that the man's hold broke loose and his father got the herder's head squeezed between his knees in a grip that made the man quit. Once he saw his father lose an arm-wrestling match when the other man held the leg of the table with his free hand. When Jean protested in tears against the man's cheating, his father pulled him into his arms, saying, "It's all right, Jean. It's not important."

Like most sheepmen, his father hated and admired

coyotes. He told stories of their ability to elude herders' traps. He'd once found tracks where a wary coyote had trotted repeatedly around a trap and then pissed on it. A coyote seemed able to sense when a man was armed and would stay teasingly just out of rifle range, but when a man happened to be without a gun, a coyote might trot right through a camp. Once his father caught a coyote pup and kept it tied to a tree, or to the leg of his chair when he sat on the back porch in the evenings. It seemed to Jean that maybe his father thought if he treated the coyote like a dog, it would become a dog. He tied the pup to a long rope and began training it. One day when the pup was half-grown, his father untied it for the first time. The pup turned and snapped at his father's arm. When his father came out of the house with a rifle, the coyote was already nonchalantly trotting out of the yard in the direction of the desert. His father raised the rifle and the coyote looked back, still within rifle range, its eyes distant and wild. His father lowered the rifle without firing. The coyote continued to lope unhurriedly toward the desert.

Sometimes, on Sundays in the sheep camps, the herders would come together, and his father would give them haircuts. Jean remembered the feel of his father's big hand, able to cover his whole head with his palm, holding him steady as he clipped with sheep shears around his ears. The smell of his father close to him was the smell of sweat and sheep wool, wine and dirt and sage, all mixed up. His father could get mad, but when he was mad, he became silent. Tight cords stood out on his neck, and he walked around talking to himself. Whipping the kids was always his mother's job. She whipped Jean for fighting in school or picking on his younger brother or sisters, but only once, when he called her a name he had heard a herder use, she slapped him in the face so hard it went numb, and she started to cry, saying he couldn't love the Blessed Mother if he didn't love his own mother. It was about that same time, when he was five or six, before he'd learned how lambs were castrated and sheep slaughtered, that he saw his father and Uncle John Laxague appear from the desert one evening. Their faces, hands, shirts, and pants were black with blood. The air was full of the hot metallic smell of blood. That night, still feeling the fright of the afternoon when he thought the blood was his father's own, he heard his parents talking in the other room, and he began to cry. He prayed that his father would not have to die for a long time, and he asked God to let him be the one to die before his father.

Everything his father knew about sheep he'd learned after coming to America, and when he said that Jean knew more at eight than he knew at eighteen, Jean felt proud. He wanted to be like his father. He was put in charge of his first summer flock when he was twelve. That summer Jean lost over a hundred sheep, and he knew it was because he had become careless. During the afternoon in the mountains, while he was alone with the flock, the sheep suddenly stopped bleating and became as quiet as the desert. Jean ran to the weak side of the flock where he found a lead bellwether, its throat torn by a coyote. He began moving the sheep out of the mountain meadow through a pass where there was a ledge that dropped eighty feet down to a stream. He knew he was pushing the sheep too hard without the bellwether to lead them. Suddenly the sheep were falling, silent as they fell, making no sound at all until their bodies thudded against the rocks below. Dogs cut off the remaining sheep, and once Jean got the rest of the flock safely into a meadow, he climbed down the ledge to those sheep that were dying. He cried as he cut their throats, expecting his father to come and grow silent in rightful anger. Instead, his father comforted him. "This has happened to me, too," he told Jean. "We always have to be careful."

It was night when Jean arrived in Eagleville. The high outline of the Warner Range in the west was darker than the night sky. Jean knew something was wrong by the number of people and horses and wagons under the cedars on the road in front of St. Mary's Church. He rode toward the church and later he had no memory of dismounting or tying his horse. He only remembered his mother on the dark steps of the church, then his aunt, and then he was holding his sister, who was crying against his neck, holding him and saying, "Daddy's dead, Jean. He's dead."

3

Nellie Lamb's train arrived in Winnemucca shortly after the noon fire whistle. Graham Lamb was waiting for her at the side of the landing where he always waited when the trains arrived. Billows of steam hissed from the engine's underbelly as Nellie stepped down from the car onto the footstool, one hand in the porter's, her face pink in the cold and wrapped in fur. She spotted Lamb and grinned. She had the long, dark eyes and high cheekbones of her father, a rancher and indefatigable hunter, but she was looking more and more like her mother, a handsome, strong-willed woman with luxuriant hair and a determined jaw. Seen walking together down the street a year ago, Nellie and her mother were almost indistinguishable from a distance, except for Nellie's limp, the effect of childhood polio. She stepped forward to hug Lamb, plumes of fog rising in the space between their faces under her big hat.

Directly behind Nellie stepped the parish priest, Father Enright, in a long black coat, the white square of his collar peeking above the V of his black scarf. The tall, thin priest stepped from the footstool, planting both feet solidly on the ground, a black valise in his hand. He stood for a moment and squinted through wire-rimmed glasses toward the bare, gently pleated Sonoma Range in the distance. He seemed to have put on some weight, his face had color. His shoulders rose as he drew in the cold air in a deep breath. In his new long black coat, he looked happier, more dignified than when he had left Winnemucca after his accident. He'd been gone now for over a month, living in Sacramento, recuperating.

Lamb shook hands with Father Enright, told him welcome back, and took Nellie by the arm toward the car, a big Austin that belonged to the sheriff's office. The packed snow on Melarkey Street squeaked against their shoes.

"That Father Enright is a strange one," Nellie said. "It took him all the way from Reno to Lovelock to get up his nerve to move into the seat next to me."

"Did you notice his eyes don't focus?" Lamb asked.

"But he seems a lot better. We didn't have much success talking until we got on to the resurrection. It's about the only thing we could agree on."

"The resurrection?" Lamb said. "You've been away a long time, Nell."

"I learned a lot of things."

"As long as you didn't learn that you'd like me to be a chicken farmer in Petaluma."

"I've got all the information you need."

"If I was a chicken farmer in Petaluma I might wake up some night choking you and not know what I was doing."

"Then we could move to Santa Clara and grow peaches. I've got that information too."

Lamb looked at Nellie. She was looking back at him from the corners of her eyes. Although no movement showed on her lips, he had come to know from the slide and the surface glitter of her dark pupils, tucked into the corner folds of her eyes, seeming to elongate her already long eyes, she was ready to smile. He watched her as she passed through the picket gate and stepped onto the boarded walk that he'd scraped clear of ice that morning. Their white frame house was the last one on Melarkey Street, at the north end of town, just before the river. A low white picket fence, put up at Nellie's request, ran between the street and the small yard in front of the house, serving no purpose other than to decorate the front boundary of their property; there were no side extensions to the fence.

Lamb noticed something puzzlingly different in the way Nellie walked, a deliberate tentativeness in the motion of her hand as she pushed open the front door and stepped into the warm living room. She stood for a moment surveying the room from just inside the door and walked slowly but deliberately about the room, still in her hat and coat, moving past the hot stove, letting her fingers lightly trail along the backing of the couch as she walked behind it, touching the window curtains as she circled the room with a concentrated steadiness that seemed to make each part of the room, as she moved through it, her own.

Despite her concentration, her face seemed calmer, more relaxed than he remembered. She was heavier. A thickening of flesh under her chin and in the lines on her face had softened her determined jaw. Beneath the hem of her coat, folds of a sage-blue skirt moved against her ankles and betrayed glimpses of the dark lisle stockings that covered her legs. It was when she stopped in the middle of the room, crooking her elbows above her head to remove the long hat pins, that Lamb realized she'd been walking normally, her back erect, her limp almost gone.

Her hair fell free from beneath her hat and swung down longer than when she had left. She shook her hair and said, "It's going to be a day before I get the motion of that train out of my head."

Nellie was out of her coat and in the kitchen when feet pounded on the boards of the front porch. The two boys, out of school, came through the front door. They stood side by side and stared at their mother.

"Kent," Nellie said, "look at you."

The boy's head disappeared behind the puff sleeves of Nellie's dress as she wrapped her arms around him and pulled his face to her breast. "You've grown like a poplar. You're going to be as big as your dad."

The younger boy stood behind Kent and twisted his face up toward his father.

"Ray's grown too," Lamb said.

"He certainly has," Nellie said as she moved her hands over Kent's shoulders and down the sides of his arms. "Come here, both of you. I want you to see the presents I brought."

Nellie piled the wrapped presents on the oak table in the dining room and the boys tore into them. There were two Buster Brown suits and two Buster Brown hats for the boys. "I hope they're not already too small," Nellie said. The boys looked disappointed.

"When do we have to wear these, Mom?" Ray asked.

"Sundays," Nellie said. "We can get you shoes to go with them here at Hoffman's."

There was a silver Chinese ear spoon for Lamb and a gold pocket watch. On the cover of the watch his initials SGL were engraved in scrolling script and surrounded by flowers of pink gold and leaves of green gold. "It's a beauty, Nell," Lamb said.

There was a book for the boys from Aunt Bess, Nellie's sister.

"Now here are the big surprises," Nell said. "They're for everyone. Here, Kent, you open this one, and Ray, this one."

Kent pulled the paper from a shiny black Kodak camera. *You push the button and we do the rest,* the instructions read. "This is great, Mom," Kent said.

"This is great too," Ray said. "They're telescopes."

"No," Nellie said, "that's a stereopticon viewer. Look, there are the pictures in the box." Nellie fitted one of the cardboard slides into the viewer for Ray. "Is it in focus? Just move this part back and forth until it's in focus. Let Kent look."

"They look like they're real," Kent said.

"It's three-dimensional," Nellie said. "That's Fisherman's Wharf. See those fish? Those are salmon."

"They're sticking out of the picture," Kent said.

"Let me see," Ray said.

"Show Ray and then we can all look at the rest of them after dinner. You boys get into your room now and do your homework."

"We don't do our homework until later," Ray said.

"From now on you do it as soon as you get home."

"I'm already done," Kent said.

"Then you start reading Aunt Bess's book." Nellie thumbed through the pages. "Here. You practice this part and then I want to hear you read it after dinner. Now get going, and no more lip."

Nellie followed the boys to their room and Lamb leafed through the magazines and newspapers left on the table amid the torn wrapping and bows and ribbons. He opened a copy of *Cosmopolitan* magazine. Advertisements filled the back pages. Side by side with cigar ads was one for No-Tobac, a tablet to break the nicotine habit. Next to an advertisement for Pabst Blue Ribbon beer was a description of pills to be dropped into a man's coffee, promising to kill all desire for alcohol. On each page there seemed to be an advertisement for an automobile and another with a black-and-white sketch of a woman in a tight-waisted corset.

Lamb looked at the *Reno Gazette* under the magazines. On the front page, a block headline read: POSSE IN SILENT COUNTRY. The article said the posse of twenty-two men and two Indians had left Camp Denio and entered the biggest expanse of land in the United States not traversed or interlaced by a railroad. Under Captain Donnelley of the Nevada State Police, the posse was headed for Soldier Meadow, eight miles from Summit Lake. The article speculated that the renegades were not Nevada Indians, but a large warring band of Oregon Modocs. If they got into the badlands, the article said, there was little hope of catching them.

Another article on the front page of the *Gazette* announced that women suffragettes planned to storm the state assembly chambers Monday afternoon to press their bill.

"Here's something the *Humboldt Star* hasn't reported yet," Lamb told Nellie when she returned to the room. He pointed to the headline about the suffragettes.

"I bet it didn't report anything about Ann Martin either," Nellie said. "There's a Nevada woman doing something that all the other newspapers are talking about and the *Star* doesn't print a thing."

"We heard she cracked a bobby over the head and got herself arrested."

"But did Herb Baker print her own story? It was in the San Francisco papers, about everything she was doing in London. I don't think Herb knows where London is. Winnemucca is never going to wake up if the newspaper doesn't help it."

"I guess you did learn some things while you were away."

"One thing is that Nevada doesn't know the first thing about real progress," Nellie said.

"I guess I don't have to tell you about these Indians then."

"That's what I'm talking about," Nellie said. "I just couldn't believe it when I read about that deal, Graham. It was bad enough to read about the murders, but when it dawned on me that one of those men was Jean Erramouspe's father, I was just slayed. That poor, hard- luck kid. First he gets the hell kicked out of him by that son of a bitch Tranmer, and then his father gets murdered by a bunch of renegade savages. It's like the clock keeps getting turned backward in this goddamn state."

"It happened," Lamb said, "and now something has to be done about it."

"It happened because people let it happen," Nellie said. "It's people's attitudes that allow these things to happen. I feel sick for that poor boy."

"I expect he'll show up here any time," Lamb said. "I imagine the state police won't let him join the posse. At least I hope they won't. So I'm sure he'll head back here."

"He's got no business on a posse. I hope you make him sit tight when he gets here."

"That's what I'd like him to do."

"And you, too. Let the state police handle it."

"That'll have to depend on what develops. We don't know who they're after or where they are."

"What difference does it make? They're murderers."

"That's how the police probably think about it, but they don't know. There has to be a reason for what people do."

"Now you're sounding like that Father Enright. Hearing him makes you wonder what kind of education Catholics get these days. Like I told him, we're talking about savages. There's only one thing to do with them."

"Maybe," Lamb said, "we'll have to see."

"There aren't any maybes about it. This country never will be civilized as long as people let Indians wander wherever they want and kill whoever they want."

Lamb left Nellie and spent the rest of the afternoon in his office. He learned that the citizens of Eagleville had formed a committee and offered a reward of two thousand dollars for the capture of the murderers of the four stockmen. The Humphrey-Cambron Cattle Company added a thousand to the reward, and the state of California put up another thousand. Governor Oddie topped them all with a reward of five thousand dollars from the state of Nevada; his request for the reward now rested with the state assembly. There was nothing new about the whereabouts of the state police and the Surprise Valley boys. As the *Reno Gazette* had said, they were now in a silent country.

That night after dinner, when the boys were in bed, Lamb and Nellie sat by the stove in the dark living room.

"What depresses me most about those Indians killing Jean Erramouspe's father," Nellie said, "is that we could've been rid of this problem a long time ago."

"It's not like this thing happens every day," Lamb said.

"What matters is that it can happen. Bess couldn't believe we're still so backwards here."

"You better tell your sister to look in her own backyard. This thing happened right on the California border."

"But it didn't happen *in* California, and it couldn't have happened in Santa Clara or Petaluma or Oakland or anywhere else around there."

"How much did you say one of those orchards in Santa Clara cost?"

"I knew that's what you'd think I wanted," Nellie said, "to pack us all off to California. But that isn't what I want. I like it here. I just want us to catch up with the rest of the country, that's all, but I'd never want to live in California."

She told Lamb about her trip to the chicken ranch in Petaluma, where one man on just fifteen acres raised ten thousand white leghorns. He stuffed the chickens with linseed meal and cleared over ten thousand dollars a year. On another day she went with her sister Bess to the Santa Clara Valley where all the orchards were laid out in flat, square grids. Rain was irrelevant; everything was irrigated. Her sister Bess, Nellie said, dreamed of owning an orchard in the valley. At night Bess sat listening to music on her Edison record player and calculated how much more she and her husband Jim would need to buy an orchard. Of course Jim didn't know the first thing about farming, but Bess read pamphlets about it, and tried to sell Jim her idea while he sat falling asleep in his chair, worn out from work, knowing that at the end of the month they'd barely make ends meet and the prices in the valley would have gone up.

"I'd try to read," Nellie said, "but that damn record player kept going around and around until it was time to go to bed, and then the moans from the woman in the next apartment would start in. I wouldn't say there was a different man every night but it was damn close." The husband of the woman next door, Nellie said, worked a night shift as a linotypist at the paper, and it seemed as soon as he was gone, his wife—her nickname was Doll—was peeling off her clothes and bedding down with a lover. She was as sweet as pie and always finding ways to help out people in the apartment building, watching their kids in the afternoon or picking up something at the store, and at night she was still doing favors for whoever wanted them. Or maybe she felt at night it was her turn and they were doing favors for her. Bess told Nellie, "When Doll was young she was in a home for 'encourageable' girls." If her husband knew anything about these nightly escapades, he didn't let on. Whenever he heard her offering to do someone another favor, he'd say, "Doll, you're just too good-hearted." He must've thought those little black curls slicked down like a row of hooks across her forehead—"beau-catchers," Bess called them—and the tight-knitted jerseys she poured herself into when she went out in the afternoons were all for him.

Nellie told Lamb that one night they were having a card party in the apartment and one of the guests was a man from England, a widower, who was traveling after the death of his wife. He'd just come from seeing the Santa Clara Valley and Bess was excited. She talked as if she and Jim already had bought their orchard. For once, Jim got angry. "Bess, there's no satisfying you," he said. "As soon as we get an orchard, you'll want something else."

Everyone was embarrassed for a moment until the Englishman said, "That's what makes progress, men trying to satisfy women." He was a real gentleman, Nellie said. He wore lemon-colored gloves and had been in countries all over the world. He claimed American women were unique. What made them different from British women, he said, was their health, and especially their energy. Bess said, "A toast to American women." Everybody raised their glasses and said, "Hear, hear." Even Jim was smiling. At that moment, Doll's howls and moans came through the walls as though she were in the same room, and everyone laughed, even Jim.

Nellie loved California, she said, when she first got to her sister's. She loved San Francisco. She liked being able to walk down the street to buy Scotch scones and eat them hot with melted butter. She liked the sound of the Alcatraz foghorn at night in the city. She liked the variety of people she met, especially the women at the Christian Science service who had such a clear idea of the principles that guided their lives. But gradually everything palled. After the storms prevented her return to Winnemucca, the streets and crowds of the city began to tire her. She was eager to get back to where she was something other than a visitor.

"I just wanted to be home," she said, "with you and the boys. I missed the snow. I missed walking in it. I wanted to kill my own chickens again and to be somewhere where people know how to play cards. I always had to twist Bess's arm to get a game going."

She began to see how many people in the city were just spinning their wheels, always chasing after illusory things. Bess sat listening to her record player and thinking about the future, the Englishman about another place to visit, Doll about the next man. They all let themselves succumb to a rut. "It's the mind that matters," Nellie told Lamb, "what we can do right now to get out of the rut we're in. But nothing can change unless we change our way of thinking about things."

"How much did you say one of those orchards cost?" Lamb asked.

"You couldn't touch one for less than five hundred dollars an acre and you'd need twenty acres. That's why Bess is so ridiculous. For less money, Graham, we could have a spread here in Humboldt County and develop it the way we want."

"That idea suits me better than plucking chickens," Lamb said.

"At least if we had our own ranch we'd be making some changes and going somewhere."

"I don't know if owning a ranch would make things that

different. But I'm not intending to keep this job forever."

"You're going on ten years now," Nellie said, "and you know you can keep getting elected as long as you want. Maybe ten years is long enough. We have to think about these things, Graham, not just for our sake, but for the boys."

Lamb stoked the fire for the night while Nellie went into the bathroom. He heard the squeak of faucets and the sound of water running into the tub. He washed in the kitchen and returned to the living room to turn out the lights. The presents Nellie had brought home, the newspapers and magazines, formed a small pile on the side of the coffee table, diminished by the larger darkness of the room. They already seemed ordinary objects from another time.

He undressed in the dark bedroom and stood in his nightshirt looking out the window toward the outline of Winnemucca Mountain, etched against a white mass of stars. The sudden sense of a presence behind him caused him to turn. Expecting to see Nellie, he was surprised by the room's emptiness and its foreignness. It no longer seemed the room where he'd slept alone for a month while Nellie was away. This was her room. The picture of her mother, looking like Nellie when she was holding back a smile, faced Lamb from the dark mahogany dresser with ivory handles that Nellie's father had bought in San Francisco. Her aunt had bought the trunk in the corner, decorated with gold leaf and shipped around the Horn during the last century. Everything in the room was hers, seemingly studied and ordered. Even the coverlet on the bed, left tossed and rumpled for the past month, had been smoothed by Nellie's hand.

He looked at the night table and recalled the strangeness he'd felt one night the previous fall when he'd gone into their darkened bedroom and a letter had been sitting on the small table. The partially folded piece of writing paper had caught his attention like an unintended disturbance in the room's order and neatness. Nellie was always so careful, he couldn't help wondering whether she'd left the letter purposely for him to see. With one hand he'd raised the top fold of the paper and saw that it was a letter she'd written to her sister, a short note beginning "Dear Sister" and ending with the words "Your Loving Sister." The appearance of the phrase "my husband" had struck Lamb with something of the foreignness of the room itself, a reminder of his distant existence to other people, totally unconnected to his own sense of himself. "My husband, as you know, is difficult to understand in certain things. He continues to be little concerned about how things have changed since Ray was born. I regret that it looks as though we will not be coming to see you after all. I thought the aviator show would attract him, but it doesn't."

After reading the letter Lamb looked out the window at the sky over the distant mountain. It seemed remote. It was as if he'd just wakened in a stranger's house and nothing eased the unfamiliarity of the room and the country where he found himself.

He remembered reading the letter and seeing the word *him*. Remembering the word in the letter made the woman who wrote it seem as remote as the sky over Winnemucca Mountain. *Him*. He felt absolutely unconnected to the man who'd earlier eaten dinner at a candelit table, and he experienced a lonely sense he once had while looking at his own dead body in a dream.

Lamb climbed into bed and thought of the posse out on the cold desert. He heard Nellie, still in the bathroom, humming. It was after reading the letter that he'd decided to send her to San Francisco even though he couldn't go with her. He wondered what had really happened there. He lay between the sheets with his hands behind his head and wondered how a traveling Englishman with lemon-colored gloves had ended up in Bess's apartment. Despite Nellie's gifts and stories, he felt excluded. They were both trying to be friendly but he felt the strain. He wondered why she'd told him that story about the woman in the apartment next door. He'd never heard her talk so enthusiastically about anyone's sexual escapades as she did about the woman called Doll with her curls and tight-knitted jerseys. He wondered if the source of her new confidence and light walk might really be religion or another man. She moved with the assurance of a person harboring a proud secret.

He was drifting into sleep when he heard the scraping of clothes hangers and saw Nellie turn from the closet and walk white and naked toward the bed. The mattress tilted from the weight of her knee next to his head. Her hands gently pushed against his shoulders and he slid lower into the bed. He felt her moving into the space at the top of the bed. She was kneeling above him, her skin warm and damp from the bath. As she leaned forward, her face came toward him, upside down.

"Remember how we used to do this, Graham?"

He looked up into her face, close to his, and saw how the curve of her forehead, upside-down, seemed to look like the lower half of a face without a mouth, her hairline became chin whiskers, her nostrils jutted upward above her eyes.

It was a game they'd played during the first years of their marriage, when lying on the floor together they accidentally discovered the grotesque features their faces assumed when they swung their bodies in opposite directions and brought their faces close together, upside down. Nellie was usually on her back and Lamb bending over her. The first time it happened, Nellie cried out, "It's like seeing a freak-show monster."

Kneeling over Lamb, her skin scented with almond bath oil, Nellie grinned and a third eye on her forehead opened into threatening rows of teeth.

"I thought this used to scare you," Lamb whispered.

Nellie's giggle was girlish. "Who are you?" she said.

"Who are *you*?" Lamb said.

Her mouth came to him with a kiss and its softness surprised him. She shivered when his hand moved between her thighs and came away wet. Lamb gently pulled Nellie to his side but before he could roll over she moved on top of him and was sitting on his bare stomach. He was in her so quickly it came as another surprise. She was slowly lifting herself up and down, her hands planted firmly on his chest, arms extended, straddling him, pushing him down while her back arched away from him, her face staring at the dark wall in front of her. Lamb reached up and let the weight of her white breasts lightly rise and fall against the palms of his hands. It was as if her rocking motion was drawing him into her, tightening the line of pleasure that ran through him like a taut string stretched between his legs to the inner curve of his skull. Nellie moaned and it was as though the string snapped away from his skull and sliced past his heart and lungs and along his backbone through his stomach and between his legs into Nellie, leaving his thighs quivering against hers. Nellie did not stop. The flesh of her thighs and hips continued to lift and fall against him as she leaned forward and lay on him, locking her mouth to his.

When Lamb awoke in the middle of the night, Nellie's mouth was against his ear. Stretched out beside him, one leg flung inertly across his, she seemed in the deepest of sleeps. He looked up at the dark ceiling and listened to the long, slow breathing of her sleeping form. As if her flesh were gathering weight in the deadness of sleep, he grew aware of the spread and heaviness of her thigh on his leg. Her body felt as different in sleep as her words and movements seemed while she was awake. Now she might be dreaming. Was she dreaming of him? He would never know. He felt himself drifting toward his own dreams as he saw images of black and white horses, running, their manes lifting in the wind. Even as a boy, he had come to know the moment when his mind signaled that it was letting go, when the thoughts and concerns of the day succumbed, as if of their own wills, to images that somehow mattered more. He had the pleasurable sensation of knowing he was awake enough to know he was beginning to dream. After weeks alone in his bed, he was drifting into another kind of sleep. With the press of Nellie's leg against his own, he felt the difference.

4

Each day Father Enright scanned the papers for more news about the massacre and for information about the pursuit by the police. On days when the *Star* didn't come out, the Winnemucca pastor went out of his way to get hold of the Reno papers. He worried about his congregation and their reactions. He worried about the guidance he was obliged to bring to his people. It was his duty, he felt, to serve as a model, to view the meaning of events in the light of God's will. Each day he scanned the papers for glimpses of that meaning.

The whole thing sickened him. The thought of those innocent men murdered and mutilated on the desert filled him with revulsion and scorn. He despised what had happened as much as he despised the situation his feelings put him in. He couldn't see beyond his own revulsion. On Sunday mornings his pale, distracted eyes stared out at his congregation from behind wire-rimmed glasses, and his vestments drooped from his thin shoulders.

He'd had such a clear sense of his mission when he'd left Sacramento. On the train trip home, at Lovelock, he'd moved into the seat next to Mrs. Lamb, the sheriff's wife. He'd tried to tell her how we know that in everything God works for good. The words were ash in his mouth. Mrs.

Lamb's disgust touched him more. She didn't want her sons, she said, growing up in such a world. She knew Jean Erramouspe, the boy whose father had been mutilated. That boy could be her son. She wanted the world rid of that possibility. Such evil, she said, had no rightful existence.

He agreed with so much of what she said that his objection sounded feeble when he tried to tell her she could not ignore the abyss that existed between divine perfection and ourselves, but she would have nothing of such resignation. In Sacramento it had been easy for him to imagine returning to his people, like St. Paul to the Galatians, with a firm sense of his mission. In solitary thought the truths of Paul's letters could be so simple, so clear, but when sitting next to a strong-minded woman of flesh and blood like Nellie Lamb, his mind went numb. He was not like St. Paul, he didn't share a love for argument that thrived on paradox and sarcasm. His only hope was that he might retain a remnant of what he had come to know while away.

He'd never found it that easy in Winnemucca. Even the two years he'd spent at the Johannesburg mission had not prepared him for the difficulties he was to have when he first arrived in Winnemucca. He remembered his time among the South African kaffirs with fondness.

The problem was that when he'd returned from Africa he thought his missionary work was done. He looked forward to settling into a Sacramento parish, near the cathedral, or returning to the diocesan seminary as a teacher. He had no interest in ecclesiastical tinsel. As a young seminarian he'd shown a knack for scriptural and historical studies, and he craved time for further study and the chance to finish some writings he'd begun on the *devotio moderna* and other contemplative movements in the Church. He wanted to put some theological iron into those pietistic quests for a more personal inward life.

Instead, he found himself on monotonous train rides between Winnemucca and Lovelock, where he said mass on alternate Sundays, or on dusty roads to mining camps like Seven Troughs and National, where he said mass when he could. He found little energy to read anything other than his breviary. His parish was bigger than the whole state of Massachusetts, but his parishioners, unlike the kaffirs who burned with the zeal of converts, asked only to be baptized, married, confessed, counseled, communed, and buried. He felt he was not cut out for that kind of work. He lacked the personal touch. He felt more comfortable giving theological sermons than counseling individuals. He was bored stiff.

"The Nevada mission is not an easy one, Jerome," the bishop had told him before he left California. "I've seen good men climb into the bottle. The loneliness is great."

Father Enright was not worried about the bottle. His temper was a greater cross to him than intemperance, but others, like the widowed parishioner who voluntarily cooked and cleaned for him, awaited his downfall. One afternoon, hovering over him like an expectant buzzard, Mrs. Garrity said, "You don't want that wine again with dinner, do you now, Father? You had that wine at noon, remember?" She brushed dandruff from the shoulders of his cassock, shiny with wear.

"I don't think a little wine will hurt, Clare. I feel a bit of a cold coming."

Mrs. Garrity sighed and looked through the lace-curtained kitchen window at the September sun beating against the corrugated tin shed next to the rectory. "It's the nights that are cold, Clare," he said.

When dinner came there was no wine. He looked down at the translucent skin of boiled cabbage flecked with tiny spots of pepper. He had to get up from the table to pour his own wine. "For Christsake, Clare," he yelled from the kitchen, "have a heart."

"Father," Mrs. Garrity said, "I am not deaf."

That was the night he first met the Basque boy Jean Erramouspe. It was the first Friday of the month, the day devoted to the Sacred Heart when he regularly took Communion to an old herder in the Basque Hotel. After dinner he entered the darkened church and in the red glow of the sacristy candle he took a consecrated host from the tabernacle and placed it in the gold pyx hanging on the chain around his neck. He paused to ask forgiveness for losing his temper with Mrs. Garrity, then tucked the closed locket into the front of his cassock, draped his neck with a small purple stole, and crossed town to the Basque Hotel. He passed through the bar where a few men at the table glanced up from their cards and their months-old Basque newspapers. He saw no change of expression as they looked to see if he might be a woolgrower in search of a winter herder. The hotel was already filling up with herders, laid off for the winter, who had no prospect of work until shearing and lambing in the spring. Through a doorway he saw one shift of men at the long tables where steaming crocks of soup, bowls of stew, and loaves of sheepherder bread passed from hand to hand.

He climbed worn stairs to where an old man was waiting in bed. "You comen," the old man said. The old man chewed the Communion wafer and stared vacantly into the room as he did every Sunday and first Friday of the month when the priest visited him.

A rosary with hand-carved wooden beads dangled from the iron bedpost by the man's head. The beads had come with him, Father Enright knew, from the Pyrenees, and they'd gone with the old man all over the country, from the south where he once wintered sheep around Tonopah, to Eagleville where he sheared sheep for Peter Erramouspe, and to the Sierra Nevada where he grazed summer bands. When the old man was once found in the mountains after a freak blizzard he had the rosary beads wrapped in one hand. Blinded and lost in the storm, the old man had groped toward his sheep and clung to the wool of a ewe for a day and a night. When the camptender found the band after the storm, he also found the old man, still alive, holding on to the ewe and his rosary. They said the old man was crazy ever since that time.

Near the doorway of the room a boy in his late teens sat quietly in a straight-back chair with a magazine on his lap. Surprisingly fair-skinned, the boy had dark hair, thin Basque lips, and the quizzical eyes that Father Enright had grown accustomed to seeing around Winnemucca. There were three other beds in the room, and in one of them two men were asleep.

The boy came to the side of the bed and the old man's eyes gathered sharpness as they focused on the boy. "Piel," he said. *"Zer gertatzen da?"*

"He knows you?" the priest said.

"No, he takes me for my father," the boy said. "He doesn't know anyone any more."

"It's a shame," the priest said, "they say he was a fine shepherd."

"He's lucky," the boy said. "His time with those animals is over."

"Are you a shepherd?"

"I hope I never have to look at another sheep's face again," the boy said. "Look at him. He left everything behind. Now he has nothing."

"Zer gertatzen da?" the old man said again.

"My father heard how you came to see the old man," the boy told the priest. "It's a good thing. He has no one else."

"It's nothing," the priest said. "You're related to Paul Itzaina?"

The boy nodded. "He's my uncle," he said. "I'm Jean Erramouspe. How did you know?"

"Paul's in the parish. He told me you were here. I understand the sheriff got you a job working on the sewer line."

"Christ," Jean said, "this place is worse than Eagleville. You can't turn around without someone telling the sheriff."

"It's better that way," Father Enright said. "Your uncle didn't want the sheriff to think you were just another tramp herder."

"I find that hard to swallow."

"That's what he told me. There are laws now, and the sheriff patrols the range to tax the tramp herds. People are getting impatient with the foreign sheep bands, and it makes it hard for all the Basques who come here."

"I'm as American as anyone else."

"The sheriff knows that, but he has a job to do."

"Who is this Sheriff Lamb anyway?"

"Let me put it this way," Father Enright said. "If you steal something, you better get out of town real quick because all the other thieves are Lamb's informants. That's how he works."

"I'm not planning to stay around any longer than I have to," Jean Erramouspe said.

"I hope I'll see you at mass," the priest said, "while you're in town."

Jean didn't answer, and the old man began to cough. "I'm sorry his mind has left him," Father Enright said.

"He's no crazier than he ever was," Jean Erramouspe said. "He's just afraid, and you can't use a herder who's afraid of the mountains. They should send him back to the Pyrenees and at least let him die at home."

Father Enright turned to go. By the doorway he glanced down at the scuffed *Police Gazette* lying on the chair. On its cover was a faded picture of a handsome, barelegged woman in a frilly black corset mounted on a high-wheeled bicycle. Her head was tipped back. Pointed toward her pouting mouth someone had penciled a long loop to look like a spurting penis. Father Enright quickly left the room.

He didn't see Jean again until after the boy got his nose broken while working on the sewer line. Then he didn't see him at all until after he'd gone to work in the mines at National. He seemed so bitter for such a young boy. Now these murders would break his life to pieces. It seemed to Father Enright as if the earth had opened and let loose some unspeakable darkness. He couldn't imagine any of the Indians around Winnemucca doing such a thing. He knew that

Sheriff Lamb was not convinced that Indians were the murderers either. He knew that they got drunk and fought but he hadn't seen any viciousness himself.

"There are Indians and there are Indians," Nellie Lamb had said on the train from Lovelock. "Graham wouldn't go tracking anyone in the desert without Skinny Pascal, but Skinny's different. Most of these Indians who wander off the reservations, they're nothing like us. Their minds are still in the dark ages."

Father Enright couldn't believe what she said was true. It sounded too much like what he'd heard again and again about the kaffirs when he was in South Africa. But what evidence did he have to the contrary? There was no question that unlike so many other tribes, uplifted and civilized after four hundred years of Christian effort, the desert Indians in Nevada still remained primitive and poor. Diggers—that's what people called them. It was no wonder that Nellie Lamb found it so hard to recognize them as children of God. Children of God! The phrase struck Father Enright as blasphemous when connected to the massacre in Little High Rock Canyon. The hideous, senseless murders made satanic mockery of God's goodness. He thought of young Jean Erramouspe and the boy's loss outraged him.

On the train from Sacramento he hadn't expected to encounter such disgust in himself and vengefulness in his people when he returned to his parish. He'd firmly resolved to finish raising funds for the new Golconda church. Plans for the church were well on their way, and his people seemed to like the idea of a church rising out of the sagebrush of Golconda, a spectacular church with a Gothic design, rose window, and mission ceiling that would rival anything on the Pacific coast. Building such a church was a form of practical prayer, Father Enright told his parishioners, for a practical people. The idea for the church and the effort to raise funds had helped improve Father Enright's relationship with his parishioners before his accident. The project gave them all something to do together.

Now the whole thing seemed derailed. The senseless murders and his people's response marred his sense of purpose. In the winter light, the words of the gospels went frail. He didn't know what to say.

Father Enright prayed: "O Lord, I ask for your help. I ask you to help young Jean Erramouspe and his family in their sorrow. I ask that you help me in my weakness and confusion. Help us through this darkness, and grant me grace to guide your people. Grant me strength to accept your will. Grant me light to speak."

5

Lamb walked quickly past mud-plastered huts patched together with willow branches and bits of burlap and tar-paper. Ahead of him, near the center of the camp, there was a musical squawling and in the firelight he could see shadowy figures. Yipping and howling dogs followed him to a shack built of sturdy railroad ties. Discarded oil cans, pounded flat, formed the roof of the shack. On the ground, among tin cans and bottles, Johnny Bliss lay holding a rag over his head. Next to him was a shotgun with the barrel broken away from the stock.

"Annie Jim," Lamb called out. "Annie Jim, it's Sheriff Lamb."

Through the doorway in the dull light he saw moving forms. The pale glow of the doorway was blocked as a seemingly neckless old woman emerged, her head covered with a wool kerchief and shoulders wrapped in a green-and-blue plaid blanket. Below a straight fringe of long black bangs, her eyes were lost in wrinkles.

"*Tsssaaa! tsssaaa!*" She hissed at the barking dogs behind Lamb. "*Tsssaaa!*" She slapped her leg and sent the dogs scattering.

Behind the old woman, three others emerged from the hut, similarly bundled in kerchiefs and blankets, skirts billowing around their legs like shapeless tents. Chattering, they fluttered behind Annie Jim like a covey of quail. They sat down with their backs against the railroad-tie shack and their legs extended straight in front of them. All three wore men's shoes. Annie Jim waved her hand for them to hush and squatted in front of them. The man on the ground groaned and Annie Jim, pointing at the man and looking up at Lamb, began to laugh. She described to Lamb how the trouble began when Skinny Pascal, who'd been drinking all afternoon, hit Johnny Bliss over the head with a shotgun. Skinny hit Johnny Bliss so hard, Annie Jim explained, that as Lamb could see, the barrel of the shotgun broke away from the stock. Annie Jim paused in her narrative to raise her voice in laughter, and the women behind her, covering their mouths, laughed with her.

Afterward, Annie Jim continued, Skinny Pascal struck at Young Charlie with a long knife, but Young Charlie ran away. He was cut only on the arm. Skinny then whipped Butch Button and Butch Button's wife, and took off all his clothes, and was last seen howling and running in the direction of the water company's reservoir.

Lamb waited until Annie Jim and the women behind her stopped laughing and asked, "Where did Skinny get the whiskey?"

"Whiskey?"

"Yes, whiskey," Lamb said. "Who sold him the whiskey?"

"No whiskey," Annie Jim said. "Vanilla exwack."

"Vanilla extract?"

"Maybe gin too," Annie Jim said.

"Where did he get it?"

Annie Jim shrugged. Lamb knew that if Annie Jim either didn't know or wouldn't tell, no one else would. She was the only woman in the camp who would talk freely with him. There were several men who claimed to be friendly and often acted as informers, but none of them ever seemed to know as much as Annie Jim. One thing she claimed to know nothing about was the group of Indians who'd killed the stockmen in Little High Rock Canyon.

"Skinny Pascal pretty crazy," Annie Jim said. "Butch Button take away his girl."

Lamb asked about the fires in the center of the camp where the squawling sounds grew louder.

Annie Jim shook her head. "Indians just make music and be happy. Everyone in town happy and drunk on Saturday, why not Indians?"

Lamb left Annie Jim and approached the circle of men and women sitting around a fire where he discovered the source of the music. Sitting in a position of prominence was the man he knew as Indian Ike, dressed in a long winter coat and a new felt hat sitting squarely on top of his head. Lamb knew that under the coat Indian Ike probably wore, as always, a white shirt and pin-striped vest, with green garters on his shirtsleeves. The old man bent over a fiddle on his lap and passionately drew back and forth the bow that was making the fiddle squawk and squeal in loud, eerie strains. The Indian closed his eyes and swayed from side to side as he worked the bow, a look of distant, rapt affection on his face.

On the outskirts of the camp, Lamb joined Deputy Muller and together they walked to the water company reservoir. Charlie Muller carried a torch fashioned from a rag soaked in kerosene and Lamb sent him circling the reservoir, muddy and splotched with patches of melting snow. From the north end of the reservoir, Lamb followed the movements of the orange flame as Muller circled the south end and began moving back toward Lamb, the black smoke of the oil fire growing visible at the flickering tips of the flame. As Muller came up the west side of the reservoir, drawing closer, a dark naked form rose from the weeds and scurried toward a clump of sagebrush twenty yards from the water. Lamb moved toward the brush, knowing that the man hiding there would be following the movements of the torch, ready to spring and run if the torch came too near his hiding place. Normally, Skinny Pascal was one of the most poised, dignified men he knew, but when he was drinking, he was something else.

As he approached the sagebrush, Lamb saw the man's glistening back. Muller came closer, moving noisily through the weeds and low brush, but Lamb, walking quickly, tried to make no sound. The man in hiding suddenly turned and looked over his shoulder at Lamb. Making no effort to escape, the man squatted motionless and naked in the brush as Lamb approached.

"Stay still, Skinny," Lamb called out. "Stay right where you are."

He moved quickly toward the man, who continued to stare at Lamb, his handsome face remaining impassive as it brightened under the light of the approaching torch. Only the man's nostrils flared and his ribs rose and fell like the panting sides of a rabbit hiding in the grass as Lamb bent over and clamped handcuffs to his wrists.

"Okay, Skinny," Lamb said. "Let's go."

It was after midnight when Lamb returned to the streets and walked downtown to get something to eat. The new electric lights stretched down both sides of Bridge Street, each bulb burning in a nimbus of late night mist. As he entered the Elite Café, a young woman in a scanty pink dress and a fur stole sat at the brightly lit counter drinking coffee and smoking a cigarette. Her hair was wrapped around her head in a turban of braids. The Chinese owner leaned over the counter talking to the woman. No one else was in the café. Under the lights the woman's streaked and caked face seemed more brightly decorated than her dress. Lamb ate a bowl of pork chow mein while the young woman complained to him about the bad effects of the new antigambling law. Her name was Cynthia. Once a dance-hall girl in Tonopah, she now was an occasional singer in a club where her husband dealt faro. She spoke, as she sang, in a pleasant throaty voice, and her trademark had become colorful, above-the-knee skirts that swished against her girlish thighs. She'd been married twice. She was nineteen.

"I know what you mean," Lamb was saying. "I don't like the new law either."

Cynthia was swinging her bare leg like a schoolgirl, tapping her toe against the wooden backing beneath the counter.

"The law is going to hurt more people than it helps," she was telling Lamb. "The trouble is that the legislators are just ignoring human nature. If my old man goes out of work, then I'm going to be going into work I don't want to be going into. But we'll need the jack."

"That would be too bad," Lamb said.

Back on the streets, he walked toward the railroad tracks in uppertown, passing clubs that were quiet except for the clicking of chips and the ticking whirr of roulette wheels. The only people on the streets were those moving out of one bar or club into another. Occasional couples came from a club and disappeared into the dark toward a hotel or a girl's crib. Everything was normal for a Saturday night. A girl in the red-light line had had to have her stomach pumped after drinking chloral hydrate, but Skinny Pascal remained the only person jailed.

Lamb moved down a side street and looked into the Silver Dollar. Through the lights and smoke he saw about a dozen men standing at the crap tables or sitting at round tables covered with faded green baize. Near the mahogany bar, a man played the piano while one of the short-skirted bar girls sang a slow, mournful tune whose lyrics Lamb couldn't make out except for the refrain when the girl lifted her chin and her voice to wail, "Hello, Central, give me heaven, mama's there." The girl seemed to be imitating the style Cynthia had brought to Winnemucca, but Lamb saw the girl straining for effects that Cynthia produced effortlessly. The difference was that Cynthia always seemed to believe in the emotions of popular songs. If she didn't, she kept the tunes and made up lyrics she could believe in.

It was almost three in the morning when Lamb was walking back through lowertown toward the tracks along the river. He liked walking through the town during the late hours of the night. Like the Indian colony, the night world of Winnemucca policed itself for the most part, and he only had to let it be known that he was around, on the edges of town, if he were needed. Bouncers and bartenders were quick to diagnose potential disruption on their own. The night world operated by its own rules and customs that those who lived only in daylight knew little about, and Lamb saw it as part of his job to keep order without infringing on one world with the prejudices of the other.

Cynthia's threat to go on the turf if her husband lost his job as a faro dealer was something that would be logically accepted by other married couples who worked in the night world, but rejected by the people who lived in lowertown's nicer stucco and shiplap houses and who ran the nine-to-five businesses in Winnemucca. To Lamb the situation was similar to his interference in the Indian camp. Skinny Pascal would probably get thirty days for his drunken behavior, but for all Lamb knew, according to Paiute custom, Skinny may have had every right in the world to bash Butch Button over the head for taking his girl. Or maybe the booze gave him the spur to do what he had absolutely no right to do, or maybe he was just drunk and raising hell. Lamb simply didn't know. The other Indians calling for him to interfere meant nothing, for they had learned to use laws of the whites to suit their own immediate needs, even when custom was violated. But perhaps Skinny Pascal really deserved praise rather than censure, just as—according to the code of the streets—Cynthia was blameless for her tricks when her husband was out of work, as long as she collected for her fucking.

Lamb passed a strip of doorways, each separated by only a narrow, oblong curtain-covered window, that formed the cribs of the prostitutes whose names were registered in six-inch letters in each doorway—Lily, Pearl, Sadie, all the typical names, whether in Winnemucca or Tonopah. Across the street in the doorway of an unmarked rooming house, under a porch light, Lamb saw a man and a woman. He recalled seeing Jean Erramouspe and Cynthia there, in the doorway, the previous fall during the Eagles Carnival. The young singer had just come to Winnemucca and hadn't yet married the faro dealer. Lamb didn't recognize her at first. He saw only a girl in a short-skirted pink dress, her mouth locked to a man bent over and obscuring her face. With the porch light falling against the man's cheek Lamb could see the movements of what looked like the girl's tongue working inside the man's mouth. Together they turned, the woman's turban of braids became visible, and side by side, the girl and Jean approached the hotel door. Cynthia wasn't married, neither was Jean. Nobody was breaking any law.

When he reached his courthouse office, Lamb shuffled through the papers and telegrams scattered over his desk. He expected Jean to be showing up any day wanting to join the hunt for his father's murderers. The latest word he'd gotten on the police posse was that they'd reached Quinn River and had split into groups. Several men in the posse had given up the search and returned to Surprise Valley. Lamb knew that the buckaroos who'd worked with the murdered cattleman would probably stay on the trail until the Indians were caught. Some would see themselves as simply doing their job, others would be looking forward to the reward, but those who were out only for the money probably wouldn't stick with it. The men who wanted retribution would be there in the end. That's why Lamb wanted to be certain that he was also there when the posse caught up with the murderers.

He'd known men like those in the posse ever since he was a kid in California working as a buckaroo for Miller and Lux. He'd tried other jobs, but after working for the San Francisco Fire Department—when he got sick and doctors couldn't figure out what was wrong—he went back to Miller and Lux and joined a trail drive to Nevada. He got along with buckaroos as well as he did with horses and for thirteen years he'd worked as cowboss of the Golconda Cattle Company in the high Nevada desert. He knew he might still be buckarooing if he hadn't met Nellie. His brother Kize still worked as a buckaroo, but as people said, Kize didn't have a pot to piss in. Buckarooing was no way to get ahead. It was Nellie who urged him to run for constable after he'd bought the butcher shop and they settled in Golconda. He already had something of a reputation as a peacemaker, the one who'd settled disputes among buckaroos at cow camps and town dances. Two years later, people urged him to run for county sheriff. Kent had been born and Nellie was pregnant with Ray at the time. She was ready to get out of the little town of Golconda and move into Winnemucca. Now she wanted to move out of Winnemucca to a ranch. He did too, but he didn't see it as a practical move for a few more years. They just didn't have the money, and he'd end up buckarooing for someone else to make ends meet.

Lamb now was convinced that the murderers were Indians. He'd gotten the reports about the discovery of the Indian camp and the corpses. Only Indians in a hurry to get away would've abandoned so many things in their camp, and no white man, not even a stock thief, would've thought to strip the dead men of their clothes or cut off a man's mustache. He just wished he knew where the Indians had come from and why they were so desperate.

The police posse was now in Humboldt County. Some reports said the Indian trail was clearly headed toward Winnemucca. Lamb knew it wouldn't be long before someone spotted them, and then he'd be ready to ride. He'd take Skinny Pascal with him. It wouldn't be the first time he'd let Skinny out of jail to go on a manhunt. Between Captain Donnelley and Skinny Pascal, he'd rather be with Skinny. His only hope was that they would meet the Indians before Donnelley did. If he could just find out *who* the hell the Indians were, he'd have a chance of figuring out *where* they were.

II
SHOSHONE MIKE
1910

6

There was a man named Jim Daggett or Daggart—no one seemed to know for sure—who left his farm and lived for almost twenty years in the far northeast corner of Nevada. Winters he moved with his large family across the Idaho border and camped in the willows along Rock Creek. There he became known as Indian Mike. He was a short, stocky man with sturdy shoulders and legs, a wide mouth and nose, and watchful eyes. He had thick gray hair, turning white, and was said to look well over sixty.

Most of the other Shoshone people who once lived in that country were now on the reservations, either to the west at Duck Valley or to the northeast at Fort Hall. Only a few continued to live around Rock Creek. One old woman called Indian Mary stuck close to the Rock Creek station and traded her buckskin work with travelers. Others like Indian Johnny and Jim Lewis—nicknamed Rock Creek Jim—built cabins and fenced pasture in the foothills. Rock Creek Jim lived in his small shack with his daughter Maggie. Indian Johnny lived alone. When not caring for their own cows, their chickens and gardens, they sometimes went to work fixing fence, haying, or grubbing sagebrush when someone needed land cleared. They were people who did not go to the reservations. Or if taken, they did not stay.

They lived as best they could in the borderlands between Duck Valley and Fort Hall.

Careless with names except for their use in distinguishing one Indian from another, some white ranchers around Rock Creek might have begun calling Jim Daggett by the nickname Mike to avoid confusing him with the other Jim. Mike had a reputation for turning out well-made ropes, bridle reins, quirts, hackamores, and sometimes he'd get some horse mane and make mecates or hair ropes and hair cinches. He had no trouble selling this equipment to ranch hands, and his wife, Nive, sold them custom-made gloves. She measured a man's hands by tying a series of knots in a long string of rawhide. Beginning with the man's thumb, the spaces between the knots indicated the lengths of the man's fingers. All the measurements of both hands were on one string, a maze of knots, but the gloves always seemed to fit.

At the cattle company store at San Jacinto, Mike bought on credit or traded for things like sugar, coffee, salt, tobacco, and ammunition. After a summer drought and a hard winter he might show up at the store looking a little gaunt and buy a tin of ham, a couple cans of evaporated milk, a can of peaches in syrup. No matter how hard the year, the little kids who rode in the back of Mike's wagon stayed plump. If someone went near while Mike was in the store, the kids scrambled to hide under canvas or hides, their round cheeks and dark eyes all in a row as they peered over the edge of the wagon. Heavy and round in a shapeless calico dress, their mother quietly sat in front of the wagon while Mike was in the store.

Once some buckaroos came across Mike on horseback during a lean year. They asked Mike why his feet were in such bad shape, and Mike said he was too poor that year and hadn't caught any moccasins. They remembered him wearing high-top buckskin boots, but that year Mike and his boys sat on their horses, their clothes and feet in tatters. "Too poor," Mike supposedly said. "No catch moccasins."

The way he said it interested the buckaroos, almost as though the reason he had caught no deer was because he was poor, not the other way around.

Or perhaps the buckaroos misremembered the whole thing. Others said Mike always wore government-issue shoes, or castoff rancher's shoes.

Mike came to know some families who moved into the country with the Sparks outfits and the Vineyard Company before it sold its stock and holdings to the Utah Construction Company. He began to trade with some of the company employees at their own ranches and homesteads rather than ride to the store. San Jacinto wasn't big, but it was getting bigger. One day shortly after the Weighalls moved into the area, Sam Weighall returned home to find his wife white a dishtowel. She said she had no idea Sam was bringing her into a country where Indians would show up on her doorstep. A dark heavy-featured man in old rancher's clothes and a broad-brimmed hat was watching closely as Sarah Weighall continued to pile the round wooden kitchen table with coffee, beans, spices, salt, sugar. "If this is what he wants," Sarah explained to her husband, "this is what he's going to get. I'd give him the ranch too, if that's what he wanted. Just to get him out of here." The old Indian continued to look at the Weighalls through what Sam saw as hard, black, intelligent eyes, the sharpest dark eyes he'd ever seen. Then the old man grinned, his eyes glinted, and he asked if Sam wanted anything in return. A few weeks later Mike came out of the hills carrying a deer in the back of his wagon for the Weighalls.

The two families came to consider themselves friends. When Mike came by the ranch, usually bringing rabbits or sagehens as gifts, Mrs. Weighall took lard buckets of sandwiches and cookies out to Mike's wife and the kids in the wagon. The first time Sarah took out sandwiches and cake, Mike's wife put the bucket on the floor of the wagon.

"That's for the kids," Sarah said and pointed into the bucket.

Nive shook her head and made it clear she was going to wait for Mike and the two grown sons who were with Sam.

"No, it isn't for the men," Sarah told her, "it's for the children."

Nive wouldn't budge.

One day Sarah saw Mike's horses floundering as they tried to pull the wagon through slick alkaline mud toward the house. Sam's irrigation water had gotten away from him and flooded the roadway. Mike and one of his grown sons sat in the front of the wagon while Nive and two of her daughters tried to push it through the mud.

Sam blew his top. He told Mike and his boy to get down out of the wagon and help those women push that wagon. Mike looked dumbfounded. He refused to get out of the wagon. Sam insisted. Eventually Mike and his son climbed down, but they refused to help the women push the wagon. Mike looked at Sam as though he were the biggest saphead in the country.

The last time the Weighalls saw Mike there were thirteen people in his family, but they were fondest of Hattie, the four-year-old girl Mike had named after the Weighalls' own daughter.

Those who knew Mike simply as another old, harmless Indian in a rickety wagon didn't know he carried with him so many strange relics from the past. In the back of his wagon he carried finely made arrows with painted shafts, spears decorated with feathers. Like his grandfather, Pandre, and his father, Cootickah, he owned drums marked with white circles and symbols from dreams. Tucked under blankets in the back of his wagon he also carried a feathered bonnet with tasseled horns of the kind that mounted Shoshone wore in the past. Crowned with over thirty eagle feathers and trailing a dozen more feathers on a bright strip of red flannel, the horned headdress was the mark of a warrior.

Shoshone Mike

Over thirty years had passed since federal troops retaliated against the last young Shoshone daredevils from Fort Hall trying to emulate the earlier raiding parties of their fathers and grandfathers. It had been over forty years since discouraged and hungry bands of Northern Shoshone buffalo hunters and their Paiute-speaking brothers and sisters, the Bannock, first agreed to relinquish their homelands. They could no longer live as they once did. "I do not know where to go," their spokesman, Tagee, had told the federal agents, "nor what to do."

Mike's people—the Hukandeka, the seed eaters or dirt eaters—were among the last Shoshone to go on reserved lands. They had been the first to strike back after the whites came into their country and now they were the last to leave. They tried to maintain themselves by foraging and hunting in the country between the Snake River and the Great Salt Lake. From these "poor people," as they sometimes called themselves, mounted bands emerged and roamed over range overlapping with the Shoshone-Bannock to the north and the Wyoming Shoshone to the east. It was from the Eastern Shoshone that they had adopted some of the ways of the people who lived on the plains.

Mike's father told him that before he was born his great-grandfather Old Tobacco Root had never seen a white man. In those days buffalo lived along the Snake River and the Shoshone people were satisfied with what they had. They watched the whites pass through the country, but there was no trouble until they began to stop in places along the Snake River. The whites were sad people, Mike's father said, apparently homeless, always wandering from place to place. The Hukandeka still stayed friends with them until they learned that many whites did not respect their word or themselves. They made promises to the Shoshone but never kept them. They tore up the ground looking for gold. They destroyed the grass, burned the trees, and drove away the animals and fish. They seemed to care about nothing.

When Mike was a boy he was afraid whenever he saw

white people. They had strange bearded faces like dogs. They seemed more concerned about cows than people. Once after whites arrested four Shoshone men because some cows were missing, they shot the Indians when the cows weren't returned. They said the Indians had stolen their cows but soldiers later found that they'd simply wandered away. They were wild, unpredictable people.

Once when Mike was a little boy his family was camped with about thirty other people in a canyon near the Goose Creek Mountains. It was fall and many men were away hunting. Early one morning the women were lighting the fires for breakfast when soldiers began shooting at them from the canyon walls. Women and children fell over each other in blood. Mike ran into the rocks and hid as soldiers came and captured four women and set fire to the wickiups in the camp. After they were gone Mike ran through the smoke and found his old grandmother and his baby sister among the dead. For days he cried with his family for all the people who were killed. His father hacked his hair short and cried with the others.

When the white soldiers later came to Mike's people and offered them a treaty to settle on reserved lands, they refused to go. The soldiers retaliated. Near Bear River where many Shoshone families camped for the winter, soldiers attacked and slaughtered hundreds of men, women, and children. Mike joined other young men to retaliate for the attack. Soon they saw that there was no way they could continue fighting against the whites. Their people were starving and they could not find enough game to live. Many Northern Shoshone and Bannock had already given up trying to live as they had and had moved to the reservation at Fort Hall.

When government officials first tried to sign a treaty with Mike's father and other Hukandeka, they could find no chief. They finally signed a treaty with nine men who seemed distinguished among the nomadic bands. Later when officials complained to Mike, who then had his own family, about continuing raids by Shoshone boys, Mike said he couldn't control the bad thoughts of young men who were determined to avenge the deaths of relatives. He was not the chief of the people. When the government officials tried to tell him that the man they called Pocatello had ordered him to go to the reservation, Mike said, "Pocatello is not my chief. I have no chief." Mike knew that the man the whites had named Pocatello would not even admit to being the chief of the band he traveled with. He was their businessman, he said, their spokesman, and he gave the agents the names of three other men who also sometimes acted as leaders.

"You people all the time are trying to make things different from the way they are," Mike told a government agent. "You make up names like Po-ca-tel-lo and Sho-sho-ne and then you think they're real. All the time you make up Indian words and tell us they're our words. We're not children. We have our own words that tell us how things have always been. Our parents and grandparents and great-grandparents have told us how things were long time before you came here."

Even after Pocatello and his people moved to Fort Hall, Mike still refused to go to the reservation. "I don't want to go to a place I don't like," he said. "Fort Hall is too cold."

He knew what had happened to the Northern Shoshone and Bannock at Fort Hall after they'd made a treaty with the whites. When they had first agreed to go to the reservation, their terms were precise. They wanted the reserved lands to be theirs forever. They wanted protection and rations promised them. They wanted to be free to hunt in the fall. In the summer they wanted to return to Camas Prairie where the flowering camas, seen from the surrounding hills, turned the meadows into a vision as blue and wide as the sky. The whites agreed to all these things. They promised the Indians the camas meadows and encouraged them to continue their fall hunts so that they might provide for themselves. But when the Fort Hall Indians returned to

Camas Prairie to gather bulbs, they found the meadows overtaken as food for droves of settlers' hogs. When the Indians at the reservation lined up for rations they were told that none had arrived and they would have to hunt for themselves. The fall hunts continued to Wyoming and Montana, but each year riders to the high country returned with fewer and fewer hides, less and less dried meat. Then they were told they could no longer hunt in the Wind River country. The government would not compensate for the lost game. Winter camps on the reservation grew shabby. The Shoshone were told they would have to grow their own food. Special farm wagons would be given to those who got haircuts.

The Fort Hall Indians cultivated 250 acres of wheat. The crop looked fine until the summer when the grasshoppers came and ate the wheat. Then the Indians ate the grasshoppers. For the next few weeks Fort Hall Indians continued to feed on grasshoppers that in turn continued to feed on the wheat. The government presented seventeen head of cattle to 1,500 Indians then at Fort Hall and ordered that the cattle be distributed only to the most deserving Indians. To the surprise of the agents, the cows did not go into the cooking pots, but in three years the seventeen head of cattle grew into a herd of fifty.

As difficult as it was to survive on reserved lands, it grew even more difficult for Mike and those who stayed away. Forgotten by the government, they began to starve in the borderlands where three states shaded into each other. Complaints came to the government about Indians loitering around towns and railroad terminals. They were seen attending baseball games. A few sawed wood for townspeople, then used the money to buy whiskey. Some hung around the local fruit stands. Others scavenged in alleys for swill. Some did nothing all day except swap horses and gamble. Several stood outside in the snow and begged for the offal from the slaughterhouses.

When Mike and his family finally moved to Fort Hall,

they settled with other Hukandeka south of the Portneuf River and along Bannock Creek. Mike said he could no longer protect his family as he once had except with other Hukandeka on the reservation. They all became known as Bannock Creek Shoshone, although no Bannock lived among them. There Mike and Nive and their young children lived about twenty-five miles south of the agency headquarters. On the reservation, Mike was enrolled as Jim Daggart or Jim Daggett or sometimes even Jim Taggart. To himself and his friends, he was still Tosaponaga, meaning Split White, or Ondongarte, meaning Sitting Light.

The government officials promised Mike and the other Shoshone that the reserved land along Bannock Creek would be theirs forever. The United States would never let them go hungry as long as they worked their land. Mike and his family planted oats and alfalfa and wheat and potatoes and cabbage. They were promised new canals and an irrigation system for their crops but the promises were not kept. Word of Wovoka's ghost dance reached Fort Hall, and Mike watched some of the Shoshone gather and dance all night in expectation of the disappearance of the white people and the return of their ancestors and the animals. Nothing happened. Growing disorder spread through the land as the Shoshone continued to give up their old ways. Mike saw what was happening to his people. They'd stopped hunting as they once had and the animals disappeared. They ate food with too much salt in it and they had sore eyes. They no longer washed their hair and skin so often in sweat baths and they caught colds in the winters. They no longer danced as often as they once did and there were fewer sego and camas bulbs to harvest. When they gathered together into large bands like the people on the plains, they could no longer sustain themselves as they did when they broke apart and scattered like their ancestors through the mountains and canyons.

Each year, as he tried to farm, Mike watched more and more ranchers and settlers move onto Indian lands. The

Western Pacific and the Utah and Northern railroad companies gained rights of way through the reserved lands. Pocatello station became their junction, in the middle of the reservation.

Mike watched as tons and tons of freight passed through the junction each day on its way to Montana and Oregon. People complained of the smell of Indians riding in open cars and they were forbidden to ride on any trains, even freights. An agreement went to the United States Congress to cede the southern portion of the reservation for settlement. Allotments of farmland would be made to heads of Indian families in the remaining portions of the reservation. The reservation had already been cut in half, and it would soon be cut in half again. Congress granted the sale to the Union Pacific of an additional two thousand acres at Pocatello junction to be laid off into lots and opened up to white settlement. The Indians were told that sales from the land would go toward an irrigation system, but the money never arrived and no system was built. A saloon, a shooting gallery, and other buildings began to arise and Pocatello became a boom town with over a thousand buildings. As hundreds of white people moved onto the reservation, Indians squeezed into less and less land. "Why do you want to crowd Indians all the time?" Mike asked the agent. "Don't whites have any homes of their own?"

Settlers spread over the land like grease stains as surveys, appraisals, and auctions of lands continued around Pocatello. Congress ratified a measure that ceded almost three thousand acres of reservation land near Bannock Creek. Mike watched in anger as his farm was taken from him.

That winter he cried when he saw his wife and children, shivering in the snow, wrapped in worn horse blankets they'd been given at the reservation. When they lined up for winter rations they were told there was no bacon, no meat. They received some coffee, some potatoes, and moldy flour. Mike and his sons left the reservation to hunt for food.

Other Indians begged in town from door to door and women sold themselves to miners in exchange for food. Mike told his family they'd leave the reservation for good as soon as the snows stopped and they'd never return no matter what the whites promised. "Too many of us are dying here," he said. "Too many are already dead."

After Mike left his winter camp at Rock Creek he made Nevada his home for the rest of the year. For almost nine months his range was around Gollaher Mountain, not far from the headquarters of the John Sparks cattle outfits. There Mike and his family hunted, fished, and sporadically worked in hayfields. Buckaroos who visited Mike's camps said there were from a dozen to fifteen people in his family, but besides Mike, his wife, and the four oldest boys, they couldn't keep track of who was who. One daughter named Wenegaw apparently left to marry a Fort Hall man. A man who seemed to be the husband of one of Mike's daughters was with the group one summer and gone the next.

Old Mike, as he sometimes came to be called in Nevada, spoke English a little bit. The buckaroos said that his son Jim, in his mid-thirties, spoke good English, when you could get him to talk. Jim also rode with a fancy rig, silver-mounted spurs and bit. He was shorter and stockier than his younger brothers, built more like Mike. He wore his hair cut short and straight in front but braided down the back. Slightly bowlegged, round-faced, and light-complected, Jim wore high-heeled boots. Like his father he was a good hand at all kinds of hair work and rawhide work.

The other older son, Jack—or Sagebrush, as he was sometimes called—was different, the buckaroos said. He didn't go around white folks very much.

All of Mike's boys were good horsemen, but the two the buckaroos knew best were two teenagers they called Jake and Charlie. Tall and slim, both boys were over six feet, dark, with large mouths and wide flat noses. Dressed in overalls and boots, they rode across rocky ground after stray steers with an abandon that earned them the nicknames Eat-'em-up Jake and Catch-'em Charlie. They were good ropers and seemed to have a knack for running horses. They kept their own large strings of mustangs in their camp. The only question to the buckaroos was whether Mike's sons would show up after payday. In the fall, when the work was busiest, they were off hunting with their father and brothers.

Mike spent a lot of time hunting, especially for deer, before the rutting season turned the meat rank. Before the cattle companies came into the country, antelope ran between Goose Creek and Rock Creek. Whitetail deer roamed along the streams of the lowlands and in the foothills. Blacktail deer grazed in the mountains both to the west and east of Mike's camps near San Jacinto. A few elk, mountain sheep, and mountain goats once could be found in those mountains, but most of them were gone from the country south of the Snake River within a few years after the arrival of the cattle outfits.

Mike had taught his sons how to make arrows as they'd been made in the past. He heated serviceberry branches in the fire and used a vice grip to straighten them into arrow shafts. Two horns were tied together with rawhide at their tips to form a hinge. He then pried the horns open and clamped them onto the heated shaft. Various-sized notches carved into the base of the horns fit the different-sized shafts.

He'd dreamed how to make arrows as a young man. In his dream he'd painted the shaft with red ocher just in front of the place where he attached the feathers. All his life he made arrows the same way. He'd learned about hunting partly from his father's teachings, but he learned most from the power that came to him in his dreams.

When he was a boy he had made his own bows and arrows and hunted in the valleys for rabbits and ducks, but he was a poor hunter. He had no luck. Whenever he played

games of throwing or shooting at targets, he simply lost his
arrows to other boys. Then his father told him, "You go up
to Black Mountain. Whatever comes toward you will come
from the north. It will be a mountain sheep. You will shoot
it and then you'll follow it southward. You will get it." Later
he had a dream and saw the thing his father told him about.
He was standing in the mountains, watching some mountain sheep coming toward him. When they were close he
took two arrows and shot, but missed. "That's strange," he
said, "after what my father told me. What he said must be
untrue."

A few years later the dream came again and he knew
his father was wrong. He saw Gollaher Mountain covered
with fog and the mountain spoke to him. "You'll always be
well and strong. Nothing can hurt you and you'll live to an
old age." He said to himself, "What my father told me is
false. After this when I'm hunting, I'll rely on my own
power." He dreamed how to paint his arrows and he went
hunting near Gollaher Mountain. He saw some deer and
started to sneak up on them, but they caught wind of him
and ran toward his mountain. Then he said, "My mountain,
I want you to help me get some of these deer. You have so
many living on you, you can give me some." He soon overtook them and was able to kill his first deer. When he returned home, he gave away the deer as he was supposed to.

Soon after this dream, when he was still a young man,
he went hunting near Gollaher Mountain and asked his
power to make it easy for him to hunt. "Now, mountain, if
you give me some of your deer, I wish you'd have them near
your foot, not too far up." He came upon some deer near the
foot of the mountain as he asked. He soon overtook them
and killed one lying under a mountain mahogany tree. As
he was packing the meat home, he saw a herd of mountain
sheep. He stopped and hid to watch them, and as he waited
one came toward him. He killed it with little trouble and
went into the valley, carrying both animals. This happened
to him again and again and he became known as a great

hunter. He could stand long and tiring trips through the mountains and could cross the roughest country.

His mountain was good to him and came to speak to him whenever he was in trouble to tell him he would be all right. Once when he was still young, someone killed a white man's cattle and there was trouble as usual. The white soldiers came and fought with some of his people. All escaped, except three, but the soldiers followed them. Everyone was afraid because most of the young men were off hunting and there was no one to fight the soldiers. But he knew his power would take care of him. An old man told the people to try to kill the captain, who, he said, would be behind the soldiers giving orders. They went toward the canyons where they found the captain, as the elder had said, behind the soldiers. They killed the captain, and the soldiers became frightened and ran away. The people took the captain's clothes. They cut off his mustache and painted their own faces black to protect themselves from the powers unleashed by the killings. More soldiers came, but the people went farther into the canyons where they couldn't be found. It was then that Mike learned something else. His mountain was strong and could carry heavy rocks on his back and could withstand storms, but the fog in the canyon had the power to appear and disappear. It could cover things, even mountains.

When Mike left the reservation he told his family that too many people lived on too little land for anyone to lead a satisfying life. Miners came for copper and galena ore. Settlers took away Shoshone farms. Government agents wanted to take the children to school. The children would become as confused as the white people. "I have never understood what the white people have wanted us to do," Mike said, "except to die. Why should we? We came to this place in peace. Who have we killed here? What have we stolen? I've tried to live in this place peaceably, but I can't sleep here any more. Bad dreams are coming to me all the time."

Mike told his family they would survive like fireflies

with the power to hide in the day and lizards who hide in the rocks at dark. They could never drive out the white people or conquer them. From then on, they would have to be careful to move around them and between them. They'd live like the blue summer haze and the winter fog.

Every December Mike returned to the same bend in the creek at the mouth of Rock Creek Canyon. Hides went back on the domed willow frame. Shredded bark and grass lined the floor. Smoke twisted from the small campfire and spread out above the river willows. The year completed, the circle of travel closed, Mike and his family were ready for the winter.

In the wickiup when the snow was falling, Mike told stories to his family in various voices as he once did during the winters at Fort Hall. To his children Mike was anything but silent. He laughed and talked into the night.

Mike's children lay on the warm, spongy floor of the wickiup and sometimes drifted to the edge of sleep. The wickiup smelled of smoke mixed with a stronger smell from the dried fish and venison stacked on the floor along the inside walls of the hut. Whether they slipped into sleep or out of sleep, they could hear the voices of Coyote and Wolf and their father, still talking:

In the beginning Wolf wanted to make everything easy and pleasant for the people, but his younger brother, Coyote, tried to make them work hard as they must do today. Wolf had all the animals shut up so the people could easily take what they wanted, but Coyote released the animals so the people had to go hunting. The people ranged through the country in individual families. There were no tribes, there were no bands. There were no chiefs. Families occasionally came together for a seasonal hunt, and an old and experienced man might emerge as a temporary leader. In the winter, groups of families camped together but went their separate ways in the spring. They all spoke the same language. To themselves and each other, they were simply the people, the Newe.

Wolf said, "The Newe shall not die."

"Why shouldn't they die?" Coyote asked. "Surely they must die."

Wolf said, "There will be two deaths then. After a man dies, he'll die again."

"No," Coyote said. "There ought to be only one death so that when a man dies, he shall stay that way."

They argued for a long time. Finally Wolf said, "Coyote, I agree with you about having only one death. It will be that way."

Shortly after, Coyote's son became sick and was near death. Coyote went to his brother and said, "Wolf, when you were giving orders, didn't you say we should have two deaths? Well, Wolf, I agree with you on that one. I like that idea."

Wolf said, "Don't be foolish."

Coyote began to cry and begged his brother to change the rule. He said, "I didn't think my son was going to die right away. Please change the rule."

Wolf said, "No, don't be foolish. When we make a rule we must keep it."

Afterward, Coyote felt sorry for the people and taught them how to cry and cut their hair when anyone died. Coyote told them that the dead go to another place. It's pleasant there, where the dead go, but they would still rather be with the living.

When Wolf and Coyote were talking, Wolf said, "Let there be no menstruation," but Coyote thought it proper that women should menstruate. So Coyote took some blood and threw it at his daughter. She began to menstruate and went to the menstrual hut where Coyote taught her what she must do.

Wolf thought people ought to be born without copulation, but Coyote disagreed. "Fucking is better," Coyote said.

"People should be born from the womb." So the world became as it was, a satisfactory place to live in.

On Rock Creek, nights were icy, the moon cold white, but the morning winds began to come through the canyon without bite. Each day the places on the horizon where the sun rose and set grew farther and farther apart. The dried food they had eaten all winter was almost gone. The boys caught a winter-starved rabbit in the snow and roasted it whole. The winds grew warmer. The ice broke up in the creek. Trout swam in the creek and squirrels pushed themselves out of the ground. Their noses quivered as they looked at the world with quick dark eyes. Green clover appeared along the stream. Shoots of wild onions and the light green leaves of young lettuce thickened on the canyon floor. After the winter, they tasted like sunlight and spring water. Birds were flying around everywhere.

Mike's boys waded into the cold water and trapped trout with their hands. In earlier years they stayed until the first salmon ran up Rock Creek. They sliced the pink flesh from the bones and hung it along the creek on drying racks made of willows. But the salmon quit coming up Rock Creek when Milner Dam was built in the Snake River.

Then Mike and his family moved southward. Timing was everything. They could not harvest biscuit root before its seeds ripened, otherwise the root would spoil. Sego bulbs could be dug up while their yellow-core lilies still blossomed, but bitterroot only after its ghostly rose flowers dried and fell. Everywhere the ground offered something to eat. Mike and his family climbed to higher country, near Gollaher Mountain. They replenished their strings of horses with mustangs captured from the wild herds. The boys went to work running horses for ranchers. The women and children dug camas bulbs with crooked-nosed sticks hardened in the fire. The stick went into the ground a few inches from the plant. The stick jerked and the white bulb popped out of the ground. The women lightly steamed some bulbs for meals and cooked and pounded others for the coming winter. As the days grew hotter, the course of the sun shifted northward each day, pointing toward the coming cold. The women dug pit ovens in the ground. On the oven floor of stones a hardwood fire burned down to hot coals. The women raked the coals and covered them with grass, then added a layer of sego bulbs. They filled the pit with alternate layers of bulbs and coals and grass, covered with dirt. After the bulbs were baked, the women pounded them into flour or flattened them into cakes to be later re-cooked in boiling baskets. They roasted camas bulbs, removed the black outer layers, and squeezed the bulbs into warm, sugary macaroons hung away from the children to dry.

Fruits ripened. The air hummed with mosquitoes. Mashed serviceberries dried in the sun. Golden currants and red currants and black currants ripened in the lower valley. They were cooked into puddings. As the fall advanced, chokecherries hung in heavy dark clusters on bushes in the mountains. The seed harvest arrived and the women moved from crop to crop to gather the seeds of the quick-blooming plants before they scattered in the wind. Sometimes a day or two made all the difference. They worked deliberately but without hurry. The women hit the withered plant heads. Seeds showered into gathering baskets. Sunflower seeds, and grains from wild wheat and rye, the round black seeds of rice grass, and the tiny seeds of pickleweed—all were parched, hulled, and ground into rich flour. Nive told her daughters that the flour of the white people tasted like alkali dust because they did not feed air to the flour. Seeds came from the ground. Fire heated them, stones cracked them. Flat winnowing baskets tossed them into the air so that wind blew away light chaff and flowed around the seeds before they were ground into flour. The same was done to crickets. In the cool mornings before they could jump, crickets lay in bunches in the grass, and children gathered them in handfuls. Roasted on hot coals, tossed in the air, they were ground like seeds into flour. Even chokecherries lay spread out on willow racks so the air could flow over and under and all around them.

In the fall, processions of clouds moved across the dark blue sky. The places on the horizon where the sun rose and set moved closer together. The women watched the sky day and night for signs. All across the land bright yellow flowers of rabbitbrush looked like lights. The men brought back fat rabbits and deer. They took sinews from the backstraps and legs of the deer; they cut the meat into strips and hung it on willows to dry. They cooked the tasty neck of the deer for the children. The women scraped hair from the hide and washed the skin. Tied to a tree the wet skin was twisted with a stick until it was wrung dry. The women rubbed and smeared the deer's own oily brains into the hide to soften it.

Mornings grew colder. It was time for the last harvest. Mike and his family moved to the mountains for pine nuts. They stopped in Tecoma, the small railhead near the Utah border where Nive's sister lived. Other families from Tecoma and Fort Hall joined them for the harvest. They struck the nuts from their hard cones and roasted them. Even as the women prepared the nuts for storage, they cracked open roasted shells with their teeth and tasted the rich nut that would be mashed into gravy during the winter. Nive and her daughter Henie also gathered yarrow and other medicines that ripened at the same time as the pine nuts. Henie was the daughter who paid closest attention to how her mother did things. She was always watching. In the evening her father played the hand game with the other men and sang as he gambled. Nive gambled too. The people faced each other in rows and their wavering voices rose and fell in pulsing rhythms. Henie felt the songs move into her body as the gamblers swayed back and forth.

Later she sat with her family where willows enclosed their camp the way a willow basket enclosed water. Smoke rose from the fire and spread over the darkening camp. The voices of the people sitting on the earth were low. Other people in the distance could be heard laughing and joking, telling stories. Mike smoked his short willowstem pipe in the dark. As he smoked, the green soapstone bowl glowed red. He'd picked wild tobacco from the earth in late fall and mixed it with tobacco from the store. Fire made the tobacco burn. Henie watched her father. Covering his head with a blanket and sitting outside facing east, he made himself into a mountain. The tobacco and fire and air around him became part of his head and rose into the cold air. Mike began to sing:

> *Old mountain, old mountain,*
> *So strong, ay, ay,*
> *Moving through fog,*
> *Ay, ay, moving through fog.*

Overhead, the white stars had gathered in thousands and covered the sky like snow.

Hard, dark days followed. Winter was long and cold. Ten of Mike's horses died. In the early spring, when Mike and his family again camped in a canyon at Gollaher Mountain, their remaining horses were weak and without feed. In late April, Dell Hardy saw five of Mike's family about two miles east of San Jacinto. They were all afoot. Old Mike was slightly stooped. He wore tattered overalls and his face was wrinkled with age. One of his sons walked beside him, a short, bowlegged, heavyset man in his late thirties. His black hair, cut square across his forehead, was braided in the back and worn looped around his neck. Shuffling behind the men were two dark-headed women, wrapped in blankets, one carrying a small baby on her back, the other carrying a bundle. They walked toward the cattle company store where they could buy on credit. At the store, Allie Patterson said that Old Mike and his family came on foot to the store several times that spring because their horses were too poor to ride.

In May, Mike's horses grew stronger and his boys were getting ready to run mustangs to replace the horses that had died over the winter. During the day they let the horses graze for feed but drove them into brush corrals at night. One day his son Jack was driving the horses to camp when someone shot him from his horse. Mike saw two of his sons carrying Jack into the camp. They put him on the ground and cut away the overalls below his knee. Blood ran into the dust, turning it black. Jack's leg bent at the knee and it bent again below the knee where the bone was broken. The bone was sticking out of the blood and skin. Nive pressed poultices of mashed yarrow against the wound but the blood kept coming, and Mike heard the blood in his son's throat as he breathed. Nive worked hard with new poultices. She and her daughters were crying, their voices rising and falling in wails. Mike looked at his son's eyes and saw that they were dead.

Mike's other sons rode out and paid death with death. When they returned they said they had found five men and a woman camped in a draw. Corralled in the draw were stolen horses, and the men and woman must have thought Jack had discovered them. They had a fight with the men and they shot one in his brains and his heart. They knew they killed him and they knew who he was, Frankie Dopp, one of the white boys they'd played with as kids. Everything was crazy now. The other men they fought were men they had worked with when they were running horses for ranchers. Frank Tranmer was someone Mike had known for the past twenty years, ever since he'd left the reservation. The other man was named Nimrod Urie. Those men shot his son. His son's blood lay on the ground. Everything was out of order.

Everyone was crying as Mike washed his son, painted his face, and dressed him. He wrapped him in a blanket and tied it. On horses they dragged the wrapped body above the canyon and buried it in the rocks. With knives and sheepshears Nive and her daughters hacked their hair short. Jim cut off his braid and threw it away. Mike cut his hair and smeared ashes on his face. He lifted his face and wailed in a high-pitched cry until his voice broke and he sobbed with his face in his hands. He burned Jack's clothing and bedding. Nive burned rabbitbrush to keep all the ghosts away. They were all crying now—my brother, my son—but no one said his name for fear he would think they were calling him back. "Go away," his mother said. "We loved you when you were here. Your place is somewhere else now."

"Don't bother our dreams," Mike said. "Just be happy where you are."

That night Mike's sons—Nogoviz, Wonig, and Hogozap—returned to the white man's camp and drove horses from their brush corrals. Riding some of the horses and driving the rest, Mike and his family rode from Gollaher Mountain toward the west under a dim moon. Mike knew what would happen to him if he stayed in that country. It would be his word against a white man's. He made his family hurry, and they left behind their wagon, some pots, the wagon jack, and everything that was too heavy or clumsy to carry on horseback. They turned loose Jack's favorite bay mare as well as some of their own weak horses. They left Jack's riding saddle and the saddle tree for his pack horse. Mike hung them in an aspen tree not far from where his son was shot.

Mike made his way westward, dropping south of the Owyhee Mountains and staying north of the Humboldt River. They stayed away from the few far-flung settlements and ranches in that open country. They had left before the spring and fall harvests and were without supplies. They moved across north-central Nevada and took what they needed from isolated sheep and cattle camps left empty during the day. They moved into the more populated country north of Golconda. They passed Paradise Valley, crossed a desert valley, and stopped at the Lay brothers' ranch to trade for some old harness. They made camp in a canyon and spent several days running horses. They now had a string of about twenty horses, including the ones taken from the stolen bunches at Gollaher Mountain. One day an Indian hunter approached the canyon but Wonig and Hogozap rode out to keep him away from the horses. In the afternoon they saw clouds of dust raised by buckaroos running horses to the south. They moved out of their camp and headed toward less populated country. They crossed the Jackson Mountains through Rattlesnake Canyon, the massive purple head of King Lear Peak hidden from view to the north. They passed pale sand dunes shaped by the wind into delicate tufts and fluted ridges. They moved into country of lava rock flows, disintegrated volcanic fissures, and steaming hot springs. They rode out onto the flat white shimmering floor of the desert. Layers of dried mud peeled up from the desert floor like paper. Crusted with salt, the ground cracked, and beneath the hooves of horses brittle salt grass near hot springs snapped like hundreds of tiny twigs. The burnt and torn hills of the Black Rock Range came closer and the volcanic rock yielded to the Harlequin Hills and the Calico Mountains. They were now over two hundred miles from home. To the south the flat desert mirrored the sky like a distant sheen of blue water. Even the hills were reflected in that waterless lake. At the ends of the vast horizon the edges of the earth fell away into a curve. The country was full of ghosts, spinning in the distance in the form of dust devils. Mike did not know where in this country he would ever find a place to live.

7

In July 1910, Lamb received a circular concerning the murder in northeastern Nevada of an Idaho boy named Frankie Dopp. The murder was reported to have occurred on May 6, 1910. The circular from the Elko County district attorney's office described how the boy, according to witnesses, had caught a few reservation Indians changing brands on stolen horses and the Indians had shot and killed him. The boy had been running horses with Frank Tranmer, Nimrod Urie, and other men from Twin Falls. It was thought that the Indian murderers had escaped to the reservation in the rugged Owyhee country. The circular requested any information concerning the murder and the whereabouts of the murderers.

Lamb wrote to the Elko district attorney that he knew nothing about the incident except what he'd read in the newspapers. He had no other information.

"That's a funny deal," Lamb told Deputy Muller. "They seem to be taking their time tracking down whoever killed that kid."

"Once those Indians got back on the reservation," Charlie Muller said, "you'd play hell finding them."

"Maybe," Lamb said, "I just think something else is going on. It makes you wonder whether the Indians really killed the kid or they're just getting blamed for it."

Lamb heard nothing more about the incident in Elko County for the rest of the summer. It was outside his jurisdiction and he had no reason to think of it. It was another of those sad incidents in the borderlands that once occurred regularly when wandering Indians and encroaching settlers clashed. Occasional disputes, an occasional death, were all that remained from what was once open warfare.

Lamb thought no more of the murder of the Idaho boy until later that fall. In early September, just before the 1910 Eagles Carnival, he was buying tickets one morning from Dora Giroux, who was running for festival queen, when he received word of a murder in Imlay. Deputy Muller took the call.

"There's been a bad murder, Sheriff," Charlie Muller said. "Somebody's robbed and shot the Quillicis in Imlay."

Two men, maybe three, wearing masks cut from flour sacks, broke into the Quillici saloon that morning and killed the saloon owner and wounded his wife while robbing the cash register. The saloon was one of three or four businesses at the small railroad stop thirty miles to the southwest between Winnemucca and Lovelock. The men made their escape on horseback across the desert to the northeast.

"I want you to get a car ready," Lamb told his deputy, "and get Dr. Giroux to go with me. We're leaving as soon as that car's ready."

Unaccustomed to such urgency, Deputy Muller stood up and removed his black bowler. He stood like an expectant schoolboy with the hat in his hands.

"I want Skinny to go with me too," Lamb said.

"You know who committed this murder?" Deputy Muller asked.

"I'm not saying they committed the crime. I'm just saying we're going to arrest them, if we catch them. That's why I'd like it if you'd get moving."

Earlier that morning Lamb had been talking to Jean

Erramouspe and another kid working on the new Winnemucca sewer line. The Basque kid had told him that two
drifters who'd been working in the sewer ditch had left
town the previous day. They'd gone to run horses near the
Blakeslee Ranch outside Imlay and wanted Jean and another boy named Gibbs to go with them.

"You're both better off here," Lamb had told the two
boys.

"Sure," Jean Erramouspe said, "we wouldn't want to be
up there where you are in a nice coat and tie."

"I'm just crazy about digging these ditches," the boy
named Gibbs had said.

"You boys've got the brains to do it, seems like," Lamb
had told them.

Now he had a hunch that the two drifters headed for
the Blakeslee ranch might have something to do with the
Imlay robbery.

After Deputy Muller left the office, Lamb called Nellie
to tell her that he might not be back in time to go to the
theater with her. They'd planned to see *The Alaskan* that
night, a benefit show to raise money for the new Catholic
church in Golconda.

"The Duckers are coming over for dinner beforehand,"
Nellie said. "Did you remember that, Graham?"

"I'm going to do my best to get back, Nellie," he said.

"If you can't, you can't," she said. "I'll see if the Duckers
have anybody else in mind to come along."

"A lot of people seem to be coming into town for the
show. I heard a slew of people are coming in from
Lovelock."

"There's a lot here already," Nellie said. "Justice Fitts
and some others have already come in."

Lamb was surprised to hear her mention Justice Fitts.
That morning he'd seen the justice of the peace awkwardly
climb down from the eastbound train, and his red eyes like
open wounds so struck Lamb that he let the man pass without calling out to him. He had no idea why Fitts should be

in Winnemucca. When he was last in Lovelock, the town had been buzzing about Justice Fitts and the woman he'd followed to Reno, but the same principle that compelled Lamb to let Fitts enter Winnemucca undisturbed had made him tell his gossiping friends in Lovelock, "It's not a crime to follow a woman to Reno."

"I know Dr. Giroux wants to go to this show, too," Lamb told Nellie. "That's why I hope we can get this thing straightened out quick this afternoon."

"That's all right," Nellie said. "If you think you're going to make it back, call ahead."

When he hung up, Lamb sensed something wrong. Things hadn't been going well between him and Nellie that summer, but she'd never asked him to call ahead if he thought he might be coming home to dinner. She'd always been one to take the irregularity of his job in stride. But it was the resignation in her voice that was most troubling. It was as though he were becoming a stranger in his own house.

When Charlie Muller returned to say the car was ready and Dr. Giroux was set to go along, Lamb told his deputy, "You can let Skinny out now."

"He's already sitting in the car," Charlie Muller said.

When the big open-top Oldsmobile pulled out of town, Lamb sat in the back seat next to Dr. Giroux while Skinny Pascal, seemingly asleep, his hat over his eyes, slumped in the front seat next to the driver. The car no sooner left the edge of town than it plunged into a hot wind and swirling alkali dust. Lamb squinted against the heat and dust. The white strip of road stretched ahead across a dull expanse of bleached sagebrush and late summer rabbitbrush. There was nothing else except light and space and distance, all the way to Imlay.

8

That evening Father Enright received a call about the shooting and robbery in Imlay. He removed a consecrated host from the church and hurried to the hospital where he found Dr. Giroux with the wife of the man who had been killed. The doctor was a middle-aged, balding man with a neatly trimmed mustache. "She kept asking for a priest every time she became conscious on the train," he told Father Enright.

The young, tiny woman looked like a bandaged doll tucked between the white sheets. She reached out, and when Father Enright took her hand he felt a wedding ring roll loosely on her thin girlish finger. She and her husband had arrived from Los Angeles with a group of Italian immigrants who intended to start a colony and grow grapes in Humboldt County. The Quillicis, in true enterprising fashion, had struck out on their own and took over the saloon about a half mile from the Imlay station. They'd scraped together enough money to bring Mrs. Quillici's eighteen-year-old brother from Italy.

"They were starting to build up a successful business," Dr. Giroux told the priest outside the room. "Now this happens. She doesn't have much chance."

"This is outrageous," the priest said. "I can't believe such savagery. Who's responsible?"

Dr. Giroux shook his head. "Sheriff Lamb will get them, if he hasn't already." He told the priest that Sheriff Lamb and his Indian trailer had stayed in Imlay and begun to hunt for the murderers northeast of town.

"It just doesn't seem possible," Father Enright said, "that people can be so barbaric."

"I'm afraid this is a barbaric country, Father," Dr. Giroux said, "no matter how much we'd like to pretend it isn't."

On his way home Father Enright walked to the edge of town where he saw the beginnings of dry, brush-covered wastes and bleak, wrinkled mountains. When he'd first come to Nevada he'd been told Winnemucca was different. It wasn't like those violent, slapdash, skeletal mining towns in the south of the state, wrenched into existence for the sole purpose of ripping ore from the earth, towns that would soon die. Winnemucca had grown slowly and naturally, people said. It supported not only roughneck miners but families of ranchers, farmers, shippers, and merchants. Here was a country not just for the rich and privileged but for the common man. People got a fair shake here, and they came to stay. Winnemucca made sense.

Father Enright looked up at the pale moon, stark as bone. He looked back down into the country of burned-out craters and valleys and mountains around him and recalled his conversation earlier that morning with Justice Fitts from Lovelock.

He'd noticed the man standing at the back of the church when he turned from the altar at the end of mass. The church was empty except for six or seven women—his regular weekday congregation—and this strange man, dressed in an expensive but rumpled suit holding a fashion-able new bowler in his hands.

"*Ite, missa est,*" Father Enright had told his small con-gregation. Go, the mass is finished.

The stranger was still at the back of the church after Father Enright had removed his vestments and returned from the sacristy to put out the candles and wash the wine cruet. The man came forward and asked if he might speak with the priest for a moment. Father Enright looked at the strange man with fashionably rolled trousers, shiny laced shoes, and rings on his fingers. His face sagged in the aftermath of drink. Red veins rimmed his eyes.

In the rectory, after Father Enright cooked breakfast, the two sat at the table, eating scrambled eggs and drinking coffee, and the man explained that he merely had been passing the church and entered on an impulse. He'd had no intention of coming to Winnemucca, but had fallen asleep on the train from Reno and missed his stop in Lovelock. The man used both hands to lift the cup, but coffee spilled over the lip and steamed up from his delicate fingers. He put down the cup, spilling more coffee, and pressed his wet fingers to his eyes. "This is embarrassing," he said. He apologized for bothering the priest, but he needed someone to talk to.

"There's nothing incapable of God's forgiveness," Father Enright said.

"It's not forgiveness I need," the man said. "I just want to square things with myself."

"I'm not sure I can help you," Father Enright said.

The man named Fitts spread his soft delicate hands on the table and told the priest of his involvement with a woman who was not his wife. Things were complicated because of his position in his community; he was the town justice in Lovelock, and his life was coming apart not because of what he did—he'd tried to be discreet—but because of people's judgment of him. "Can it be such a sin," he asked, "for a man to realize he no longer loves his wife? Isn't it enough that something has broken inside me? I've tried to be a gentleman, but this is a barbarous country."

"I hope you understand that if you were a Catholic,"

Father Enright said, "this would be a matter for the confessional. This is a difficult situation. I can't presume to judge."

"But there are those who do judge," Fitts said, "and they're the ones who should be in a better position than you of knowing what it means to be drawn to a woman."

Father Enright took off his glasses and wiped his hand over his brow. "I'm sorry to be blunt, Mr. Fitts," he said, "but you're talking to a man, just like yourself. I know what you're talking about."

"But you're not married."

"But I can know temptation. I can know your feelings to that extent. My vows wouldn't make any sense unless I did."

"I'm sorry if I've irritated you."

"It's my choice," the priest continued, "to be as I am, just as it's my choice to fast even when I'm hungry. I wish I could help you, Mr. Fitts, because I can pity you and your wife and the other woman, too. I can only tell you that you mustn't forget them. You're not alone in this."

For the rest of the day Father Enright was bothered by his response to the man. So long preoccupied with schemes for raising money, he wondered if he'd completely forgotten how to direct those fallen from grace. He hadn't wanted to become legalistic with the man, and he didn't want to become trapped into condoning adultery, but his response seemed misguided, and he had become annoyed. As Fitts was leaving, he'd said, "I feel deeply sorry for all of you, for what you're suffering," and the man seemed touched, gladdened, but Father Enright later stood in his room and stared at the copy of *The Imitation of Christ,* lying on his dresser, unopened for weeks. He felt somehow he had failed.

That night Father Enright walked alone to the Nixon Opera House. He knew he would have to stand in the lobby and thank people for attending this benefit for the new Golconda church. His heart wasn't in it. The robbery in Imlay was a shock. There had been other crimes since he'd come to Winnemucca, but nothing quite so brutal. His encounters with the wounded woman and with the Lovelock justice had drained him. Building a church seemed far from the real work of his vocation. Churches were important, but the souls of his parishioners were more important.

He passed open ditches where the installation of the new sewer system had left the streets in shambles. Red lanterns glowing from all the wooden blockades in the torn-up streets made the town seem a disaster area. At the Nixon Opera House a crowd was entering the lighted doorway. Glaring in the light, a bright poster displayed a chorus of young women, dressed as Eskimos in short-skirted fur parkas, singing and kicking their long bare legs across a snowy Alaskan landscape. Arched over the chorus line in bold red letters were the words: THE ALASKAN—A COMEDY WITH THE PRETTIEST, SAUCIEST, DAINTIEST CHORUS OF GIRLY-GIRLS IN THE U.S.A.

Father Enright felt uneasy. He looked at the crowd and considered the nearly empty church he faced every weekday morning. He saw the district attorney, Edward Ducker, and his wife in a long lilac coat walking toward the doorway. Under the lights appeared the sheriff's wife, Mrs. Lamb, her pretty dark hair pinned up, the silk-faced lapels of her coat and the white ruffles of her blouse shining in the light. Next to her walked the strange man the priest had talked to that morning in the kitchen of the rectory. Shaved, his eyes clear, his hair combed, the man named Fitts looked happy as he entered the opera house gently holding Mrs. Lamb by the elbow.

9

On Monday morning the front page of the *Humboldt Star* announced:

ATROCIOUS DOUBLE MURDER AT IMLAY—MURDERER CAPTURED

One of the most atrocious and brutal crimes ever committed in Humboldt County was perpetrated last Saturday morning when Eugene Quillici was shot dead and his wife mortally wounded by masked bandits.

The assassins, with masks of flour sacks covering their faces, entered Quillici's saloon, which is situated about a mile west of the railroad station at Imlay. The robbers commanded the proprietor to throw up his hands and when he hesitated one of the robbers aimed a rifle at him and fired, the bullet entering the left shoulder. Quillici then started for the door when a second shot was fired, killing him instantly. The fatal bullet struck the victim close to the right ear and came out at the left ear, tearing away almost half of the man's face. After killing Quillici the assassins directed their attention to Mrs. Quillici, who had just come back from the bedroom in the back part of the house. She was about to enter the barroom when one of the robbers fired at her, the bullet entering

[93]

her back. The robbers then placed a pistol against the head of Mrs. Quillici's brother, the only other person in the saloon. The latter only recently arrived from Italy and cannot speak English, yet the bandits made him understand that they wanted him to locate the money for them. The brother is only 18 years of age and while the robber was threatening him he began to cry and the robbers proceeded to search the house.

In the bedroom the four-year-old son of Mr. and Mrs. Quillici was standing up in bed and the little fellow said to the robbers, "You killed papa; don't kill uncle."

The cash register was emptied and it is said the robbers carried away a considerable sum of money that was hidden under a pillow of the bed, but they overlooked about $400 in coin that was in the proprietor's pocket. After completing their dastardly work, the robbers then made their escape.

ONE BANDIT CAPTURED

Sheriff Lamb was notified of the crime and he left immediately for the scene, taking with him an Indian trailer, "Skinny" Pascal. At dusk Sheriff Lamb and his posse took up the trail of the bandits which led them toward the Humboldt River where they discovered on the ground a flour sack with eyeholes lined with cardboard. At that moment a man rode toward them, evidently searching for something he had lost. The man was arrested and taken with the posse. The trail of the robbers led to the Blakeslee ranch on the river, but the cabin was empty, the other bandit having made good his escape along with most of the money. In the cabin were found a 30-30 rifle and an old rubber coat used in the robbery as well as a tobacco can of coins, such money as would likely have been in the cash register. As it was then dark, the posse returned to Imlay with their captive for the night.

The captured bandit gave the name of Nimrod Urie. He is only 23 years of age and is from Twin Falls, Idaho. He had been working on the sewer in Winnemucca until the day before the crime. Urie has been positively identified by Mrs. Quillici's brother as one of the men who committed the crime. The fellow raised his flour sack as he was looting the cash register and the young Italian caught a glimpse of his face.

The captive has refused to give any information about his partner in crime. Sheriff Lamb has notified Elko and Idaho authorities that the escaped murderer may be headed toward the fastnesses of the rugged Owyhee country. Sheriff Lamb has returned to Winnemucca to direct the hunt for the second bandit.

DOUBLE FUNERAL TOMORROW

Mrs. Quillici was taken by Dr. Giroux to the county hospital in Winnemucca on Saturday night where she died early the next morning. The remains of Mr. and Mrs. Quillici are now being cared for at Alter & Alter's undertaking parlors. The double funeral will take place at St. Paul's Catholic Church when Father Jerome Enright offers mass for the dead at 9:00 tomorrow morning.

10

Lamb stepped over the low picket gate in front of his house and removed his dusty hightop shoes on the porch. Two shorthair cowdogs ran through the Virginia creepers and rubbed against his legs. Behind them his son Kent walked through the unfenced side of the yard carrying a single-barrel shotgun cocked open in the crook of his arm. "You caught 'em, didn't you, Pop?" the boy said.

"One of them as much as caught himself, Kent," Lamb said. "We'll catch the other one, too. They're both about as dumb as they come. Get anything?"

"Just rabbits," the boy said. "I gave 'em to Skinny. Pop, it sure would be more fun to hunt with a rifle."

"We'll see," Lamb said. "We'll see what happens when you get to be twelve."

"I'm almost twelve now," the boy said.

"Almost is almost," Lamb said.

The boy appeared to think for a moment. "I sure do wish we were living on a ranch."

"Sometimes I do too, Kent," Lamb said. He looked north to where scraggly red brushwillows marked the Humboldt River. In the late afternoon light, the tawny grass on Winnemucca Mountain glowed like a cougar's pelt.

After his bath, his bare feet slapping damply against the hardwood floor, Lamb walked down the hall to the bedroom where he fell asleep on top of the bed, naked, until Nellie called him for dinner. Dressed in a clean white shirt, his hair combed and still wet, he came to the table where Nellie was lighting candles. "I guess I'll have to be taking Kent deer hunting before too long," he said.

"I hope he gets it out of his system early," Nellie said. "I wish that boy liked doing his schoolwork just a tenth as much as he does hunting and riding."

"It must be that Perkins blood," Lamb said.

Nellie looked at him and Lamb grinned. Her father, Richard Perkins, had been a hunter all his life and had died the day after he returned from a bear hunt when he was seventy-five.

"I guess if Kent gets to be a boy when he's still a boy," Nellie Lamb said, "he won't have to keep being a boy when he grows up."

"Like your pop, you mean."

"I suppose Mom knew what she was doing letting him go off for days with a gun," she said. "She straightened him out in every other way."

"There's nothing wrong with hunting," Lamb said, "it's just how you do it."

"I expect Kent and Ray will be more like you than Pop," Nellie said. "At least I hope so."

From the kitchen she brought a plate to the table. A dozen wet oysters in half-shells glistened in the candlelight. "I got these for you today," she said, "because you missed them on Saturday. I hope they're all right."

Lamb was delighted. The cool, clean taste of oysters reminded him of the sea, filled him with a sense of the sea's freshness and its wind, just as mushrooms always brought him a taste he identified with sunlight and earth.

After dinner, when the boys were in bed, they sat in the dark living room, and Lamb felt the coolness of the night beneath his loose cotton shirt.

"Where do you think that other killer's gone, Graham?" Nellie asked.

"I don't know," Lamb said. "I'm going to wait until this Urie kid tells us."

"What a terrible thing that was. All for a few dollars, too. I wonder what got into those two. It seems they could've robbed that place without killing anybody."

"I think these guys have been in trouble before. There was a telegram here from Elko saying Nimrod Urie was probably mixed up in a deal with some Indians near Idaho last spring. I wrote to Twin Falls to see what they could tell me."

"They're not going to tell you where the other guy went."

"No, but they might tell me who he is. I talked to Jean Erramouspe and another kid the other morning and they thought the guy's name was something like Trammer or Tramley. He just went by the name Idaho when he was working on the sewer line with this kid Nimrod Urie. The trouble is we're going to need evidence to arrest him even if we know his name, and this kid Urie won't talk. At least not yet."

"It's funny," Nellie said, "the son of a bitch is probably somewhere sleeping like a baby right now, while a civilized man like Justice Fitts suffers the tortures of the damned for doing next to nothing."

"What brings up Fitts?" Lamb said.

"I guess you heard that he was here for dinner Saturday night," Nellie said.

"Nobody said anything to me," Lamb said.

"I just thought people would be talking," Nellie said. "He came here with the Duckers and I let him escort me to the show."

"If we were in Lovelock, they'd sure be talking."

"People talk everywhere," Nellie said. "Mom always said people who feel littlest about themselves will always be the biggest talkers about other people."

"We got enough of those kind in this town," Lamb said.

"What was that thing Jim Butler told you in Tonopah that time?"

"About people talking?"

"No," she said, "something about not caring what people say but something about what they do."

"Wasn't there something about keeping up with the Joneses?" Lamb asked.

"Not keeping up with the Joneses," Nellie said, "but there was something about the Joneses in it. What the hell was that?"

"And the Smiths," Lamb said. "Something about not caring what Smith said to Jones. I'll think of it in a minute."

"It doesn't matter," Nellie said. "I just figured that Fitts is getting a raw deal in Lovelock, and I don't think he deserves it. If people want to talk, let them talk."

"You mean because I wasn't with you?"

"It might have been worse if you were there. You're the one up for election."

"If people voted for those reasons, I'd say to hell with them and to hell with their job."

"But they do. That's what's happening to Fitts in Lovelock. It's not fair. He's trying to be a gentleman about it."

"If he's doing his job," Lamb said, "that's all that matters."

"He can't be doing his goddamn job very well with all that's happening to him."

"He has to do his job, no matter what's happening. If he isn't, then he has to go."

"Now you're being too hard," Nellie said.

"That was the point of what Jim Butler was saying, I think. It's what you do that counts, not what you say. But I can't remember how he said it."

"Mom always said if people were a little more sure of themselves, they wouldn't be so damn busy judging everyone else."

"I don't know if I'm following you."

"I'm talking about Fitts. He said that Father Enright made him feel human again, just talking to him that morning. And being able to have dinner and go to the show with us helped him see how he could straighten out his business in Lovelock."

"I'm sure he felt that way when he was with all of you," Lamb said, "but I doubt it lasted past the night. I know Fitts and I like him as much as anybody does, but he's a wormy-headed man. He's trying to be something he ain't."

"He was still all right when he left the next day."

"You saw him then too?"

"Sure. I put him up on the couch here. The Duckers were full up with people who came from Battle Mountain to see the show."

"I'm glad I wasn't here then," Lamb said. "I couldn't put up with Fitts that long."

"You're probably just going by what people say about him."

"I remember how it went, Nell," Lamb said, "what Jim Butler told me in Tonopah. 'I don't care what Smith says of Jones; it's what Jones does to me that counts. We are all here to get rich, and your dollar is as good as mine.' That's how it went, Nell."

While Nellie was in the bathroom getting ready for bed, Lamb looked out the window toward the dark outline of Winnemucca Mountain. It was hard to imagine that only a day had passed since he was out there on horseback tracking down a murderer. He undressed and put on his cotton nightshirt. It was then that he noticed the letter folded on the night table. With one hand he lifted the top fold of the paper and read Nellie's note to her sister saying how much she'd like to visit San Francisco. He refolded the letter and looked back out the window to the mountain. It looked remote. The distance between the man who'd been out in the desert and the man eating oysters seemed unbridgeable. He felt as distant from himself as from the woman who had gone to the theater with Justice Fitts from Lovelock. He imagined her laughing and talking with Justice Fitts as they walked together to the opera house. He wondered whether she'd found dinner with Fitts and whatever they talked about more pleasant than the evening she'd just spent with him talking about murderers.

11

At noon Jean Erramouspe climbed out of the sewer ditch and took his lunch bucket to a strip of shade cast by a single poplar in front of the Masonic and Odd Fellows Hall. The boy named Gibbs, followed by Frank Tranmer, a lean, bare-chested man in his mid-forties, dropped cross-legged into the dirt in front of him, the three of them forming a triangle on the ground with Jean at the apex, sitting against the trunk of the poplar. The man named Tranmer had returned to work on Monday after missing work on Saturday. Up and down the street men were leaving the ditches and looking for shade under trees or behind piles of dirt and gravel.

"What's for dinner today, Basco boy?" Gibbs grinned expectantly. He wore a tight felt hat that made his head look like a misshapen jug. Trails of muddy sweat snaked down his grimy face and bare chest. Even his teeth looked muddy.

"I bet it's sheep's balls," the man named Tranmer said. He pushed his railroad engineer's cap to the back of his head and stared at Jean. He had a long weathered face and a scruffy, drooping mustache.

"Bound to be sheep's balls one of these days," Gibbs said.

Jean looked down and popped the lid of the lard can.

From the first day he'd brought his lunch from the Basque Hotel and uncovered two lamb chops, wrapped in a towel and still warm, along with sourdough bread and a corked soda bottle refilled with wine, the two men had followed him at noon, frustrating his attempts to eat alone. Gibbs had left him alone on Saturday when Tranmer was gone, but as soon as Tranmer was back on Monday, he and Gibbs started up where they'd left off. It was now Wednesday. Jean was reaching his limit. He pulled a crusty chicken wing from the bucket and tore at it with his teeth.

"What do you figure happened to his tongue?" Gibbs asked. "He hasn't said two words in three days."

"Used up all his United States in one day," Tranmer said. "Must be all he's got left are them Jap Basco words."

Gibbs fell back on the ground holding his stomach in mock laughter. "Whooee!" he yelped.

"Yes, sir," Tranmer said, trying to extend the joke, "either that, or all he knows is sheep talk. *Baaaa, baaaa.*"

Jean stood up. "All right, Tranmer," he said. "I've had it. Get up."

Tranmer tilted his face up, his body motionless, his lips parted but unsmiling. Gibbs pushed himself back into a sitting position, grabbing for his hat. Glancing at Tranmer, he emulated the other man's sorrowful expression.

"One at a time, or both of you at once," Jean said. "I don't give a damn. Get up."

Tranmer continued to squint at Jean, his face a mask of sadness. "We were only funning, Jean."

"Funning, hell," Jean said. "Get up, or I'll kick your teeth where you sit."

"What do you think, Gibbs?" Tranmer asked, not taking his eyes off Jean.

"I think we ought to pound the piss out of him," Gibbs said.

"Naw, you got it wrong, Gibbs. It's all in good fun. Come on, Jean, sit down and finish your dinner. I ain't looking for a fight."

"You've been looking ever since you started working here," Jean said, "and now you got it."

"Come on, Jean," Gibbs squeaked. "We knowed you could take it."

"We want to be friends, Jean. We're not fighters," Tranmer said.

"Yeah," Gibbs said.

"Shut up, Gibbs," Tranmer said. "Look, Jean, I got ribbed when I come to work here, and Gibbs did too. It's nothing to fight about. I got mad too, so did Gibbs, but then we got to laughing about it, and nobody hurt nobody. Look at how I was ribbing Gibbs last Saturday."

"What are you talking about?" Jean said. "You weren't here Saturday. You didn't rib nobody."

"You got it wrong," Tranmer said. "I've been here every day you have. Isn't that right, Gibbs?"

"That's right," Gibbs said. "He was digging this shit ditch just like you, Jean."

"The hell he was."

"You're just not remembering right, Jean," Tranmer said. "You're all mixed up."

"You can tell it to Sheriff Lamb. He was here on Saturday and knows you were gone."

"He ain't got no witnesses except you, and you must've got me mixed up with somebody else."

"All we have to do is ask the foreman," Jean said.

"He don't keep track," Tranmer said. "How's he going to keep track of seventy guys coming and going? That's why they pay us every day, just like niggers picking cotton."

"We're just trying to be your friends, Jean," Gibbs said, "and you're trying to make trouble. Maybe you should learn not to talk so much around sheriffs. Ain't that right, Idaho?"

"Ah, shut up, Gibbs. Just try to be nice for a change. Maybe Jean will see here what friends he got."

"Horseshit," Jean said. "No friends treat people the way you do."

"Come on, Jean, it's just a joke," Tranmer said. "Let's be

friends." He slowly stood up and put out his hand, continuing to tell Jean that there were no hard feelings, they didn't intend to get him so upset, they only intended to rib him a little until they got to know each other better and then they might settle down and become good buddies. They'd just let the teasing pass now, shake hands, and hold no grudges.

Jean hesitated, then took Tranmer's hand. "That's it," Tranmer said. "You're a good egg. Now shake hands with Gibbs and let's forget about it."

Jean shooks hands with Gibbs, and Tranmer put his hand on Jean's shoulder. "Now we'll bury the hatchet." He suddenly clutched at his crotch. "I got to take a piss," he said.

"Me too," Gibbs said, and his stumpy legs did a little three-step run to catch up with Tranmer, the top of his hat bobbing next to the other man's shoulder as they disappeared behind the Masonic Hall.

Jean leaned back against the tree and drained the wine from the soda bottle. When he folded his arms across his chest, he was still quivering. Trickles of hot sweat ran down his stomach. He didn't trust Tranmer any more than he had before, but if he'd just leave him alone and let him work in peace, he'd be satisfied. Gibbs reminded him of a slug turned up under a rotten log, annoying but harmless, but there was something about Tranmer, mean and unpredictable, that reminded him of a rabid coyote. Maybe he did get mixed up on Saturday, and Tranmer was working somewhere else on the sewer line, but he was pretty damn sure that he'd left with Nimrod Urie and he was mixed up with Urie in the Imlay murders. Tranmer was smart, though, and it would be hard to corner him. The sheriff had already come to Jean's hotel room and asked about Tranmer. He asked Jean to tell him if Tranmer ever left town, or even talked about leaving. When Jean asked Lamb whether he thought Tranmer had been in on the murders, the sheriff just said he was working on it.

Tranmer and Gibbs returned, carrying their shovels,

and they dropped back down, finished their lunches in silence and stretched out in the dirt. Gibbs lay on his stomach, and Tranmer, lying on his back with a hand behind his head, sucked the amber liquid from a pint bottle. "What you think is going to happen to Nimrod?" Gibbs asked Tranmer.

"He's fucked," Tranmer said. "He should've stayed here digging this shitline with us."

"I guess he just thought he was going to make himself some big money."

"He needed to think a little better, seems like. He had a future here. They'll be putting in these lines in every town from here to Salt Lake City. He'd have work till hell freezes over."

"He just didn't enjoy this line of work the way we do, I guess."

"Ain't nothing better," Tranmer said, "except maybe going into the restaurant business. People always got to eat, too."

"Nimrod never had no sense to see that."

"And look what happened. He had a future here, and now he's going to get himself hanged."

"I don't know," Gibbs said, "I bet he'll confess and then they'll give him a break for singing."

"Nimrod Urie never got a break in his life," Tranmer said. "I never met a dumber son of a bitch. At least, I never met a dumber *white* man."

Jean opened his eyes to squints and looked at Tranmer. He was still on his back.

"Nimrod would be better off if he just keeps quiet and never says nothing," Tranmer said, "but they say Lamb always gets confessions. That's how he works."

"What's he do? Break their fingers?"

"Only if he has to. Usually he just sweats them. But you wait and see, that other guy will get off. I read in the paper that he's up in the Owyhee somewhere. He's long gone. It's going to be Nimrod who gets it in the neck."

"Lamb shot that guy Taylor in the back of the neck," Gibbs said. "He's going to get his someday."

Jean heard Gibbs squirm in the dirt. "Look at that!" he shouted.

Jean opened his eyes. Gibbs was sitting up and looking at a pretty young girl with blond hair crossing the street with her mother. She seemed to know she was being watched.

"Wouldn't you like to plug that little pussy?" Gibbs asked.

"Must be jelly under that skirt," Tranmer said, "jam don't move like that."

Gibbs stuck two fingers into his mouth and whistled. The girl started to turn her head but kept walking.

"She's about as juicy as that Edna Purvey girl," Gibbs said in an excited, high voice.

"You dumb shit," Tranmer said, "that *is* Edna Purviance."

Gibbs scowled at Tranmer. "The hell it is. That's that doctor's daughter."

"That's all you know," Tranmer said, "'cuz you'll never get any closer than you are right now."

"Look who's talking."

"I'm getting mine," Tranmer said.

"None of that stuff, though. I'd make that little pussy smoke."

"What do you think, Basco boy?" Tranmer said. "Would you like some of that?"

Jean sat up against the tree. "She's all right," he said.

"'All right?'" Gibbs asked, feigning surprise. "Is that all you can say? I thought you wanted to be our friend."

Jean folded his arms and looked at Gibbs.

"Here we been carrying on a nice conversation," Tranmer said, "and you just sit back icing us out, saying nothing except 'all right.' What the hell are you up to, anyway?"

"Maybe he's just looking for another fight," Gibbs said.

"I'm not looking for a fight," Jean said. "I just didn't have anything to say, that's all."

"Maybe he didn't know what to say," Gibbs said, "'cuz that little skirt didn't have a sheep's tail hanging behind it."

"Naw," Tranmer said, "if Jean fucked his sheep, he'd lose respect for 'em, and you can't work with someone you don't respect. Ain't that right, Jean?"

"You're asking for it, Tranmer."

"He's threatening us, Tranmer," Gibbs said.

"Well, you upset him talking about his sheep that way," Tranmer said. "Everyone knows they put Bascos out with the sheep 'cuz the smell keeps the coyotes away. It's their dogs they fuck."

Jean lunged forward and felt a burst of pain in his shoulder as he fell to the ground clutching Tranmer. Scrambling to his feet, his fist struck bone, a bright splotch of blood appeared under Tranmer's nose. He rushed forward swinging and found himself on his back with Tranmer holding him down, teeth bared, shouting, and Jean saw Gibbs swing the shovel a moment before the metal blade struck flat against his face.

12

Lamb was in a good mood on Wednesday when Captain J. P. Donnelley of the Nevada State Police was to arrive to explain the new Bertillon system to him. That morning he'd once again interrogated Nimrod Urie without success, but the noon mail brought a letter from a prosecuting attorney in Idaho that seemed to throw some light on the Imlay murders. "Looks like we got our lead," he told Deputy Muller, who waited with him in the courthouse office for the arrival of the state policeman.

"It's about time," Charlie Muller said. "I don't know what's keeping Urie from talking. He's a nervous wreck."

"He'll talk when he hears this," Lamb said, "if his mind doesn't snap first."

Lamb read the letter to Muller.

My Dear Sir:

Yours received regarding the arrest of Nimrod Urie. There is absolutely no doubt that this same Nimrod Urie was mixed up in the Indian murder affair in Elko County last spring. I hope you will help us ferret that abominable outrage to its just conclusion.

These facts so far appear: Last spring it was reported that some buckaroos had come across a family of Indians stealing horses in northern Nevada, and that a fight ensued, in which a white boy named Frankie Dopp was shot and killed. The boy's body was found, but no trace or signs of Indians were secured.

Nimrod Urie, who was with the white men, and Frank Tranmer, the white man who had told the story, disappeared. Right on the heels of this, the dead boy's mother announced her belief that Tranmer's outfit had been caught by her son while stealing horses and had killed him to prevent exposure.

Four months went by before three Indians of the Shoshone Tribe came to my office to report that fourteen of their kinsmen, mostly women and children, had gone over into Nevada sometime in May, to trail around for the summer, as Indians will. Not one of them has ever come back, and their white neighbors at Rock Creek have heard no word from them. Their relatives have scoured the country for them and could get no trace of them except a story that they had been killed by white men, and their remains concealed or burned.

Last month, some Nevada ranchers discovered in the vicinity two long trenches, hastily covered, in which some twenty horses had been shot and tumbled in. They did not investigate the bottoms of these pits, or look beneath the carcasses. Despite frequent requests by us, Elko County authorities have failed to investigate the bottoms of these trenches where Indians in this area are confident the bodies of their missing relatives will be found.

Now this tells the whole story to us here. There is no question of a doubt that these Indians came across Nimrod Urie, Frank Tranmer, and the others with them who were out stealing horses, and fearing exposure, the horse thieves murdered the Indians and piled their bodies along with their slaughtered horses in these pits; later they killed the white boy, fearing he would give the crime away.

My Indian visitors told me that their relatives "are gone from the face of the earth." They have vainly tried everywhere to get some action taken, and have complained that the Government did not care what became of them, even alleging they had been told that the Indians had been killed by order of a Nevada sheriff. I immediately assured them that such was impossible and promised to take up the business with the Attorney General at Washington. I have listened to such a tale of horror from these outraged wards of ours who are pitiably dispirited over their inability to secure information from Elko officers whose obvious lack of interest I am at a loss to un-

derstand. My own hands are tied, for the state
line blocks me.

The missing Indians were docile, law—abid—
ing good Indians, who owned ranches and stock,
were respected by their white neighbors, and
never harmed anybody. The murdered white boy,
Frankie Dopp, played with them as a child, and
they were fond of him. I believe that Nimrod
Urie will tell the whole miserable business of
this Indian outrage, if pressed. I have been
digging on this thing for months back, and ev—
erything goes to connect him and the others
with the disappearance of these Indians, and
killing young Dopp last May. Many white people
around Rock Creek country are unified in pro—
claiming the Tranmer and Urie gang the real
murderers.

Everyone here is wrought up over this affair
and eagerly await any information you can pro—
vide so that justice can be accomplished.

> Respectfully and sincerely yours,
>
> T. Bailey Lee
> Prosecuting Attorney
> Cassia County, Idaho

"Let's get Urie in here and see what he can tell us about
this deal," Lamb said. "It looks like this guy Tranmer's our
man."

"Seems like those Indians got some friends up there in
Idaho."

"Tranmer and Urie's got some enemies, too."

Charlie Muller pointed toward the window behind

Lamb. "Captain Donnelley's coming, Sheriff. He's crossing the street with Herb right now."

Lamb turned toward the window. "I guess we'll have to hear his two bits first," he said, "but bring Urie in here before he leaves. Maybe he can help us get the kid to talk."

Charlie Muller pulled up chairs for Captain Donnelley and Herb Baker, the editor of the *Star,* who had come to cover the captain's sales pitch for the paper. Lamb leaned back and lighted a cigar as Captain Donnelley began to explain the new Bertillon system to the men.

"A professional crook fears a camera and the Bertillon measurements worse than prison," Captain Donnelley told the men. "Knowing this system is used here, they will naturally keep away." The captain's gray eyes turned toward the editor. "Do you want to write that down, Mr. Baker?"

"Herb never writes anything down," Lamb told the captain. "He's got the kind of memory that will make your words come out sounding better than the way you said them."

Donnelley turned to Lamb and tried to smile. He kept his long dark coat buttoned all the way to the top button, and a small, tight knot in his narrow tie pinched against his neck. Only at Lamb's urging had he removed the hat that had kept his eyes in shadows. When managing a smile, his face seemed to be going through some difficult procedure. He pressed his lips back and exposed only his upper teeth. He directed toward Lamb the bleak look of a hanging judge.

"It's important for people to have a clear idea how the system works, Sheriff. Part of the system's effectiveness is the way it scares people away from committing crimes."

"Well, why don't you go ahead and explain it," Lamb said, "and we'll have Deputy Muller here take some notes."

"You're the one who will have to make it work, Sheriff," Donnelley said.

"But it's the county commissioners who have to approve it," Lamb said. "They're the ones who shell out the money. I just work for them."

"It's your recommendation that will make them decide."

"Maybe," Lamb said, "but they've got minds of their own. Like I say, I work for them."

Captain Donnelley explained that the Bertillon system, now used in almost every country in the world, was presently being installed in several Nevada counties. Photographs were kept of every man sent to the Nevada state prison, and with indexing of body measurements the matter of identification was made very simple. No two humans had exactly the same dimensions in certain parts of their bodies. Measurements of a person's head were classified on index cards and divided according to their general sizes. These classifications were then subdivided into groups according to the lengths of the left middle finger and the left little finger. If the lengths of the left forearm and left foot, as well as the length and width of the left ear, were also taken of any person suspected of a crime, the sum total of measurements would lead to the photograph and the positive identification of the criminal.

"Then what?" Lamb asked.

"Then the officers in other parts of the country would be able to identify suspects or to notify you of a criminal's past record and his present status, whether he's wanted elsewhere, for instance."

"I've got a joker locked up back there right now," Lamb said. "Do you mean I'd have to go back and measure his ears?"

Donnelley said that a picture of the left ear would suffice. Since the whorls and loops of the ear were unique to each individual, the convolutions of the ear provided one of the soundest means of identification. Close-up photographs of distinguishing marks and characteristics of the face also helped ensure positive identification.

Lamb turned to his deputy. "Charlie, did you notice any distinguishing characteristics on the person of that fellow locked up back there?"

"Urie's got that purple birthmark on his neck," Charlie Muller said, "where it looks like a mule kicked him. I didn't notice anything else."

"I know it's hard at first to see the value of *bertillonage*," Donnelley said. "We've had problems in counties where some of the older sheriffs are set in their ways. But we're living in changing times, Sheriff. The world isn't simple any more. You've got your foreign element filling up this country, and you've got outsiders from other states coming and going every day. There's no way to keep track of all these people without a scientific system."

"You mean you want to get everyone classified on those little index cards," Lamb said.

"That would be the ideal," Donnelley said, "but right now we have to concentrate on the criminal element. But if everyone was classified at a single location, the state police could identify victims of crimes, too, and even the victims of natural disasters."

Herb Baker interrupted to say that the Nevada State Police would be more effectively located if its headquarters were in Winnemucca rather than Carson City. In Winnemucca the police would have a central location from which to fan out to all areas of the state. During the troubles at the McGill copper mines, Baker pointed out, Donnelley could have gotten his troopers to Ely in half the time it took them to get there from Nevada's present capital on the far western border of the state. He certainly hoped Captain Donnelley, as the ranking captain of the Nevada State Police, would put his political support behind the upcoming legislative bill advocating the transfer of the state capital to Winnemucca.

Lamb lighted a cigar and Charlie Muller left the room. Baker and Donnelley continued to talk, agreeing that the next big mining boom would no doubt be in north-central Nevada. Tonopah and Goldfield were about played out, Baker said, and every township in Humboldt County contained indications of rich mineral deposits, not just of gold and silver, but of copper, borax, iron, manganese, cobalt, and antimony. The Stall brothers of the National mining district had just hit a ten-inch vein on their Radiator Hill property that was assaying out at eight hundred ounces of silver to the ton. It was just a matter of time until the future arrived in Humboldt County.

And the troubles, Donnelley added, maintaining that Ely and its copper mines were pointing out the direction of the future. What had killed the mines in the south, Donnelley said, was not the lack of ore, but the I-won't-work Wobblies who had come from Colorado to stir up trouble. If the Bertillon system had been in effect, it could have been proved that these were the same Wobblies who were agitating the Greeks and other riffraff in the Ely copper mines. The conditions of the strike were something the sheriff's department in Ely simply wasn't trained to handle—few county sheriff's departments were. It wasn't until the governor declared martial law, and Captain Donnelley arrived with ninety men and closed the smelter and the saloons, and disarmed both the strikers and strikebreakers, that order was restored. It was lucky that the whole incident had passed without erupting into violence. Strikebreakers had killed a couple of Greeks before Donnelley arrived, but nothing major had occurred. Even though the power of the unions was pretty much broken, Humboldt County would have to be ready for other efforts to disrupt the natural supply and demand of mining. Modern society was vulnerable to these mobs. Once one factory or mine went, they all went. People of property and enterprise were endangered. Foreign mobs, industrial strikes, and union agitators were things that called for trained and efficient control by state police. Didn't the sheriff agree?

"Now if I say yes," Lamb said, "you got me siding with the Guggenheims and those Philadelphia fatcats who are getting rich off our mines. Maybe it's time the workers got their share. Everybody's just trying to make a buck."

Charlie Muller returned to the room. "I think that kid's ready to talk, Sheriff," he said.

"Bring him out here. Maybe Captain Donnelley and Herb can help us."

Charlie Muller led the handcuffed boy into the room and seated him in a chair facing Lamb. Muller removed the handcuffs and the snub-nosed boy, his sandy hair flying in all directions, nervously rubbed his wrists. His damp face, except for the birthmark, looked colorless, his pale skin translucent with fear.

"Nimrod," Lamb said to the boy, "I think it's time you did some talking. This is Captain Donnelley of the Nevada State Police and he's seen several men like you in the penitentiary swinging from a rope. It's not pretty, Nimrod. Sometimes the rope breaks and a guy has to be hanged all over again. They take pictures and their necks are all stretched like sausages. Do you want your mother to see a picture like that?"

The boy's eyes looked electrified. Tiny threads of dried blood lined deep cracks in his chapped lips.

"We got a witness now, Nimrod, a man who says he heard you planning that robbery. He found your Colt revolver not far from the Blakeslee ranch, near the river, and the shells match the murders. He said he was with you running horses but left when you tried to get him to rob that saloon. The game's up, Nimrod. This fellow's willing to testify against you and see you hang. What's his name, Charlie?"

"Frank Tranmer," Charlie Muller said.

"That's right. Frank Tranmer. He's the witness we needed to see that you get the rope around your neck."

The boy's watery eyes looked glazed. "It's not true," he said. "He's the one who done the killing. He told me if I didn't come with him he would kill me. I didn't shoot nobody."

"Now who am I to believe, Nimrod, you or him?"

"I'm telling you the truth. I told Tranmer I didn't want to run horses and was going back to work on the sewer line, and he said we could get some easy money by robbing that Dago saloon. I said I didn't want to do it, and he said if I ran off he'd follow me and kill me, even if it took him ten years."

"Now why couldn't you tell us that before?"

"Tranmer said he'd kill my mother if I ever said anything against him. He said he could shoot her just as easy as he shot that Dago lady. I don't want to swing for what he did."

"And was it Tranmer who killed those Indians off the reservation last summer?"

Urie looked stunned. "Nobody killed no Indians. We come across some Indians with stolen horses and they attacked us. They killed Frankie Dopp. We reported that to the deputy sheriff up there."

Lamb slapped the kid hard across the mouth.

"Sheriff," Captain Donnelly said, "I don't think you should."

Lamb slapped Urie again. "Don't lie to me," he said. "You were doing good till now. Tell me the truth."

Urie began to sob. "I am telling you the truth. I swear it. I wouldn't lie about no ratty Indians. They jumped us when we found them camped up there changing brands on some horses."

"Get him out of here," Lamb said to Charlie Muller, who'd been writing down Urie's statement. "We got to pick up this guy Tranmer."

"The problem's finding him," Charlie said.

"If you can find that Basco kid, you'll find him," Lamb said. "He's right here in town working on that sewer line. We'll bring him in so Captain Donnelley can measure his ear."

Captain Donnelley stood up as Charlie Muller led Urie out of the room. "Maybe you can use your methods to get a kid like this to talk, Sheriff," Captain Donnelley said, "but in the future things will be more complicated. I need your support to help us get the Bertillon system set up in this state."

"I don't like it," Lamb said.

"I didn't either at first," Donnelley said, "but I accept the fact that we're living in a changing world. We have to curtail the professional criminal with the best scientific means at our disposal.

"It isn't the criminal I'm worried about," Lamb said. "It's who's going to be running these systems that concerns me."

"That shouldn't worry you," Donnelley said, "the Nevada State Police will be in charge."

13

Lamb sat alone smoking his cigar. Captain Donnelley had said the future was coming to Winnemucca and the state police would be in charge. Or the captain might have said the state police were in charge because the future with its automobiles, telephones, business interests, mining corporations, and real estate deals had already come to Winnemucca. Where towns grew up along the railroad, promising to become cities, Lamb knew that people had come to depend on the kind of law and order the state police represented. But he also knew that out in the cow camps and mines there was still a world where men like Tranmer and Urie grew up thinking they did not need such law.

"You're always going to have your criminal element," Donnelley had said, "your dangerous classes, those who just won't fit in. If they don't cause trouble, fine. If they do, they have to be controlled, and force is the only thing they know. But you're aware of that, Sheriff. You and I both know what we had to do when we went after Jim Taylor. And that was only one man. Today the problem is even greater because you're dealing with mobs, and mobs are insane."

Lamb imagined that Jim Taylor and Frank Tranmer were probably alike in a lot of ways. They probably weren't much better or worse than many buckaroos and miners in northern Nevada and southern Idaho but they always wanted their own way and they couldn't stay out of trouble. Before he shot and killed Taylor on Rodeo Flat northeast of Kelly Creek, Lamb had already arrested him twice before. The first time was after a man in a slouch hat and corduroy coat had robbed the Biggins Club saloon at four o'clock in the morning. Lamb had enough leads to be sure the bandit was Taylor, but he had no hard evidence. Like Tranmer, Jim Taylor had stayed around town, probably thinking his openness put him above suspicion. Lamb sweated him, released him, and after gathering more evidence, arrested him again, but a grand jury ordered Taylor's release and the judge admonished Lamb for bringing Taylor to court with only circumstantial evidence. He was always careful afterward to have evidence certain to stand up in court before making an arrest. When leaving the jail, Taylor told Lamb, "You're a pushy guy."

Two years later when Lamb and Sergeant Donnelley waited in the dark tent while Taylor talked to two buckaroos outside, they heard him tell the buckaroos that he'd like to shoot Lamb in the guts and watch him double up. Lamb remembered Donnelley's face slick with sweat in the flickering firelight. The state policeman lay on the floor of the tent rubbing the barrel of his gun. His hands were shaking. Lamb felt a coldness run through his own arms but he kept his hands rested on the stock of the shotgun. When he stepped out of the tent, Donnelley remained inside. Only after Taylor lay dead in the brush did the state policeman leave the tent. Lamb didn't know if he could've taken Taylor alive, no matter what he might've done that night. He only knew if he had it to do over again, he'd try something different.

Deputy Muller poked his head into the doorway of the office. "Sheriff," he said, "there's been some trouble down the street. We got Tranmer, but that Basque kid's been hurt."

When Lamb arrived in front of the Masonic and Odd Fellows Hall, a man in Levis knelt in the dirt pressing a handkerchief against the boy's nose. The wet handkerchief was exchanged for a clean one and a gush of blood ran down the boy's bare chest. People passing in the street looked in the direction of the few men who now gathered around the boy. Lamb squatted down next to the man in Levis; flecks of sunlight and shadows dappled the boy's dirty chest. The man said he'd seen two others kicking this one in the head until they grabbed their shovels and ran away.

"You say this kid was taking them both on?" Lamb said.

"Looked that way," the man said. "I guess he better get to a doctor."

"We're closer to my house," Lamb said. "Some of you men just haul him over there. No use paying a hospital when there's no need."

Nellie Lamb sponged the boy off in the kitchen and told him to take off his pants and put on her husband's nightshirt. Jean said he was all right now, but when he stood up from the chair where Nellie had been washing him, he grabbed for the sink and fell to the floor, causing his nose to bleed again. She stopped the bleeding with cotton and continued washing him. The boy seemed unconscious until his fingers weakly fluttered over Nellie's hands as she unbuttoned his pants, and then he closed his eyes again. She hooked his arm around her neck and helped the boy up. Washed and draped in Lamb's large nightshirt, he lay on the couch in the living room.

"Maybe he should go to the hospital," Charlie Muller said. "His face looks a mess."

"He's all right," Lamb said.

Dr. Giroux arrived and inserted two metal prongs into the boy's nostrils and twisted the nose until the bone popped. Jean, groaning, arched his back up from the couch.

"He's going to have a bump," Dr. Giroux said, "but he'll be able to breathe, once the swelling goes down."

That night, when Nellie looked in on Jean, he lay on his side facing the Isinglass front of the wood stove, and the light from the fire played across his face. The skin around both eyes was black.

The next day she went to the Eagle drugstore and returned with leeches floating in a jar of water. She placed a cool, spongy leech on the darkness under each of Jean's eyes and then returned them to the water to be cleansed and used again. When Jean's uncle arrived the following morning, the swelling under his eyes had gone down and the skin was greenish gray. "Why don't you move over to our house?" Paul Itzaina said. "We have the room and your aunt would like to see you." Jean shook his head and said he was all right and would return to the hotel.

Father Enright came to visit and gave him a set of rosary beads.

"What am I going to do with these?" Jean asked.

"You certainly know how to say the rosary," Father Enright said. "You might find a few prayers doing you some good."

"What I need is a gun," Jean said, "to get those sons of bitches."

Father Enright laughed. "You better leave them to the sheriff. It seems you have enough problems taking care of yourself."

As he left the house, Father Enright said to Nellie, "I hope you can talk some sense into this boy. He's certainly bitter."

"He has reason to be," Nellie said, "just look at his nose."

Late that afternoon, when the two Lamb boys, Kent and Ray, returned from school, the younger one, Ray, called into the kitchen, "Mom, something's wrong with Jean." He lay shivering on the couch, his body rigid under the blanket, his chest rising each time he struggled to suck air through his mouth. She stoked the fire and held a damp towel on the boy's forehead. With a spoon she fed him clear salty broth followed by a little brandy diluted with water.

The next day he was up, walking around, ready to leave, but Nellie asked that he stay one more night and watch the boys while she and Graham went to the musical in Golconda. Jean agreed to stay with the boys but wanted to get back to work the following morning. Then word came that there would be no more work for him on the sewer line. He had already been replaced and could draw the pay coming to him. The foreman didn't care who was right or wrong, he just didn't want any troublemakers on the job.

"We got Tranmer," Lamb told Jean. "He was at the stables looking like he was planning to leave town, but that kid Gibbs got away. Do you want to press charges?"

"No," Jean said, "I'll settle things myself."

"Best forget the whole thing and go back home," Lamb told him. "I'll want you to testify against Tranmer, but I'd just as soon not have Gibbs confusing a jury with his lies. As long as he stays out of town, I won't even think about him."

"Is it better if I pressed charges?" Jean asked.

"No," Lamb said, "you can if you want, but it wouldn't do any good. A fight's a fight."

"It wasn't a fair one," Jean said.

"They rarely are," Lamb said. "Let someone else catch up with that bum. It just wouldn't be smart to try to do it yourself."

That evening, the boys, Kent and Ray, taught Jean how to play five-card stud while their parents went with the Duckers to the Saval Opera House in Golconda to hear the singer Richard José. When Lamb and Nellie returned home they found a note from Jean. It said that he was writing the note ahead of time but was waiting until he heard them return before leaving through the back door. He thanked them for their help but just couldn't stay any longer. The boys were in bed, and they were fine.

"That's odd," Nellie said. "You'd think he'd at least stay to say good-bye."

"He must've made up his mind," Lamb said, "that he didn't need any more advice."

"It's still odd," Nellie said.

The next day, Lamb learned that Jean had left the Basque Hotel and was heading north to look for work. By the time of the Eagles Fall Carnival he was a mucker in the mines at National.

14

It was a high pop-up. The white ball climbed into the sky while the sound of the whack that sent it flying was still in Father Enright's ears. He stood to the left of home plate, and the man who'd hit the ball was running away from the priest, his back retreating, his blue-striped cap lifting from his head as he ran. The ball reached the peak of its upward climb, spinning for a moment like a planet or dead star before it slid into its downward arc and passed into the glare of the sun, no doubt causing a minor eclipse unobserved by everyone whose attention was more rigidly fixed on the outcome of this moment in the morning's history. A cheer went up. Father Enright scanned the flat outfield, spotted in the distance with greasewood and shadscale, where the white ball now rolled innocently along the cracked ground. The sweating man who'd lost his blue-striped cap stood on first base, drawing a mug of draft beer from the keg that awaited those who safely reached base. It was the third inning, and the score was Battle Mountain 5, Winnemucca 3.

"Have leisure and know that I am God," Father Enright had read in Psalms that morning. "Unless you become as children you shall not enter my Kingdom," he now thought as he watched the baseball game in the growing morning heat. He liked seeing these men playing like children. It made him feel that some things were right with the world. For a time the double murder in Imlay had flung him into depression. During the murder inquest he'd gone to the courthouse and heard the testimony of Nimrod Urie. The boy repeated the confession he'd made to Sheriff Lamb. Urie's youth and contriteness stunned the priest. He seemed so much like other kids around town, nothing like a murderer. The older man, Frank Tranmer, also reminded him of others who worked on ranches around Winnemucca. Tranmer insisted he was working on the sewer line at the time of the murders, and he claimed Nimrod Urie was trying to frame him. The man's passionate sense of being wronged disturbed Father Enright. He had to force himself to recognize that these men were killers.

After Battle Mountain won the baseball game, Father Enright found himself moving with a crowd to where the rock-drilling contest had already begun. It was getting hotter. The priest craned his neck to look over the sea of men's hats and women's parasols to the scaffolding that rose above the crowd. It reminded him of a gallows, and the shouts and intensity of the crowd, sweating in the blazing desert sun, reminded him of a gallows crowd. Two men were on the platform, and while one held the octagonal steel hand drill with its cutting edge against a solid block of granite, the other man swung the double-jack—an eight-pound hammer—striking the end of the steel drill and driving it into the granite. After each blow of the hammer, the man holding the drill gave it a partial turn. The speed of the jacker's swings was incredible, the head of the hammer a blur, and the blows of steel against steel produced a clanging that bore all the rapidity of a machine-driven trip-hammer. Father Enright could see how a good jacker might swing and strike the drill from any angle inside a narrow mine shaft, sometimes swinging the hammer and scarcely missing the head of the holder. Although pneumatic drills had replaced professional jackers in all the big mines, they had not replaced a good double-jacking team's pride in its ability to hammer a three-foot hole into the hardest rock in thirty or forty minutes.

A man shouted close to Father Enright's ear, his voice carrying a margin of hysteria that seemed connected to the mad clanging of the hammer, "Drive it, Daly, drive it, you cocksucker, drive it." People pressed against Father Enright. They pushed him closer to the platform where the clanging was louder and the shouts of the crowd more urgent. Over his head hung a hot airless vacuum. He felt panicky, unable to draw enough oxygen into his lungs with each gasping breath. He thought it was the wine; he shouldn't have had it so early in the day.

The scaffolding was badly built. Under the weight of the granite block and the violence of the swinging hammer the platform shook and swayed as if it were going to collapse. "They won't come into the money, Dickie boy, they can't slam right on that fucking platform. There's no leverage." The voice was that of a Cornishman, a Cousin Jack, as they were called. Father Enright had seen the man with the other contestants earlier that morning. He was solidly muscled and sunburned, stripped to the waist, covered with sweat. Grinning widely beneath a thick mustache, the man seemed to look through the priest as if he were a ghost while he continued to shout to his companion, "Damn me, but they're trying, Dickie boy, ain't they?"

"They can't find the hole," the other man said. "It's like diddling with a limp cock."

"Is that how it is with your Janie, Dickie boy? Does she make your cock go limp?"

"Damn you, Lou, me wife is better diddling than you got."

"She ought to be, mate, I broke her in meself." The man's laughter was convulsive, virulent. When Father Enright saw him earlier that morning he had been with the other jackers in front of a blacksmith shop where they were dressing and tempering the steel bits to be used in the contest. Steam hissed from the water tub where men plunged the hot drills. One of the Cousin Jacks was tossing what looked like pieces of raw liver to a pair of tame ducks in the street. The big man with the grin was hammering out a bar of red hot iron on an anvil. He chopped off small chunks of the iron and flicked them into the street along with the pieces of liver. Laughter overcame him as the hot pieces of metal, eaten by the unsuspecting ducks, burned through their crops and dropped to the ground.

Father Enright had felt sickened, and now he again turned away from the man and tried to push himself out of the crowd. He hated the way these men brought work into the carnival. Baseball was one thing, this was another. People pressed against him, and a roar rose from their throats. He turned to see that one of the men on the platform, while changing a drill, had flung the bit away and struck Daly, the jacker from Winnemucca, on the mouth. Daly spit blood and resumed hammering against the new drill. With the hammer flying against the bit and sounding like a clanging bell, the men on the weak platform looked like men trying to maintain their balance in a swaying rowboat. The crowd continued to cheer as inch by inch the bit drilled into the block of Gunnison granite, and the jacker continued to swing the hammer without pause while bright blood ran from his mouth.

On Railroad Street, he found another crowd in front of the Lafayette Hotel, where on a raised platform, District Attorney Ducker was leading the crowd in the "Yea! Yea!" cry of the Fraternal Order of Eagles. In a row behind him stood the five candidates for queen of the carnival.

"Isn't it a wonderful day, Father?" Mrs. Giroux, the mother of a queen candidate, clutched the priest's fingers into her wet palm and pulled him toward her as she spoke into his ear, pressing close against him and forcing him into the thick, sweet aureole of perfume rising from her moist skin.

"I'm sorry I'm not feeling well, Mrs. Giroux," he said.

He remembered Mrs. Garrity's face coming up to him

in a similar way that morning after she had snatched his hat off the foot of the bed. Her gray lips parted and her tongue quivered as she told him that it was bad luck to put a hat on a bed. Since he had grown up in a household ruled by superstition, there lingered in him a vague tolerance for Mrs. Garrity in her daily battle against the forces of darkness. She was careful never to step over a broom or sweep dirt out the front door or leave her house if she heard an owl hoot. Once after a visit from Dr. Giroux and his daughter, she showed Father Enright the inside of Dora's coffee cup where coffee grounds had formed a ring on the bottom of the cup. "She's going to be kissed," Mrs. Garrity said.

Father Enright now looked at Dora standing with the other girls on the platform as District Attorney Ducker extolled the virtues of the queen candidates. "Each of these great little gals is a dead game sport," the district attorney said, "and each of them is a real queen, but for the next three days the one who will be our queen, the royal queen of Humboldt County, is Miss Dora Giroux."

A cry of the Eagles' "Yea! Yea!" went up from the crowd as Dora accepted her prize of a fifty-dollar all-silk dress. She moved to the center of the platform to be crowned. Standing in a white satin dress with her thick hair piled high on her head, she received a long kiss from the district attorney. Next to her stood the blond-haired and dark-eyed princess, Edna Purviance, holding the crown on a velvet pillow. Dora turned to face the audience. Father Enright was looking directly at the girl above him, on the raised platform, as she sat down, and he found himself staring at the crotch of bright bloomers, exposed like a white star, between the girl's two brown knees. Father Enright watched transfixed as District Attorney Ducker took the crown from Edna Purviance and placed it on Dora's head.

"In the name of the people of the empire of Humboldt," he said, "I crown you queen of the carnival. As this crown encircles your brows, it will also encircle your throne with a wall of patriotism through which treason cannot enter. It will encircle your empire with a wall of strength through which no foreign foe can come. Long live the queen!"

People cheered and clapped. He felt Mrs. Giroux, in her excitement, grab his arm. He jerked away with such violence that his hand accidentally flicked sharply against her cheek. "Oh, Father," Mrs. Giroux said, holding her hand against her cheek, her eyes pained and astonished.

"I'm sorry, sorry," he said. "Really, I'm unwell, so I must. Go." His face flushed and sweaty, he pushed himself through the crowd.

He found himself on the edge of town. The sun flared against the sky like a blowtorch. The voices of children drifted from a field where boys in a three-legged potato race kicked up puffs of alkali. A dull dusty haze hovered over the town, and crowds milled through the streets with a late-summer apathy.

He felt a tug on the sleeve of his cassock and turned to see a tall, young Paiute, obviously drunk, wearing a dirty yellow shirt and a baseball cap. "You help him Johnny," the Paiute said. "Need money to eat."

Father Enright so rarely encountered Indians in town that he was taken aback. The Paiute pushed a piece of paper into the priest's hands. Father Enright unfolded the worn piece of paper, splitting at the creases. Scrawled in pencil was a smeared message: "This here Injun is name Jonie Bliss. He wold be a good Injun if someone kilt him—Ha ha!"

"Do you know what this says?" he asked the man.

The Indian grinned, showing black stumps of broken teeth. "He say Johnny Bliss good Indian. Give him money."

"I can't help you get drunk," Father Enright said. "You can come to see me when you're sober."

A scowl crossed Johnny Bliss's face. The devilish grin vanished. Glaring at the priest were flat, black, inhuman eyes.

Father Enright shoved the piece of paper into the man's hands and walked quickly toward the safety of the crowd. A row of shouting children startled him. They wore capes and masks from the morning parade, looking like creatures of the night, strangely out of place in the sunlight as they howled at the priest and ran toward the boys' three-legged race in the open lot.

Father Enright held his forehead as he hurried toward home. He felt as though a slab pressed against his skull. He wasn't sure what was happening to him, why he'd hurt Mrs. Giroux's feelings, why he'd shunned Johnny Bliss. He couldn't believe how different he felt from earlier that morning when he was watching the men play baseball. The Gospels were right. It was children we must become like. Our Lord had said so.

He was scarcely aware of where he'd been walking when he looked up to see piles of dirt along the open sewer trenches of West Second street. A small child, no more than three or four years old, knelt precipitously over an open trench while he pushed an imaginary car or truck through the dirt. "Oh, my God," the priest said. He felt given a providential sign.

Calling to the child in a low, controlled voice, he hurried toward him. "Don't move, sonny, stay right where you are." He took the little boy by the hand and led him away from the mound of dirt. It was then, when the child seemed on firm ground, that Father Enright felt himself falling. His body slammed against the ground and he found himself looking up to see framed by the edges of the trench the faces of two older women who were looking down at the priest, covered with dirt at the bottom of the ten-foot sewer trench where he had fallen and now sat bruised, his face twisted with shock, holding his ankle and looking up at the women, as he said, trying to sound calm, "I think my ankle is broken."

15

During the night, after hearing of Father Enright's accident, Lamb received word of Justice Fitts's suicide. The justice had entered the Silver Dollar and dumped eight ounces of strychnine into a tumbler of whiskey. He fell to the floor in convulsions. The saloon singer Cynthia got her finger bitten to the bone while trying to keep the man from choking. Dr. Giroux arrived with a stomach pump and a hypodermic needle, but the dose of strychnine had been too large. It was learned that Fitts had already made arrangements with an undertaker in Lovelock for his burial, and had sent his money, watch, and diamond ring to his mother in Kansas.

"What a waste," Nellie said when Lamb told her. "He was such an elegant man. Who would've thought he'd kill himself in such a way?"

The next morning, after three hours' sleep, Lamb was back in his office when the district attorney and the district judge from Elko came to question his prisoners—Tranmer and Urie—about the Indian murders in northern Elko County the previous spring.

"I'm glad you fellows didn't let our fall carnival get in the way of your investigation," Lamb said. "I'm sure you couldn't have waited a day or two until it was over. After all,

Tranmer and Urie have only been locked up for over a week, and another day or two would've made all the difference in the world."

"We didn't know," the district attorney said.

"Didn't know what?"

"About the carnival," the judge said.

"You're here now," Lamb said, "so let's get on with it."

The district attorney from Elko, Jay Dysart, did most of the talking, explaining that the man in jail by the name of Frank Tranmer was most likely the same man as the J. F. Tranmer from Idaho who'd been reported killed in northern Nevada earlier that spring. "You've got a dead man locked up there, Sheriff."

"No wonder he didn't want to give us his name," Lamb said.

The judge explained that while Tranmer, Urie, and some others were running wild horses near the border the previous spring, Tranmer's sixteen-year-old nephew, Frankie Dopp, was reported murdered. A few weeks later word came that Tranmer himself had been killed.

"We want to know why he wanted people to think he was dead," the district attorney said. "Some people think he killed that Dopp boy. There was also a robbery in Jackpot about that time, and we think Tranmer had something to do with that, too. If people thought he was dead, they wouldn't be looking for him."

"He's all yours," Lamb said. "You just tell Deputy Muller here who you want to talk to and he'll fix you up. But I'd talk to Nimrod Urie first. He's the one who spilled the beans about the murders in Imlay. He's a scared kid and he might sing."

Lamb went downtown to eat breakfast. He met Dr. Giroux and learned that Father Enright's ten-foot fall into the sewer trench had left him with a dislocated ankle and some bruises, nothing serious. During the night, though, the priest seemed in a state of nervous shock and Dr. Giroux thought he should have a period of recuperation away from Winnemucca. The bishop gave permission for the priest, as soon as he could travel, to leave for a week's rest with his sister in Sacramento.

"It's been a busy carnival," Dr. Giroux said.

"Fitts got things off to a good start," Lamb said. He told the doctor that people in Lovelock, a week before the suicide, had learned of Fitts's embezzlement of county funds for the past year. "It's funny how long he went before people found out he was stealing their gambling fees," Dr. Giroux said.

"He collected the fees," Lamb said, "and he pocketed 'em. Who would know?"

"If he could've gotten by a few more months, he might've gotten away with it. If that new antigambling law goes through, he wouldn't have had any more fees to embezzle."

"Something else would've happened," Lamb said. "Fitts had a lot of problems."

"It's funny how people will react to things. As soon as Fitts gets threatened with losing his job he kills himself."

"That's right," Lamb said, "and as soon as people find out he's been taking their county funds, nobody gives a damn whether or not he's chasing after some young actress in Reno. They just want to know how much of their money he got."

"He might've gotten a little more sympathy if he'd killed himself over a woman."

"Maybe," Lamb said.

When Lamb returned to his office, the Elko district attorney and the district judge were getting ready to leave.

"They stuck together on this one," the judge said. "Tranmer now claims that Frankie Dopp was actually his stepson, and he was outraged that anyone would suggest he killed his own stepson."

"Nimrod Urie supported everything he said," the district attorney added. "They both insist they came across some Shoshone with stolen stock and the Shoshone panicked and murdered Tranmer's stepson and ran off with some of Tranmer's own horses. Urie and Tranmer took off after them but couldn't catch them."

"How could a bunch of Indians, especially women and children, disappear like that without leaving a trace?" Lamb asked. "Why in hell doesn't somebody dig up those pits where people say those Indians are buried? If it was my county, I would."

"Deputy Sheriff Grimm is the one who found those pits," the district attorney said, "and he didn't report seeing any bodies. If Tranmer and Urie killed any Indians, I don't think they'd bother burying them."

"If you thought some ranchers were buried up there, you'd be digging them up."

"All the information we've gotten supports what Tranmer and Urie have been telling us."

"What did Tranmer have to say about being dead?" Lamb asked.

"He claims he didn't know anything about it. Urie didn't either. Tranmer figures some friends assumed he'd been killed when he took off after the Shoshone and didn't return to Twin Falls."

"I'll tell you what the problem is," Lamb said. "When we caught Urie after the robbery in Imlay, we found that kid's bedroll crammed full of magazines about outlaws and rustlers. That's the problem right there. Those guys think they're in a magazine story."

"Maybe so," the district attorney said, "but they're sticking to the story."

"So you fellows haven't learned a thing," Lamb said. "Coming all this way on a holiday, too. And now you're going back not knowing any more than you did when you left. It's just too bad."

"We did learn something," Judge Tabor said. "That Indian you got locked up back there says the pine nuts in the mountains have shells twice as thick as usual and we got a cold winter coming."

"I wish it would hurry up and get here," Lamb said. "This heat is making everybody goofy. It's curdling their brains."

"We appreciate your help today, Sheriff. We know you're busy, but this visit has helped us."

"You boys might try talking to some of the Indians around Elko, they always know things you'll never know."

"I think we've learned as much as we're going to learn, Sheriff. Whether those Indians are back on a reservation or dead in those trenches, they're gone. It's not official, of course, but as far as we're concerned, this case is closed."

16

Mike and his family were on foot, hot and thirsty, leading their horses west through low greasewood and saltbrush. Lizards, their throats pumping in the heat, stood motionless under spiky bushes. Ahead, between low dark cliffs, the dark fissure of Little High Rock Canyon split the hills. Shiny obsidian glass covered the white cracked ground. At the entrance to the canyon hawks began screeching, and their screams echoed from the rimrock.

The canyon opened into marshy meadows of Indian rice grass. A breeze smelling of mint blew through the river willows. A pair of ducks flew up from behind a beaver dam. Kinglets and blackbirds and meadowlarks buzzed and trilled from the reeds. Wild roses grew among the sage. Hundreds of sagehens, flashing their salmon-colored feathers, whirred out of the grass and up the canyon sides.

Mike's sixteen-year-old daughter, Henie, carried the youngest baby on her back as she walked along the grassy bank of the stream on the canyon floor. A crashing noise came behind her when an antlered buck broke from the brush where he'd been hiding as she passed. With his neck curved into an arrogant S, the deer pranced unhurriedly up the sloping canyon side. Halfway up the draw, he stopped and turned his rubbery neck to look back over his shoulder at the people. After they made their camp, Henie's brothers went out and came back with the deer to eat. That night, the high-stepping deer came to her in a dream and he was singing, but she did not know what the singing meant.

Now over three hundred miles from where her brother had been murdered and buried, Henie camped with her family in Little High Rock Canyon. For the first time since leaving Gollaher Mountain she crawled into a wickiup and lay with her face against the warm sage on the floor of the hut. Everything had been out of order since they'd left their home. They had had no wickiups to sleep in, no menstrual huts for her and her sisters, no sweat huts for baths. They'd just kept running across the desert toward the west.

In Little High Rock Canyon her father said they would make a wickiup and stay for a while. "We'll camp up there," he told his family, "where it looks like Rock Creek Canyon." There was plenty to eat in the canyon, and while her brothers hunted, Henie helped her mother. She hated to see her mother and father so tired. She wondered whether they would ever go back home, but her father said nothing about it. He just said they'd wait now in Little High Rock Canyon, and see what happened for a while. At night he smoked his pipe and told his family, "This is a good place, this canyon where we are now. It's a good place to spend the winter."

Henie helped her mother repair the children's clothes and shoes and tan the hide of the deer her brothers had shot. She also began making a cooking basket from river willows. She'd learned the proper way to make things after she came of age as a woman. That was when she began going to the menstrual hut. She'd watched her mother go to the hut regularly every month, but the first time she went she had to stay for thirty days. They were living at Rock Creek then, and her mother made her go to the hut as soon as she knew Henie's blood was coming. It was a strange time. There was a power loose, and Henie could feel it in the hut. After her first day in the hut, before dawn, her sister, Wenegaw, came to her and said, "Wake up, Henie. Let's run and get some water at the other side of that mountain."

"We can get water here," Henie said.

"Don't be so lazy," her sister said. "You'll end up with a good-for-nothing old man."

Every morning during that time Henie gathered water and firewood and stacked the wood outside her father's wickiup while he was still asleep. Her mother later brought food to her, but no meat and nothing with salt in it. Sometimes her sisters came to the hut secretly to talk and play with her, but it was a dangerous time and the men stayed away. They were afraid of women's blood. Henie had watched how carefully her own mother went to the hut for two or three days as soon as the time came every month. She went right away and did not touch or even look at Mike's rifle or knives or spears. The power that came to a woman could so weaken her husband that if he had to fight at that time he would be killed. Henie was careful not to touch her own hair with her fingers for the power visiting her could so weaken the power that made her hair grow it would die and fall out of her head. Her mother came to comb it for her, and it continued to grow long and dark, even when she was asleep.

Once there was an old woman Henie liked because she was fat and laughed all the time but the woman was actually a witch. After she was near this woman, Henie became sick. She felt about to die. The sage tea her mother gave her did no good. A stick doctor came from the reservation. He was a poor man and wore only rags, but he had great power. He asked Henie, "How are you? Are you still there?" The blood came into Henie's mouth when she said, "I'm almost gone." The man twirled his fire drill until the tip was hot. He pressed the hot stick against Henie's stomach and left it there until it made a mark. He then worked her body with his hands. His hands felt strong and warm. She felt the pain moving out of her stomach.

"Soon the morning star will rise up," the man said. "After that, there will be a star brighter than the morning star. You'll feel better then."

The man left and everything happened as he said. The morning star rose, Henie got up from her bed, a brighter star appeared, and the following morning she was playing and laughing with her sisters.

Henie knew the real world was full of powers and their forms were always changing. It was not possible to judge only by appearances. She had to learn to read signs, to discern good from harmful powers. Her older sisters teased her when they came to her hut. "What was that hot stick the doctor put on you?" they asked. "Tell us again about the doctor who put the hot stick on your belly." Then they all laughed at her and she chased after them.

Henie did not know whether she would like to be a married woman. She knew on the reservation married people seemed to have a lot of trouble with each other. When young men came from the reservation it was her oldest sister who threw dirt at them and then ran away through the sagebrush as they chased her. Henie saw how when her sister sat with young men, she sometimes lifted her legs when she got up and showed everything, and the young men could see all the way up to her teeth. Her mother told them, though, they must never sleep with men until they were married. Henie heard how men sometimes used a strong, sweet-smelling root to attract deer when they were hunting. It made women come, too. Once when they were gathering pine nuts a young man from Tecoma came and at night she could smell the sweat on his hands and it made her afraid. She told her mother, and her mother said it was all right, all good women were afraid of men, but there was no need to be too afraid because women were strong too. They made the men.

During the month Henie spent in the menstrual hut the days were long and boring. Without other people sleeping close to her, the nights were cold. When she finished her morning's work she returned to the small hut and crawled alone through the open doorway. By then the sun was high in the sky. The hut was full of the warm smell of shredded sagebrush on the floor. Henie lay down. The sagebrush pressed against her face. Dust specks hung in the sunlight in front of her eyes. The voices of her brothers and sisters lingered in the distance. A sage sparrow fluttered to the ground in the doorway of the hut and cocked his head, as if ready to speak. Behind the sparrow the world stretched away into a deserted plain of sagebrush and greasewood. A spider weaving her thread from the willow doorway stopped, as if she understood something, and looked at Henie. It seemed as if the light of innumerable days glowed in that morning's sunlight. In the distance the dark rimrock on the hills was pushing itself out of the folds of the earth. Through the door of the hut Henie looked out and saw the world as it was, a place where Wolf and Coyote and all the powers of the earth still moved and breathed.

In the dark of morning her mother came and took her out of the hut to Rock Creek where Henie waded into the water and washed herself. The cold made her skin bumpy and numb. Her mother gave her a new dress and shawl to wear. She painted her face and they returned to the camp where all the men, her father and brothers, waited.

She learned from her mother how to boil small willows, split them, and weave them into a water bottle the shape of a falling raindrop. She learned to coat the inside of the bottle with pitch to make it hold water. She learned how to scrape hair from the skin of the deer by using a bone from the deer itself. She learned how to wash the hide and to soften it with the deer's own brains, to pull and stretch it until it was ready to be smoked over a fire or rubbed with clay until it was white.

Now, far from home, camped in Little High Rock Canyon, she again helped her mother while her brothers helped her father. Her father and brothers made arrow shafts and chipped obsidian into points. It was easy to find lots of obsidian in the canyon. As Henie watched her father and brothers work, it seemed at times that everything was as it had been when they lived at Rock Creek and Gollaher Mountain. But it wasn't the same. She couldn't forget that her oldest brother wasn't there. Her father and other brothers looked different as they worked, and her mother and sisters looked different, too. Her oldest brother was gone, and the sadness of missing him made them all look different.

As the summer ended, buckaroos and herders began driving their stock through Little High Rock Canyon. Every day more men appeared on horseback and Henie's father said they had to leave.

Too many people were coming through the canyon, Mike said. They frightened away the animals and it was harder to hide. If something happened to these men's cattle, they'd be blamed for it. Henie knew her father was angry.

"There's nothing else to do," he said. "These people are too unpredictable. They can never be trusted. The only thing to do is to get away from them."

They left Little High Rock Canyon and rode with their strings across Surprise Valley to Cedarville. Mike went with two of his sons into town to the store for flour, sugar, and cans of milk. Henie stayed with the rest of her family and the horses. When some white men came near, her brothers Wonig and Hogozap rode toward them and told them to get away. Henie was afraid whenever she saw white people. She always thought they would try to kill her or take her away. She'd learned that whites didn't respect themselves or their word because they had no respect for what came before them. They killed animals from great distances with their rifles. They ripped up the camas fields and blew up mountains to get gold and silver. They made the land look sad. They were wild, always going against the way things were. Henie knew this was true because they took things out of the earth without putting anything back. It was just like in the story her father told about Coyote who took beads from the rock without giving the rock something, as he was told to do. "I'll never pay," Coyote said. The rock rolled down the hill and crushed him. Only Coyote's tail stuck out from beneath the rock.

When they left Cedarville, they rode into the low junipers and piñons of the Warner Range. The evergreens grew taller, rising high above their heads as they crossed Cedar Pass and continued westward, riding toward the high country of the Sierra Nevada. Now they changed horses more often. They rode through mountain mahogany. Aspen leaves, stirred by the wind, green on one side and silver on the other, set whole groves shimmering. They rose into high forests of spruce and fir that hid the sun. The ground grew soft with thick layers of decaying pine needles. The air cooled and darkened. They worked their way through ridge after ridge of the Sierras until the sky opened up and they saw falling away to the west the descent of the forest into rolling hills of yellow grass and scattered oak trees. Even farther west there came into view a shimmering line coursing through the valley toward a broader sheet of water. On the other side a low blue range of hills marked the horizon. Beyond was the ocean. Mike and his family were as far west as they would go.

They dropped south into the Sacramento Valley and helped themselves to the late summer fruit in the orchards and melons in the fields. Harvest crews of Indians and Mexicans moved through the valley picking peaches and apricots and cantaloupes. In the evenings the air thickened with the warm smell of fruit. The earth gave off a fertile black odor. The sun itself seemed to be ripening as each day it flared swollen in the west before it died, and the evening glow in the fields and orchards deepened.

The nights grew cooler, and with hints of winter in the air, Mike and his family left the valley and circled back toward Nevada. There was nowhere else to go. Hogozap told Henie that in the Nevada canyons they had the best chance to live as they once had at Rock Creek, but her father said they would stay there only for the winter. Henie wondered if then they would go home. In the spring it would be a year since her brother's death. She'd seen other families do the same thing, leave the scene of violent death until order was restored. They'd done what they were supposed to do. She wondered if they'd now return.

As Mike and his family left the California foothills, aspen leaves now flashed yellow in the sun, lighting up the hillsides. They climbed toward the white granite and dark green pines of the Sierras. It began to snow steadily and when it was not snowing the wind still filled the air with snow. Across the main range of the Sierras, their horses were buried belly-deep in snow drifts. Wind whipped off the glacial expanses above them. They huddled together for days and burned fires in dead tree trunks. The men took turns breaking trails through the snow, frequently changing horses as they drove them to exhaustion. In the mornings they began to find the horses dead. Their clothes grew ragged. More horses died. Their feet and hands, wrapped in rags, looked like bruised rocks. They smeared charcoal under their eyes and wrapped their faces in rags as shade against the hard glaring ice fields. As the sun softened the ice, the horses broke through crusts into deep drifts. Henie took turns with her sister carrying the year-old baby on her back.

With only a few horses left, they reached the Warner Range and climbed to Cedar Pass. The sky behind them was dark, ahead it was pale and clear. They descended toward the warmer tan and gray rolling hills and snow-patched flats of Surprise Valley. They passed Eagleville and headed southwest until the Calico Mountains parted and opened into the western entrance of Little High Rock Canyon. Deep in the canyon where the walls grew steep, Mike returned to where they'd camped the previous summer, high on the north-facing wall. Lichen on the dark wall grew like moss. On the opposite side of the canyon, lichen streaked the wall like rust.

They bent and tied cut willows into a frame for the wickiup. They built a rock fireplace and a low rock wall that extended down to a semicircular lookout shelter. They moved rocks on the sloping scree field west of their camp to form a level path running from the lookout to the side canyon where the path then switchbacked down to the canyon floor. The basalt walls echoed with the scraping sounds of rock. Shredded sagebrush bark on the path muffled the hooves of horses led up to the camp. High up on the ledge the wintry wind sounded like the rumble of thunder. When the wind stopped, a stillness filled the air. Pure and piercing notes seemed disembodied from the tiny wren singing on the distant rock wall. On the canyon floor the sagebrush grew like trees, but from the camp three hundred feet high, Henie looked down to where the sage seemed no bigger than tiny clumps of winter bunch grass.

Now they were warm at nights in the wickiup. A fire glowed in the shielded rock pit. Plenty of animals still lived in the canyon, and Henie's brothers brought back rabbits and sagehens. They went into a line shack one day and took salt, flour, some tins of evaporated milk, and ammunition. From an old rock blind built by Indians years in the past, they waited for deer to come. Her brothers hunted and Henie helped her mother and sister cook and repair the clothes they had torn and worn thin while crossing the Sierras.

In January, blizzards hit the canyon and the earth became frozen and white. There was no food. Henie's brothers scurried down the canyon wall to where bawling cattle wandered aimlessly through drifts. They slaughtered and butchered a steer on the canyon floor and returned to the camp with the shoulder quarters. They killed five more steers as they needed them and let the snow fall on the carcasses.

One day a lone rider approached from the east and rode along the south side of the creekbed directly toward where slaughtered cattle lay partially buried in drifting snow. He dismounted and looked closely at the carcasses. Henie's brothers wanted to shoot him, but her father said no. They would wait to see how much this man cared about these cattle. Her father must have known there would be others because the next day the same man was seen from the distance returning with three other men on horseback. Now it was clear that the men were returning to go after whoever killed the cattle. Henie's brothers hurried down the side of the draw to hide in the willows south of the cattle. The four men rode along the rimrock above the canyon until they reached the side canyon west of the camp. They dismounted and led their horses down the draw, oblivious of the people watching them as they passed Mike's camp. They continued down the draw and out of sight from those in the lookout. Henie was in the camp with her mother and sisters and the younger children. She saw nothing of what happened as the men reached the canyon floor and led their horses toward the frozen beef and the willows. The four men continued to walk toward the red willows where her brothers lay hidden with their rifles. High on the ledge in the sheltered camp Henie heard through the wind the popping of guns in the canyon before everything was silent once again.

III
BATTLE AT
RABBIT CREEK

17

Mort West was with the group of men who found the bodies. He'd come over the pass from Alturas to see his friend Frank Perry who was laid up with the pleurisy. Not much was happening on any of the ranches where Mort had worked in the fall, and he'd decided to stay in Surprise Valley and spend a few midwinter afternoons around the stove in the Eagleville store. He liked to visit the homestead where Frank Perry lived with his parents and twelve brothers and sisters. Although Mort had distant cousins and relatives on the other side of the Warner Range, his own father, mother, brother, and sister had all burned to death at a community Christmas tree party when he was nine. His father had pushed him out a small window just before the burning hall collapsed. Ever since then Mort had been pretty much on his own, moving from ranch to ranch, getting what work he could. His friend Perry usually worked the homestead, where he had more than enough to do with all his brothers and sisters, but he sometimes took on side work as a teamster to help bring in money for his family. Perry was twenty-two, the oldest in the family, but he looked younger lying on the couch with his dark eyes and long eyelashes like a girl's. Mort was twenty-four.

"I've been thinking about looking for some steady work

for a change," Mort said. "Maybe with one of the outfits over here."

Perry started to smile. He had a soft voice. "I was thinking the same thing, Mort. Only I was thinking of going over the pass to where you were."

The thought of them both simultaneously changing jobs and again ending up on opposite sides of the pass struck Mort as funny, even probable. "I guess it doesn't much matter which side of the pass we're on. We're both going to be doing the same thing anyway."

"But we're not making no progress," Perry said.

"Who the hell ever said we would?"

Perry started to laugh, but his cough took over. His lungs sounded like churning washtubs until his sister came from the kitchen with hot brandy and water.

Mort had heard about the missing stockmen at Brown's Joint, where he sometimes shot pool. A woman outside the Eagleville Store told him, "It's Harry Cambron and three others. They went out to check on their stock three weeks ago, and they never have come back." At the pool hall, Mort ran into some vaqueros who were getting ready to look for the missing men. They were talking about horse thieves who'd been seen near Little High Rock Canyon. "We're afraid they might've met Cambron's party and killed them," a man told Mort.

Mort recognized a few vaqueros who worked around Eagleville, then he saw his friend Henry Hughes, a buckaroo on the Bare Ranch, who smiled and said, "This is another man we want. Get your gear, Mort."

Mort wasn't well known around Surprise Valley, and a horse wrangler, Joe Reeder, a tall, unsmiling man in his mid-thirties, glowered at him. "You'll have to furnish your own outfit."

"He's a good man, Joe," Henry Hughes said. "I'll answer for that."

The next morning it was snowing when Mort rode out of Eagleville with the search party. There were ten of them altogether, including Dr. Kennedy, and six packhorses with supplies. By noon they were out of Surprise Valley, pushing their horses through drifts over the East Warner Range. Mort rode behind the cowboss Ottie Van Norman. He watched snow pile on the haunches and melt down the dark flanks of Van Norman's horse. From morning to after-noon, there was no change in the day's dim light. The horses moved eastward. The snow continued to fall. The men rode draped in coats, their shoulders white with snow, hunched on their horses in immovable curves, as if asleep. Over the edge of the scarf covering his nose and mouth, Mort's eyes fixed on Van Norman's recent haircut where the razor had scraped clean white lines in the skin behind Van's ears.

They spent the night at the Cambron home camp from where Harry Cambron formerly oversaw company cattle running east into Nevada. The men at the home camp cal-culated they'd last seen their boss and the two sheepmen heading toward the Denio homestead in the middle of Janu-ary. Now it was the second week in February.

The next morning the sky was blue, brilliant with white clouds, and Mort was again riding behind Van Norman, gazing at the white lines of Van's scalp and the white glare of sun on ice. In the afternoon, a leafless cottonwood rose against the skyline as the men approached the small house and sheds of Billy Denio's homestead, about five miles from Little High Rock Canyon. The temperature dropped as it grew dark, and the men pulled sagebrush to make fires. Billy's wife called them into the small house for hot beans and bread.

Billy Denio, a stocky, dark man of fifty, told them that one day, about three weeks earlier, a Basque camptender named Bertrand Indiano had arrived at the homestead from the muddy playa called High Rock Lake, where sheepmen grazed their stock during the winter. The camptender was on his way to Eagleville for supplies. He'd left the winter range and was riding through Little High Rock Canyon when he came upon some dead cattle covered with snow. He dismounted for a closer look and found that the beef had been shot in the forehead. The upper quarters had been butchered, and the remains lay frozen to the ground.

On the same day that the camp tender was telling his story and drinking coffee in the Denios' kitchen, the cattleman Harry Cambron arrived from Eagleville with the two Basque sheepmen, Peter Erramouspe and John Laxague, riding east to check on their stock in the winter range. The camptender told Harry Cambron about the cattle, but Harry, who was young, happy, and about to be married in Eagleville, said he'd heard the same news from a rider earlier in the week. He laughed and said they'd all have a look in the morning.

The camptender seemed spooked. It was only at the insistence of his bosses, Erramouspe and Laxague, that he joined the stockmen the next morning instead of going into Eagleville for supplies. They intended to ride along the high windy north rim of the canyon rather than try to fight through the snow on the canyon floor. They would then cut down into the canyon to where the camptender had seen the butchered beef. When they rode out toward the mouth of the canyon, none of the four men carried weapons, except the cattleman Harry Cambron, who had only a thirty-eight-caliber pistol. That was the last Billy Denio saw of them.

Two weeks passed before another sheepherder rode into the Denio homestead from High Rock Lake. He reported that he'd become worried when the camptender never returned with supplies for the sheepcamp. Concerned that the men hadn't even reached High Rock Lake, twelve miles away, Billy Denio wrote notes for the herder to carry to Mrs. Erramouspe and Mrs. Laxague in Eagleville. About the same time the girl in Eagleville engaged to Harry Cambron also became alarmed. When Harry had left he told Laura he'd return in two weeks, plenty of time before their wedding. But the two weeks came and went. Laura persuaded young Warren Fruits, a friend of the family, to ride to the Denio homestead to see what he could learn. When the boy returned to Eagleville, news spread through town that three Basques and the young cattleman Harry Cambron were missing in the canyons of the Calico Mountains.

The morning after their arrival at the Denio homestead, Mort and the other men rode to Little High Rock Canyon, its mouth a jagged black gash in the mountains. They agreed that anyone finding signs of the missing men should fire three shots into the air. Mort rode and walked through pale rye grass along the frozen creek that curved and turned for seven miles through the canyon. The sage grew like low trees, shoulder-high, sometimes head-high. On the ridge of the canyon above him, the outline of Ottie Van Norman's hat appeared against the sky before it dropped out of sight. The afternoon light grew thinner. A covey of sagehens burst from the grass and flew up the side of the canyon, their fluttering wings lit like flying halos. At noon, the men found the remains of the six butchered cattle, dead now for over a month. A cottontail moved through the grass in tentative hops and then huddled motionless under the sagebrush.

It was Warren Fruits, nicknamed Fruity, the youngest and smallest of the group, who was looking through some scrubby red willows near the south wall of the canyon when he saw what looked like tracks in the snow and a man's cap. He dismounted and led his horse through the brush when he saw a frozen hand and arm sticking out of the snow.

Sounds of gunfire scattered up and down the canyon walls. Mort cocked the lever of his rifle and rode toward the shots. A riderless horse stood stiffly in the cold, its head drooping, a back leg cocked. The other men rode forward to where Fruity knelt in the snow. On the ground lay steaming cartridge casings the kid had fired in panic. The boy's back was quivering. Mort knelt beside him. Partially buried in the snow were the bodies of the four missing men, on their stomachs, frozen together side by side.

The men lifted Fruity to his feet. The sandy-haired boy was muttering, "My God, my God." His face was white, his eyes pale as water.

Mort scraped away snow, careful not to touch the bodies. The four dead men lay head to foot, their undershirts pulled over their heads, arms extended. Each man looked to have been shot several times. One man's frozen buttock was exposed in the snow. Mort pulled ice away from another man's face. It was the Basque sheepman Peter Erramouspe. Under his nose was a jagged notch where his thick dark mustache and upper lip had been cut away from his face.

Mort cleared more snow from around the dead men's faces until a voice said, "It's best just to leave them the way they are." It was Dr. Kennedy, who'd just walked into the circle of men. "There'll have to be an inquest," he said.

"Can't you do it?" Joe Reeder asked.

"We're in Nevada now," the doctor said. "Someone will have to come out from Reno."

"It'll be days before they get here and get these bodies out."

"What difference does it make?" Mort said. "These boys are as dead as they're going to get."

The men decided that the kid Fruity, warmed with whiskey and eager to be on his way, should ride to Eagleville with the news.

"Fruity won't stop until he gets there," Henry Hughes said.

"His horse will stop," Joe Reeder said.

"He'll get a fresh one at the home camp and keep going."

The men returned to the Denio homestead, and the next morning they continued their search of the canyon. The men figured that whoever killed the stockmen must have been hiding in the willows where the creek bent close to the south wall of the canyon. The killers probably watched the four stockmen ride along the north rim to where there was a break in the rimrock. The men must have come through the break in the rimrock, down a draw along the canyon wall, to where the butchered beef lay about seventy-five yards from the willows. No doubt the attention of the four men was fixed on the dead cattle when those in the willows began shooting. The four men never had a chance. Their dead bodies were dragged by their shirts to be hidden in the brush and covered with snow. Shirts and undershirts were left jerked over their heads and extended arms in the way they'd been dragged. It was Harry Cambron's gloved hand, raised stiffly over his head, fingers curved downward, that had drawn Fruity's attention. The men's heavy coats were gone. Three of the men were stripped of their pants, leaving drawers tangled around their knees and ankles. Boots and socks were gone. Only Peter Erramouspe's blood-soaked overalls and one boot were apparently left as useless. The big Basque must have stood for some time after he was shot. The boot on his left foot was filled with frozen blood. The other foot was bare.

The men separated, and some climbed the canyon walls. East of the draw on the north rim, three hundred feet above the canyon floor, two men found a wide natural shelf in the rimrock. Under an overhanging jut of rimrock stood the remains of a deserted camp. The skeletal frame of a wickiup, made of bent willows lashed with rawhide and resembling in shape an overturned basket, remained upright, its floor thickly covered with shredded sagebrush bark. The hides or brush that once covered the conical willow frame were gone. A trail led from the wickiup to where a semicircular rock wall had been built forty feet away. Spongy sagebrush bark covered the trail, and behind the curved rock wall lay a bed of soft bark. A person could lie there concealed as a lookout and survey the canyon. The camp itself, situated in a depression and blocked by a slab of basalt, could not be seen from the canyon floor or from the rim above it.

Mort stirred the cold wet ashes of the campfire, long dead, mixed with snow and dirt. The men said little as they moved through the camp, picking up a piece of rawhide here, a scrap of jerky there. The wind pounded in the rimrock and the red river willows swayed on the canyon floor. Far below, magpies and ravens swirled in the wind. Bones and remains of butchered beef lay on one side of the ledge. Coyote tracks showed that no one had been in the camp for a long time.

With his pocket knife, Mort nicked the wickiup poles and saw that some of the poles had been cut long ago; they were partially dry, but where repairs had been made, fresher green willows had been latticed into the wickiup. The work was not that of white men.

Obsidian flakes lay scattered near the side of the camp. Van Norman found what looked like dolls made of clay and sagebrush, and Joe Reeder picked up what he thought were combings from a woman's hair. He turned the wad of hair over in his hand and held it out for the others to see, his palm extended as if in a tentative offering. The men looked at each other with uncertain expressions.

They knew there'd been some Indians camped in the canyon earlier in the summer and fall but they'd paid little attention to them. Hunting groups from the reservations often used the old rock shelters in the canyon as deer blinds. Van Norman, who worked a small claim near the canyon, got the closest look at them but assumed they were a family from the reservation. Women, kids, and an old man were with them. They'd stopped for supplies in Cedarville the previous summer but they seemed to be on their way to the California Sierras. They might have been the ones who passed through Little High Rock Canyon and stole some rifle cartridges from Van Norman's camp. But after looking through the remnants of the abandoned camp and especially after finding snowshoes fashioned from willow reeds, the men concluded that these Indians were not like any they knew. The camp seemed like something out of the past.

That night, the men returned to the Denio homestead. The homesteader Billy Denio said he'd seen a few Indians roving through the country but no more than usual. In the late summer a couple of families came in wagons with some fish from the Summit Lake reservation to sell to ranchers. In the fall, a few others showed up with braided riatas and gloves for sale, but there were never more than four or five together, and they never bothered anybody. There were always Indians working for various cattle outfits, and despite their superstitious and funny ways, most of them made good vaqueros. They all dressed pretty much like any other buckaroos, and after working with them for a while, the men didn't even think of them as Indians. It was hard to imagine those men massacring anyone or living in the camp the men had found in the canyon. The massacre and camp resembled stories old-timers used to tell when the men were kids.

Mort volunteered to take the news about the Indian camp to Eagleville. A storm was threatening, and some of the men were convinced that Mort, who was less familiar with the country than any of them, would surely be lost. "Then we'll have to hunt that damn fool," the wrangler Joe Reeder said.

"Let him go," Van Norman said. "Somebody's got to get through."

"I guess," Joe Reeder said, "it's best to send somebody with no brains."

Early the next morning Mort rode into a storm blowing from the west. He'd paid close attention to the country on his ride to the canyon, but he found himself unable to make out many landmarks. His big bay Hambletonian struggled against the wind, broke through drifts to its belly, and sent Mort's back knocking against the cantle. Wherever he looked there was blowing snow, but in the late afternoon he reached the Cambron home camp. He'd covered twenty-five miles through the storm. Against the warnings of the men at the camp, who said he was crazy, he decided to try to push on over the summit of the East Warner Range. Night fell, and in the darkness the snow was blowing so hard he lost the trail and had to return to the home camp until the next morning.

When he'd volunteered to take the news of the Indian camp to Eagleville, Mort had simply told the men that his horse was strong enough to make the trip. What he didn't say was that somehow, for him, as an outsider in the group, going to Eagleville was a way of justifying his being with the group at all. He was getting tired of the way the wrangler Joe Reeder was making him feel like some kind of freeloading kid. The cowboss Ottie Van Norman just gazed at him as though he were a stranger with snot on his nose. He was going to prove that he was as game as them even if he hadn't known any of the murdered men or hadn't ties with anyone else in Surprise Valley. He knew what it was like to lose a family. Ever since that night as a kid in Silver Lake when he'd fought his way through a roaring wall of fire, leaving behind his father, mother, brother, and sister, all he had in the world, he'd felt himself a loner, on the fringe of groups. He was never able to put that tragedy into a sensible scheme. It seemed just luck that his father had pushed him, rather than his brother or sister, through the window before the burning hall collapsed. Ever since then he felt that some connection had gone out of his life.

At times Mort wished he could settle down to a steady job. He wished he could have his own cattle outfit and work for himself, but he knew it wasn't likely. Nobody paid a buckaroo enough to buy cattle. A sheepherder had a better chance of going out on his own by taking out his pay in ewes and building up his own bands. A buckaroo was a person who was always dependent on someone else. Every spring, after cutting and branding calves and driving summer stock into the high country, Mort sometimes got a job fixing fence or haying, though he didn't like working when it was too hot, especially as a hay slayer. After shipping out fall steers and getting snowbound horses into the valley, he'd sometimes get a winter job, cooking somewhere, or feeding weak cattle, or hauling wood or coal. He usually just got by, but he wasn't alone. Buckaroos were mostly all broke during the winter.

Whenever he thought of working full time for a big outfit, rather than scratching around for seasonal work and then facing winter unemployment, he remembered that a steady job meant you always had to be doing something, even in the off season, when there was only shit work to do. It also meant having somebody telling you what to do every damn day of the year. He preferred to take what work he could get when he needed it, and except for haying and fixing fence, he liked the work he got.

He knew it had been different in the old days when his relatives settled on the other side of the pass. To his grandfather, father, and uncles, fresh from the Civil War, settling that country—as Mort's grandmother had told him—was duck soup. Now a valley—West Valley—was named in their honor. Mort wished he'd been there when his grandfather, father, and uncles first left Minnesota to join Grant's army, when they rode into battle with the cavalry in Tennessee, and when they all moved west into what was new, open country. He'd heard stories about how the Modoc and Pitt River Indians were on the warpath in those days and the government paid a bonus to settlers. It was as though he'd missed out on something fine.

It was like marriage. Mort simply assumed that marriage was something that happened to other people. He once had his eye on a dark-haired girl in Eagleville, but she refused even to dance with him at a tag dance. It was typical. Of all the men in the search party, it seemed to him that if anyone was lost while trying to make it to Eagleville in the storm, his loss would be felt least. He was on the fringe of the group, but he was bound to show the men that he was game. When he'd uncovered the faces of the dead men, he felt an odd sensation, a strange sense of excitement. Unlike the tragic fire that had wiped out his family, here was a wrong he could do something about. It seemed something large, something important, was happening, and he was going to be part of it.

He arrived in Eagleville the next day, five days after the search party had left in the storm. The small town seemed transformed. Hitch rails were crowded with horses. Wagons and buggies lined the streets. Mort soon learned that Fruity had made the ride from the canyon in a day, just as the men had predicted. Telegraph messages immediately went to officials in Reno about the murders. Within a few hours Captain Donnelley and three other officers of the Nevada State Police were on their way to Carson City to catch a special train to Alturas. The sheriff of Washoe County, Charlie Ferrel, along with the Washoe County physician and the county coroner, had joined the special train in Reno. Harry Cambron's brother was on his way from Constantia. A contingent of thirty men lined up in front of St. Mary's Church in Eagleville to have their picture taken before beginning the ride to the Denio homestead. The cowboss of the Miller and Lux ranches, Charlie Demick, began gathering a cavvy of horses for the men to use. Dick Cook sent a four-horse sleigh from Cedarville to carry the bodies from the canyon. As Mort was riding into town, a caravan of men passed him, headed for the Denio homestead.

At the Eagleville store, men and women gathered to hear about the Indian camp. As Mort talked, he noticed the dark-haired girl who'd refused to dance with him two years earlier. She moved through the crowd toward Mort, but he turned away and went up to his friend, Frank Perry, who stood near the door.

"This place has been going crazy since Fruity showed up," Perry told Mort. The boy was still coughing, but he was off the couch and ready to ride with the men. His clean-shaven skin looked pallid in the light of the store.

"There's going to be a hundred men out there," Mort said.

"Not everyone's going to be going," Perry said. "Elzie will start sorting out those who can and can't ride real quick." He meant the Modoc County sheriff, Elza Smith, who would have jurisdiction over the men from California, at least until they were in Nevada.

"I expect the state police will want the sheriffs to know they're in charge."

"They might unless they get into Humboldt County," Perry said. "People say Sheriff Lamb doesn't like the state police and they don't much like him."

At nine o'clock that night, Mort and Perry rode together out of Eagleville, each loaded with a fifty-pound pack of ammunition. Mort had traded his rifle for a lighter Winchester. Perry was coughing as he rode. Mort knew he should still be in bed, but the kid was worried about his parents and twelve brothers and sisters in Wall Canyon.

"If this could happen to Harry Cambron," Perry said, "then it could happen to us, too."

"They say the son of one of those Bascos is coming to town and will be wanting to go," Mort said.

"He's probably one that will get himself left," Perry said.

"How come?" Mort said. "Harry Cambron's brother will be going."

"Ben knows how to ride. What makes you think a Basco kid would even know what to do on a horse? The boys can't be waiting on burros or mules."

"So what?" Mort said. "If he falls off, he falls off. They ought to let him try, for Christsake. It's his father what was killed. How would you feel if your father was killed and you couldn't ride?"

Somewhere in the darkness ahead of them over fifty men rode with guns, ammunition, and a pack train carrying food and supplies. Telegrams and letters and phone lines were carrying the news Mort had brought from the canyon about the Indian camp. Newspapers throughout Nevada, California, and Oregon were setting the news in headlines. Buckaroos in the cow camps of Surprise Valley and southern Oregon and northern Nevada were learning about the massacre in Little High Rock Canyon. They were learning that a large band of outlaw Indians had killed and badly mutilated four California stockmen.

18

Mr. G. L. Matthews, the professional photographer from Cedarville, took a picture of the bodies before they were unpiled from the snow. He climbed to the canyon ledge and photographed the willow frame of the abandoned wickiup. Several men posed behind the wickiup for the photograph. He took a wide-angle picture from the canyon floor to show the camp in relation to the slaughtered beef and the willows where the murdered men were found.

The bodies were hauled through the canyon on stretchers fashioned from two-by-fours and horse blankets. Mort West and Frank Perry were glad to see them go. The two kids were the ones stuck with guarding the dead men while the rest of the posse stayed at the Denio homestead. Mort and Perry had stayed alone in the canyon with the bodies for two nights until the others returned with Lee Davis, the Washoe County coroner, and Dr. Morrison, the county physician. The men worked for nearly an hour getting the frozen bodies pried up from the ground and unstuck from each other.

They hauled the bodies over rocks and through brush for a mile and a half to where a four-horse sleigh waited. Mr. Matthews took another photograph of the four men stretched out on the snow in front of the light sleigh. Behind the sleigh stood almost twenty-five men, all looking into the camera. Two men held rifles and one was on horseback, others stood with their hands in their pockets or cocked on their hips.

After the photographs, the men debated whether the light driving sleigh could support the four bodies through the rough canyon without losing a runner.

"We got no choice," the cowboss, Ottie Van Norman, said. "Let's get them in."

The men hesitated again when they saw no way for the four bodies to fit into the sleigh except piled on top of each other.

"I don't think they'll mind," Mort said. "I guess they're used to it by now."

With men walking by the side of the light sleigh and supporting it with their hands, the sleigh carried the bodies to the mouth of the canyon where they were transferred to a wagon and driven to the Denio homestead.

Almost sixty men were gathered at the homestead. Night was falling. The men pulled sagebrush for fires but the deep snow was crusted over. It was decided to have a full inquest that night so the men could be on the trail in the morning. Billy and Mattie Denio cooked supper in the small house and served men in platoons. The mercury was at seven degrees below zero and falling.

Mort and Perry were working outside grubbing sagebrush for a fire. The two kids had stayed together since riding out from Eagleville. They both wore big, high-crowned hats. Ottie Van Norman and Ed Hogle, their faces flushed from the warmth of the house where they'd just eaten, joined the others pulling sagebrush. They pulled together on a resisting bush. Like most of the other working buckaroos, Van Norman and Ed Hogle wore battered, low-crowned hats.

"It wouldn't be so bad if this happened in summertime," Ed Hogle said. He was an excitable young buckaroo from Nevada City in California and worked as a camp cook for the Humphrey-Cambron outfit. He knew the murdered cattleman, Harry Cambron, as well as anyone.

"If it was summertime," Perry said, "we wouldn't be grubbing brush for a fire. Wake up, Ed."

The other man looked at Perry, seeming surprised to hear the brooding, dark-eyed kid say anything.

"I guess since Ed's paid year-round," Mort said, "he don't know what it's like to work except in the summer."

"I like working in this weather," Van Norman said, his bright blue eyes glancing from man to man. "Your body don't sweat too bad."

Nevada officials swore in three men to serve on the inquest. The men attempted to thaw out the bodies enough for Dr. Morrison to examine them, but the fast-burning sagebrush seemed of little help except for some light. Mort held a lantern close to the bodies as Dr. Morrison examined the wounds.

Peter Erramouspe had been shot four times—in the head, chest, and both legs. One bullet had entered his left thigh, passed through his scrotum, and come out through his right thigh. It looked as though a bullet had dislodged Indiano's eye. In some cases it was impossible to tell entrance from exit wounds because snow mice had gnawed the wounds. Snow mice had gnawed the tissue holding fragments of Indiano's fractured skull so that the bone had collapsed into the brain, leaving a gaping hole where the eye socket and cheekbone had been. Dr. Morrison said the only wound not caused by a bullet was where a knife had cut away Peter Erramouspe's heavily mustached upper lip from his face.

Inside the Denio house, the kid Fruity, his sandy hair falling across his eyes, told the coroner and Captain Donnelley of the Nevada State Police how he'd discovered the bodies. Mort told about finding the butchered beef on the canyon floor and the deserted Indian camp three hundred feet up on the wall of the canyon. Van Norman guessed that these Indians were the same ones he thought took some cartridges from his camp the previous November. He'd gotten a pretty good look at them but didn't pay any more attention to them than to other Indians moving back and forth from the reservations. There was an old man, four Indian bucks, two or three squaws, and three or four little kids. Because of the snowshoes they found in the camp, the men supposed the Indians weren't local. Possibly they were Modocs from farther north.

Other men were willing to testify but the coroner said that he had enough evidence to rule that the four men probably had been killed by a band of unknown Indians for some unknown reason. He said as far as Nevada law went, the bodies could be released and returned to California.

In the morning while it was still dark, the men loaded the bodies into the wagon to begin the two-day trip to Eagleville where they would be laid out in St. Mary's Church long enough to be thawed and placed in coffins.

19

Jean's mother, her eyes black in the lamplight, begged him to forget about joining the police posse.

They sat at the kitchen table. Jean's sister lay curled in a soft chair in the darkness of the living room, her head turned away, not saying anything. Across from her sat her father's empty chair. At the table were Jean's aunt, Dominica, whose husband was one of the dead, and his Aunt Marie, who had lost her brother. All day the kitchen door banged open and shut as relatives and friends came and went, spreading food onto tables and counters—chickens, pies, beans, cakes. Jean was watching his thumbnail peel the black eagle from the paper label on a can of milk. A few Carnation corn flakes floated in a bit of milk left in the bowl in front of him. It was all he would eat.

He felt out of place with these women, his sister, mother, aunts, with their black hair tumbling from their heads, their peasant arms, their dark worried eyes and quick tongues. All this female flesh encircling him.

"You're all *we* have, Jean," his mother was saying. "We can't lose you, too."

"I'm not all you have," Jean said. "There're four of us." He turned to look in his sister's direction. She sat with her chin cradled into her chest, her hair obscuring her face.

Light clung to wisps of hair growing from her temple. The wet skin stretching over the little ridge of bone between her eye and temple seemed delicate in the lamplight, so vulnerable.

"Without him, you're the man I have," Jean's mother said, "the man we have."

"Listen to your mother," his Aunt Dominica said. "Stubborn as you are, you're all the same."

"What is this?" Jean said. "'Do this, Jean. Do that, Jean. I don't want you to go, Jean.' What about me? Am I supposed to sit here while everyone else gets revenge except me?"

"Always we're fighting with ourselves," his Aunt Marie said. "Isn't it enough that others fight and kill? Look at you, Jean, at your nose."

"That's right. I let a man break my nose and I didn't do anything about it. I'm not going to make the same mistake again. That's why I'm going."

"Take care of your family here, Jean. They need you."

"I'm going to go," Jean said. "He was my father, goddamn it. Can't any of you see that?"

"*Astakilo*," his aunt said.

Outside, elms loomed black against the sky. The night was like an ice house. His eyes and nose ran in the cold as he walked to his father's corrals. Stars became blurred blobs in the sky. He knew it would be worse, colder, sitting on horseback, but when he got to his father's barn and corrals, he found no horses.

Jean turned back into town and walked to Brown's Joint where he found one of his uncle's part-time workers and a part-time hand at the livery stables, Paul Mendive, shooting pool.

"I can get you a horse," Paul Mendive said, "but it wouldn't be worth shit. All the decent horses are already out there."

"I'll take a mule then," Jean said, "just to get me out to Denio's."

"Forget it," Paul Mendive said, "your mother doesn't want you to go. She's the boss now."

"Don't trouble yourself, Paul. I'll get my own goddamn horse."

"They don't want you out there, Jean. They don't want anybody except men that can ride with them."

"I can ride as good as any state police."

"They're paid to be there, you aren't. But they're going to have knots on the balls of their ass as big as marbles. Sheriff Smith's the only one to ride with those boys. Charlie Ferrel hasn't been out of a desk chair since he's been sheriff. And those state police don't know what a horse is."

"I'll just hurt along with them."

"No you won't because they don't want any Bascos out there. Do you think those boys would go on a trail if only three Bascos was killed? Get that through your head. To those boys' minds, they're out there 'cuz a white man was killed."

"Thanks for your help. I'll remember it."

"Save yourself some trouble, Jean. You might get out to Denio's but those boys are already on the trail. You'll never catch them. They're gone, Jean."

Two days later, Jean brought his face close to the rocking train window and the cold sweaty smell of wet glass. Outside, the snowy hills in the distance with their twisted sagebrush looked scabrous. The passing hills became part of his own faint reflection in the window as the train chugged toward Winnemucca. He thought of his sister sitting in the dark living room and his father's empty chair. Wisps of grass sticking through smooth surfaces of snow mixed with the image of his sister's skin, taut and almost translucent, covering the little ridge of bone between her eye and temple. Again and again the image came back to him until with all the force of his earlier grief he realized what had been floating on the periphery of his thought for the past two days. That place was where he'd been told his father had his head shot open. For two days he'd held back from thinking clearly about his father. Each time his father's face drifted into view, he'd seen instead the face of one of his uncles, or Sheriff Lamb, their upper lips laden with thick curving mustaches like his father's. Now an image came into his mind of his father lying in the frozen canyon with his body blown apart, his mustache cut off. He was dead. He was dead forever. He was buried in the ground and he did not even know he was dead.

20

Lamb was sitting in his office on Monday afternoon, the day after the stockmen's funeral, when the telephone rang with a message sent from Captain Donnelley of the state police. Charlie Muller took the call. Captain Donnelley and the posse were now at the northern head of the Black Rock Desert, at the Miller and Lux home ranch. The caller had ridden forty miles east to the Western Pacific station at Amos to make the call. Some of the posse had picked up the trail of the Indians on the desert fifty miles south of where Donnelley and the rest of the men now camped. Donnelley and his men were getting fresh horses that morning and heading out to join the others. They believed the Indians to be hiding in the Jackson Mountains, northwest of Winnemucca.

The afternoon sky looked lowery and cold, threatening more snow. Charlie Muller spat into the spittoon by the desk while Lamb leaned back in his chair and looked out the window. Slaps from the spittoon punctuated ticks of the schoolhouse clock above the desk and the hissing of the steam radiator.

Ten days had passed since the bodies were found in the canyon. From the position of the posse, Lamb figured the police had followed the trail east from the canyon until they lost it in the Black Rock Desert. Down the east branch of the Black Rock Desert, void of vegetation, ran a channel of the Quinn River, flowing from the north before it spread and dissipated on the desert flats. At the river the posse apparently had split into two groups. Donnelley and his group had headed north to the stock and wagon bridge at the Miller and Lux ranch; the other group had moved south until they picked up the place where the Indians had crossed the river. Apparently the Indians were in the lower end of the Jackson Mountains, moving farther southward than anyone expected.

Lamb had kept his thoughts to himself while everyone waited for some word from the posse. The editor of the *Star*, Herb Baker, had badgered him to reveal what tribe he thought the Indians belonged to and where they might be headed. Lamb saw no reason to add to the speculation that already filled the papers. The *Nevada State Journal* had dragged out old Colonel Reddington to talk about his adventures with Cutmouth John while serving as an army scout in the rough Salmon River country thirty years earlier. Other old-timers talked as if the slaughtering of the Modocs had happened only yesterday, and renegade bands still roamed the country.

None of it made any sense to Lamb. Even if some surviving Modocs had maintained their hostility for the past forty years, they wouldn't be found wandering in Little High Rock Canyon. That was Paiute country, and Lamb's hunch was that a group of Paiutes had killed the four stockmen. He didn't believe the Indians could be the ones Tranmer and Urie had supposedly fought near the Idaho border. Those Indians were Shoshone, mostly women and children, and they weren't likely to end up three hundred miles away in western Nevada. Things were usually simpler and more banal than people wanted them to be. The southward turn of the Indian trail supported his hunch that the Indians were renegade Paiutes. Donnelley assumed the Indians would continue eastward and head toward Winnemucca, but Lamb thought it more likely that once out of their territory they would eventually circle back in the direction they had come. Indians stayed in their own country. The Paiutes in Winnemucca and the Shoshone in Battle Mountain never crossed over Golconda summit into each other's territory.

If the Paiute renegades really had a month's head start on the police, it was also unlikely that they would still be in the Jackson Mountains. If they had continued in a south-westward direction they would be heading back toward the home of the Paiutes at Pyramid Lake on the western edge of the state. Or they might be headed toward the reservation at Summit Lake in the northwestern part of the state.

That was as far as Lamb would speculate. Either the Indians were in the Jackson Mountains or they were not. He could no longer delay finding out for sure. He just wished he knew more about what was really going on in the desert before going out there. If he was right and the trail heading into the Jackson Mountains was cold, he'd be off on a wild goose chase while the Indians were safely a hundred miles to the east or west. But Donnelley's report would soon be in all the papers, and there was nothing to do except go find out for himself. He couldn't take the chance of having Donnelley catch up with the Indians in his own county without being there. If the Indians were in his county, he was the one who was going to bring them in, not the state police.

Lamb told Charlie Muller to telegraph Donnelley's message to Governor Oddie in Carson City and to tell the governor that he would be going out that night to join the state police. The governor wanted to be kept posted on the pursuit, but if he wanted to do anything, Lamb said, he might keep his eye on the Paiute reservation at Pyramid Lake. Lamb would take a freight to Sulphur in the southern part of the Black Rock Desert and ride from there to the Jackson Mountains, taking his brother Kize and Skinny Pascal with him, no one else.

"What if somebody else wants to go?"

"Fine," Lamb said, "as long as they take their own horses, their own grub, and their own money to pay for the trip."

Lamb said that whatever Indian trailers Donnelley had with him would be getting nervous now that they were out of their own territory. Kize knew the country, and Skinny would quickly read the trail. He suspected there would be little more to do than to figure out the Indians' movements. He didn't want any ramrods getting in the way. He told Charlie to get in touch with Superintendent Ogilvie at the Elko office and have a car added to the night freight for them and their horses. In the meantime he would get hold of Skinny and Kize.

"What about Herb?" Charlie Muller asked. "He'll be pestering me any time now."

"Tell him what we know," Lamb said, "and tell him that's all we know."

The streets were dark when Lamb reached home at suppertime. The boys were in their room doing their homework and Nellie stood at the stove frying chicken. The afternoon *Star* was on the table. The headlines read:

INDIAN MURDERERS ARE HIDING
IN FASTNESSES OF JACKSON MOUNTAINS
Sheriff Lamb Will Leave Tonight with Posse
and Join in Pursuit at Sulphur

News of the capture of
the Indian murderers
may be expected at any time.

"I guess Herb held up the paper to get his news in," Lamb said. "I didn't think he would have time."

Without turning from the stove, Nellie asked, "Who's going with you?"

"Just Kize and Skinny."

"No more?"

"No more."

"I wish you were taking more men."

"There's already enough men out there to round up the whole Paiute tribe," Lamb said.

"You're not always right, Graham," Nellie said. "You always think you can do things yourself. It's stupid to take a chance."

"If the Indians are out of the county like I think, I'll get Donnelley on the trail and be back in a day or two. There won't be any trouble."

"That's not what the paper says. Read it. It says you're in for trouble, and that's what you must have told Herb."

Lamb read in the article that a special car on the night's train number 1 would be loaded with horses and a local posse. They would leave that night over the Western Pacific for Sulphur, an oil drilling camp in the Black Rock Desert and the nearest railroad point to the place where the murderers were supposed to be hiding. Sulphur was about thirty miles distant from the southern end of the Jackson Mountains. Sheriff Lamb and his men would take up the pursuit bright and early in the morning and a junction with the state police would be effected sometime tomorrow. Sheriff Lamb and his brother, the article said, knew every foot of that section of the country where the murderers were supposed to be and it seemed impossible that the murderers could evade capture longer than a day or two, unless it happened that the state police posse were following a cold trail, in which event the Indians might be far away from the Jackson Mountains by this time. Once Lamb left Winnemucca, there was no possible source of news since the area was isolated in the extreme.

"I guess Herb just can't help himself," Lamb told Nellie.

"The Erramouspe boy wants to go with you," Nellie said. "He was here this afternoon."

"He was at the office, too," Lamb said, "but I wasn't there and I won't be here much longer either."

"I don't want him going," Nellie said, "but I'd rather have him go than just the three of you. I don't understand why you don't leave the whole thing to the state police."

"I'd rather they left the whole thing to us."

After dinner Nellie wrapped the remaining pieces of fried chicken in waxed paper and packed them into an empty lard pail for Lamb to take. Lamb was in the bedroom changing his clothes when he heard Nellie talking to someone in the living room. He finished dressing and found Jean Erramouspe sitting on the couch. Hunched forward with his elbows on his knees, the boy looked up at Lamb through reddened rims, his dark eyes angry and pleading.

"There's no posse," Lamb told the boy. "The paper's wrong. If there was a posse I might let you go, but there's no posse."

"But you're going," Jean said. "I have as much right to go as you do. He was my father."

"Then go," Lamb replied, "but you're not going with me."

Nellie called from the kitchen. "Come in here, both of you, and have some of this pie before I throw it out the window. Don't waste any more of your breath, Jean. You're not going to change Graham's mind once it's made up."

At the table, Lamb said, "There are certain things I can do, and certain things I can't. The same's true for you. There's always riffraff who don't want to follow any rules except their own, like your old friends Tranmer and Gibbs, but if you don't deal with them according to laws, then you just become riffraff yourself."

"That's horseshit," Jean said.

"It would be horseshit if there weren't any laws in this country. This whole thing is now a matter for law officers."

"You can appoint them. Ben Cambron is no law officer but he's out there because his brother was killed."

"I didn't appoint him and I wouldn't. The only people

that should be out there are the police and the sheriffs and the men that they've worked with before. I can't control that situation but I can tell you that I don't like it."

Jean clenched his fist next to the dish of apple pie. "It's not fair to me."

"I'll tell you this," Lamb said. "If we locate those Indians and we form a posse of people from this town to get them, then I'll appoint you, but not before."

"You say that because you don't think it will happen."

"I don't know what will happen, and neither do you. One thing you can be sure of is that I'll be back here before anything does happen."

Jean shook his head but appeared relieved. "I guess there's nothing else I can do."

"That's right," Lamb said, "not now anyway."

"I'll be at the Basque Hotel. I have a room."

"I know how to find you."

At the door, Jean asked, "Do you know where that guy Gibbs hangs out?"

"I haven't seen him since the sewer was finished," Lamb said. "I think he was running horses with Tranmer and Urie up in Idaho, but he wasn't involved in the Imlay murders. Forget Gibbs. Thinking about that kind of scum isn't worth your time. It'll make your mind rot."

After midnight the whistle of the approaching freight sounded down the track and the engine's white eye appeared blinking on and off in the distant darkness. At the end of the station a man stood swinging a red lantern as the locomotive, spitting sparks, rumbled into the station. Lamb led his horse up the wooden ramp of a cattle car and followed Skinny and Kize into the cold darkness of the caboose. Skinny seemed to fall asleep instantly, sitting upright on the hard bench, his angular face placid under a straight-brimmed hat, his secondhand, double-breasted army coat buttoned across his chest. Across from him Kize stretched out on the bench with his hands behind his head and his hat over his eyes.

Couplings gripped the car with a succession of jolts and Lamb slid the bucket of fried chicken to the back of the bench. At twelve-thirty, the coach lurched again before coasting forward, and the train rolled out of Winnemuccca. The darkness in the car looked blue. Lamb folded his arms and sensed a familiar ease that formerly came to him in the company of men on dark mornings before going to work. He felt relaxed in the clarity and simplicity of an old routine from the past.

The train rolled slowly into the west. It would still be dark when they reached Sulphur and rode from the south across the desert to meet the police posse coming from the north.

21

On Wednesday morning when Father Enright ran into Nellie Lamb at Mose Rhinehart's butcher shop, she was complaining to the butcher about the last live chickens he'd sold her. "When I went to pull their damn necks they were already half dead," she said. "I want some birds with kick in them, Mose."

Father Enright almost left the butcher shop. He didn't want to get involved with Nellie. He knew she'd get around to talking about the Indians and he didn't want to argue with her. Her vehemence always left him with nothing to say. At the same time he couldn't just walk out. The butcher had already noticed him, and young Dora Giroux, the girl he'd seen crowned queen of the fall carnival, came into the shop behind him and said, "Good morning, Father."

Heads turned. Nellie looked at him and nodded without smiling. "Morning," she said. She looked grim, so different from the previous fall when she had walked to the Nixon Opera House with Justice Fitts. How handsome she'd looked that night, how elegant Fitts seemed. Now Fitts was a dead man, remembered as an embezzler and a woman-izer, and Nellie was a grim-looking woman with an ashy complexion. He wondered if Nellie felt duped by Fitts, as he did. Such civilized elegance was nothing more than the sheen on a whitened sepulcher, yet he'd heard Nellie say nothing unsympathetic about the man. She didn't seem to care that people were talking about her.

Now she had other things to worry about. Her husband had gone into the desert after the Indians, and no one had received any word since he'd left.

Nellie took a package from the butcher and turned back toward the priest. "If you see that Erramouspe kid," she said, "try to talk some sense into him. He's wanting to go after those damn renegades and he's going to get himself killed. Maybe he'll listen to you. He damn sure doesn't want to listen to anybody else."

"I don't know whether there's anything I can really do," Father Enright said. "If he won't even listen to Sheriff Lamb, I don't know what I can do."

"You're his priest, you know," Nellie said. "You should do something."

Her clear and compelling demand stunned him. *You should do something.* Ever since he'd returned from Sacramento he'd brooded over the murders and the pursuit by the police. He'd prayed and meditated and worried, but he'd done nothing, said nothing, except to ask his congregation to pray for the souls of those who had been killed. But what about the Indians? What had he said and done about them? He was a pastor, and pastors gave guidance. He'd given no guidance.

Nellie was still talking to him. "I hope Jean doesn't even get a chance to get out there," she said. "I hope they're cleaning up the whole goddamned works of them right now so this thing will be over."

"But what about the Indians?" Father Enright said. "They're people, too. They have to be judged by the same laws as we are." He'd spoken before he knew it. He couldn't believe he was confronting Nellie in the very way he'd intended to avoid.

"How can you compare those savages to us?" she asked. "What laws did they follow? What justice did they show to

those men in Little High Rock Canyon? If you want them
treated like us, then they'd better act like us." She pointed
to young Dora Giroux who stood next to her. "Imagine one
of those murdered men as Dora's husband or son. Could
you look her in the face and say we should let those savages
go? We're not talking about civilized people, Father."

Father Enright looked around the shop. He knew he
shouldn't have let himself get into this situation and now he
should get himself out. He could simply tell Nellie he sym-
pathized with her and prayed for God's will to be done.
Then he could leave. Instead, he said, "Do you want justice,
or more murders, Mrs. Lamb?"

His unexpected question clearly startled Nellie. She
glanced at Dora and back at him. "I can see I'm wasting my
breath here. We're talking about apples and oranges, Father. You haven't been in this country very long, but all you
have to do is look at Dora and then look at one of those
Indians, and you'll see what I'm talking about. I'm not talking about *all* Indians, mind you, I'm talking about these
particular Indians. I'm talking about savages."

"I know you are," Father Enright said, "that's the whole
problem."

Later that morning Father Enright began working on
his Sunday sermon. It was the first time since returning to
his church after his accident that he'd worked with such
resolve. He saw his duty with a clarity that he hadn't known
since his recovery in Sacramento. *You should do something,*
Mrs. Lamb had said. Of course. How could he have forgotten? That was exactly what he'd come to know while he was
away. But it had come slowly, his awakening from
confusion.

During the first week after falling into the sewer ditch
and leaving Winnemucca, he'd lain in bed at his sister's
house in Sacramento wracked with alternating chills and
fever. When he felt well enough to climb from his bed and

move about the house, an inquiry came from the bishop about his possible return to his parish at St. Paul's. He found himself back in bed, tortured with headaches and a throbbing in his leg. Another message came from the bishop telling him his only obligation was to get well; he should not think about returning to his parish until he was better. It was like a cross lifted from him. He cautiously rose from his bed and moved about the house on crutches. He spent hours sitting listlessly in the living room, his days marked only by the arrival of breakfasts, lunches, and dinners that his sister insisted he eat. There were no books worth reading in the house except St. Augustine's *Confessions* and a Bible, but he never opened them. He ignored the newspapers his sister brought to him.

He began to take short walks down the street outside his sister's house. Other days he sat in the living room and stared out the window. His sister's house was on the edge of town. Through the window he could see orchards in the distance and beyond them the soft folds of straw-colored foothills. He looked out the window and often fell asleep in his chair. In the mornings fog twisted through the trees and over the hills in the distance. During warmer afternoons he moved a chair to the back porch and watched the sky fill with pale ocean light and sudden fiery changes at sundown. Nights were mild, starlit, quiet in the stillness of the long valley and its sluggish river waiting for winter rains.

One morning crews of men with ladders moved through the orchards pruning branches. The outlines of the bare trees began to change shape. Father Enright turned from the window and looked blankly at the calendar above the writing desk. It was now December, but the word meant nothing. He realized that he did not know whether it was Tuesday or Thursday or Saturday. He returned to his chair and a calmness entered him. He had no desire to know what day it was. He had lost touch with nothing but a series of black numbers marked on leaves of paper. Beyond his window the men left the orchards and the valley darkened. Days came and went, and in the distance the bleached hills turned pale green, but their shapes remained the same. Killdeers and blackbirds and sparrows appeared before his window, disappeared, and returned again. Beyond the hills, unseen, the Pacific rolled against the coast as it had to, unconcerned about the comings and goings of men.

Father Enright now remembered himself as another person who had once lived in a small Nevada town in a country with too much sun, too much space. He saw himself on those white empty stretches among people like himself who vainly moved from here to there, passing each other with distracted eyes. He saw now that in that empty country, a day six thousand years ago, or a hundred, was as near the present as yesterday. He saw himself as a feckless man who once dreamed of a church and who appeared and disappeared in an instant under an unchanging sky. He saw himself as a pitiable creature who gave truth to St. Paul's warning that for the worldly ambitious there would be wrath and fury. Now all such desire left him. He wanted nothing. Outside his window, the comings and goings of birds and men, grass and leaves, fog and rain didn't matter. What remained was invisible and unchanging glory. The winter grass pushing out of the wet hills, the bare outstretched branches of trees, the swirling and cries of birds in the wind, became manifestations of the divine mercy that suffused him and the world with equal regard. His sense of that mercy moved through him as a wave through the sea, as light through stillness. Nothing else was real except that lambent outpouring of divine mercy. There was no boundary to it; the same light and stillness stringing the stars linked the spaces of his nerves and skull. When his sister found him in his chair by the window, the glass streaked with afternoon rain, his face happy with tears, he recalled Aquinas and said to her, "All that I have known seems to me nothing but straw."

"What's wrong with you, Jerry?" his sister said. "Here, you haven't touched your soup. Come into the kitchen. I'll heat it up."

For days he felt light and free. His former torments and concerns no longer seemed imaginable; it was as if they belonged to someone else. He felt removed from the troubled priest in Winnemucca, distant from the man who sat by the window in his sister's house. In the mornings it was as if he could enter the living room and actually see his former self sitting inertly in that chair. The vision bemused him, but one morning he looked at the chair and window and saw something else. A strange sense of loss sliced through him. The view in the windowframe looked like a static picture on the wall. He felt devoid of any feeling for it. He could not understand why he felt so utterly abandoned. Once he had been able to look through the window and love what he saw. But something was missing from the view. He had pulled back and the world beyond the window went on, but he had no part in it. His chair was empty. He had become like a dead man. He was more than a dead man. He sensed only the vacancy of his own absence in the room.

The next morning he made his way to St. Anne's rectory, spoke to the pastor, and said morning mass for the first time since leaving Winnemucca. He returned to his sister's and sat at the kitchen table. He stared at his hands folded on the shiny red and white checked oilcloth. Light spilled through the window, and beyond the kitchen doorway he sensed the dark presence of the living room like a shadowy cell. His sister was out shopping. She'd left a note and some sweet rolls on the table. He picked up a roll, spread it with butter, and began to eat. Outside the kitchen he heard the sounds of birds and the voices of children on their way to school.

In the afternoon he found himself on the back porch reading St. Paul's letters. He felt a sudden affinity for St. Paul and his letters. He comprehended St. Paul's chronic illness, his temptations, his conversion. He couldn't account for his own transformation except to know he had experienced a darkness like death and through a goodness greater than himself he had returned. The goodness that let him live humbled him. It was like a residue of what he'd felt so keenly in his chair. But it was enough. He knew it was a mistake to think he could absorb the world without the inconvenience of being in it. St. Paul hadn't spent his life sitting in a chair staring out a window at other men fishing or cutting grapes. He hadn't withdrawn from the world to fret about his own redemption. He acted in the world. He argued with the rabbis in synagogues. He harangued the Greeks in the markets. He worked to bring about the transformation of the world into the kingdom of God. He traveled the roads and seas to Antioch, Corinth, and Rome, collected money for the famished, celebrated festivals, comforted the frightened, admonished the confused, went to weddings and funerals, and wrote letters to those he longed to see until he was dragged away in chains. Paul did not live outside time. Time was all he had.

Father Enright knew that time, too, was all he had. He had to make his people see, both in his congregation and outside, that to be a Christian meant total belief in the certainty of God's kingdom coming into the world. It meant possessing the will to work for it. It meant the desire to work for the transformation of the world. He had to tell people that the Gospel was like straw unless a hope for such communal renewal dominated their lives. He had to tell them that their faith and hope and actions had to fly in the face of the hard facts of their daily lives. They had to think like children. They had to change the world. He had to tell them.

His sense of purpose had faded after learning about the brutal murders of the stockmen, but now, back in Winnemucca, after talking to Nellie Lamb in the butcher shop, he felt renewed. He worked on his sermon until noon and left the rectory when Mrs. Garrity arrived to clean the house. He didn't want to hear any more about his failure to build the new church in Golconda. He knew that building new buildings was no longer what he was to be about.

He walked to the Basque Hotel to find Jean Erramouspe but the boy was not there. His things were in his room, so he hadn't left town. At least Father Enright hoped not. Rumor around town was that the state police had cornered the Indians in the Jackson Mountains. No one really knew what was going on out there. The only thing he did know was that if the posse had caught up with the Indians, a massacre was possible, simply because so many people thought the way Nellie Lamb did. He hoped that Sheriff Lamb had reached the posse and could make a difference. The state police and their posse were expected to arrive in Winnemucca any day. They'd know then whether Sheriff Lamb had reached them in time.

22

Mort was beginning to think they'd never catch the Indians and he almost didn't care. The Eagleville buckaroos were crowding out everyone else and he'd about reached his limit. They kept splitting off from the posse and heading in different directions so that he had about as hard a time keeping track of the posse as he did the Indian trail. The only time he sided with the Eagleville boys was when they got after Captain Donnelley and the other state policemen. Sergeant Stone and Private Buck were all right; they kept mostly to themselves. But Mort disliked fat Sergeant Newgard as much as some of the Eagleville boys.

When they'd left the frozen gray sump of Little High Rock Lake, where the Indians had crossed the ice at night, the state police couldn't maintain the vaquero trot of the Eagleville boys on the flats. Mort kept up easily, but the police walked their horses until about to lose sight of the buckaroos, then galloped to catch them, only to curse as the buckaroos again left them behind.

"Damn the sons of bitches," Sergeant Newgard shouted to Captain Donnelley. "What are they doing now? Look at them."

"Forget 'em," Joe Reeder said to the other buckaroos about the state police. "We'd be better off without them."

"They can just go to hell," Perry said to Mort.

"Donnelley looks sick," Mort said.

"His horse looks sicker," Perry said.

Mort climbed into the Black Rock Range with Perry. At the top of the pass, the boys helped Sheriff Charlie Ferrel off his horse. At the end of the first day's ride, Sheriff Ferrel had continued to sit on his horse after the other men dismounted until Mort realized that the fiery, red-haired sheriff, more at ease at his desk than on horseback, couldn't dismount. Each day the men had to pull the immobile sheriff, saddle-galled and stiff-legged, from his horse.

"Let's put him over here," Perry told Mort.

The likable Washoe County sheriff was in agony, his blue eyes glazed, as the boys put him down on an outcropping in the snow. His cracked lips wiggled into a painful grin. "If I get back to Reno alive," he announced, "I'm going to get me a string of horses and ride forever."

"You look right where you're sitting, Sheriff," Mort said.

Below them stretched the burnt, bare slopes of dry washes and broken volcanic rock that looked like dead cinders in ice. A frigid wind slapped Mort's face and clawed around his ears. Snow started rolling over the crust. Captain Donnelley looked like an old man as he removed his hat from his balding head. "Damn fine county you have, Sheriff," Donnelley said.

"Damn the county," Sheriff Ferrel said. "It's Lamb's, not mine. Let's go."

They'd found two abandoned camps that day, about twelve miles apart. At one they'd found a dead dog; at the other, bits of cloth from the dead men's coats, apparently cut to fit children. The Indian trailers had stirred the dead campfires and squeezed the cold wet ashes between their fingers. The camps were at least a couple weeks old, maybe a month.

Rather than follow the trail into the desert, the police and sheriffs had decided to take a safer and quicker route

directly over the Black Rock Range and drop down into a
Miller and Lux ranch near the main expanse of the Black
Rock Desert. The posse had already lain over for two nights
at another Miller and Lux ranch at Soldier Meadow to re-
shoe their horses and load a pack train, and some of the
buckaroos were complaining.

"How the fuck are we going to catch up with these sons
of bitches if we don't stay on the shitass trail?" Joe Reeder,
the wrangler, asked.

The posse split, and Joe Reeder led a group of Eagleville
buckaroos south, directly onto the desert.

Mort was glad to be rid of Joe Reeder. The glowering
horse wrangler always seemed to be looking at him with
disdain. The way Reeder's hat, too small for him, sat cocked
high on his head, and the way his lips pouted and his eyes
narrowed made Mort want to smack the arrogant son of a
bitch. Fruity and Perry were both smaller and younger than
Mort, but Reeder didn't ride them as much, even though he
didn't particularly like Perry's new, high-crowned, black
buckaroo hat any more than he liked Mort's white one.
Fruity was all right; he wore an old driving cap like Sheriff
Smith and some of the other men.

It didn't help matters when Joe Reeder learned that
Mort didn't smoke or drink. "This is what comes when you
have kids doing a man's job," Joe Reeder said.

Mort had called down Fruity back at Denio's when the
sandy-haired kid mocked him for not gambling with them.
The scared look that came into Fruity's eyes under his cap
showed Mort that he would gain nothing by crowding the
smaller kid further. Joe Reeder and Ottie Van Norman were
the ones he had to get. Several of the men worked for Van
Norman on the Bare Ranch, and if the cowboss came
around to accepting Mort as game, others might follow suit.
Until he saw his chance, he decided to stick with Perry and
his friend Henry Hughes, who always smiled and defended
him against Joe Reeder's criticisms.

That night on the edge of the Black Rock Desert the

wind was like a wavering groan, whipping the campfire first one way, then the other. Mort took off his boots and tried to warm his feet. Like his hands, they were so cold they burned, as if submerged in coals. He felt something wrong with his stomach as well. The first day out of the canyon his hot bowels had gushed with diarrhea. Weariness and coldness then seemed to settle in, turning his stomach to lead, and after two days of constipation, hard dry pellets dropped from him like small stones.

A few of the men took turns sleeping in the small ranch quarters at the meadows, but most, along with Mort, climbed full-dressed into their bedrolls to endure the night on snow. As the sun dropped, shadows moved up the Jackson Mountains. In the shadows rocks turned black and layers of dry grass looked like hair on the mountains. A few delicate yellow and rose-colored clouds, bright blue at the bottom, hovered in the mockingly pale eastern sky. In an instant the light went out of the clouds and they floated in the sky like smudges of ash. When Mort awoke in the night, the noise of the wind was like a scream. To the south the Black Rock Desert shimmered like an enormous white lake with a mist rising.

The next morning when Joe Reeder's group rejoined the posse, the pack mules acted owlish, and one of them, objecting to its load, rolled and bucked loose the squaw hitch from its pack and scattered frying pans, tinware, and canned goods far and wide over the desert. "Let's get rid of the shitters," Joe Reeder said. "What good's a pack train if we don't stay on the trail?"

The men found where the Indians had camped on the edge of the Black Rock Desert. Not far from the camp, they found the remains of dead Miller and Lux cattle, shot in the head. Some of the men speculated that the Indians had shot the cattle at night and let them freeze; in the morning they took only the front quarters, leaving the back quarters frozen to the ground. It looked as though the Indians had camped for at least ten days, maybe longer, before venturing across the Black Rock Desert. Their trail led directly across the desert toward the Jackson Mountains and King Lear Peak.

Joe Reeder, who was in charge of the cavvy, then refused a change of horses to the buckaroos who were not from Eagleville.

"Those are Miller and Lux horses," Mort said, "and we have as much right to them as you do."

"I'm in charge here," Joe Reeder said, "and there's not enough shitters for everyone. That's all there is to it."

Some of the men from Cedarville decided to turn back since their horses were worn out from the hard ride over the Black Rock Range. Twenty-four men had left Little High Rock Lake, but one had dropped out at Soldier Meadow. Now four more were ready to turn back. They tried to persuade Mort to join them. They said the trail was cold and the Indians were too far ahead. "We'll never catch 'em so you might as well join us."

Mort looked down at his weary horse and was about to go with them when he told the men he'd come out on Harry Cambron's account and as long as he had any chance of catching Harry's murderers he'd stay with the posse.

"But you can't go on with no change of horses."

"Yes I can," Mort said, "'cuz I'm going to get a change of horses and I'm going to get it right now."

Mort dismounted and walked toward the cavvy.

"What are you going to do, kid?" Joe Reeder said.

"I'm going to catch that pinto," Mort said.

"Well," Joe Reeder said, "you're not."

Mort rushed the wrangler but Henry Hughes quickly got between them, pushing them apart and telling them to knock it off. Henry said he had two horses and Mort could take one of them.

"I don't want your horse," Mort said. "I'm after that pinto."

Mort again tried to get at Joe Reeder, and Joe at him, but Henry remained between them, laughing all the time, and finally got both men to settle down. Mort let Joe Reeder know he was sick and tired of the Eagleville boys trying to crowd out the others, and he was going to get his change of horses from there on. At Henry Hughes's insistence, the wrangler relented, but four of the Cedarville boys still decided to turn back. Nineteen remained on the trail.

The posse split again. Mort and four others followed the renegade trail east across the salt flats, while the main body of the posse rode north toward the bridge at Quinn River Crossing. There, at Miller and Lux headquarters, Captain Donnelley's group would get supplies and notify Sheriff Lamb that the Indians were thought to be hiding in the Jackson Mountains.

Mort rode across the dreary salt flats behind Sergeant Newgard. The big Swede irritated him, the way he swayed back and forth on his beleaguered horse as he broke trail. The large, slope-shouldered state policeman—the tallest and heaviest man in the posse—struck Mort as an unformed man in the overgrown body of a child. The night before, the idiot Swedish sergeant had put saltbush into the cooking fire, causing the fire to explode and shoot cinders into Ed Hogle's face as the camp cook was bent over a cast iron pot of buckaroo beans. Mort had jumped all over the Swede until the cowboss Ottie Van Norman intervened. Like some others, Van had taken to calling him "kid." The less Mort had to do with either Van or the big Swede, the happier he'd be.

Mort and the other men followed the Indian trail due east to the Quinn River where the Indians apparently had crossed on ice. Now the river was thawing and the ice broke under the horses' hooves. Mort, Perry, and Henry Hughes rode up the bank looking for a place to cross. Sergeant Newgard and Jim Taham, the Indian trailer, rode downstream. The men rejoined and decided one place was as good as another. The Indian trailer rode in first and drove his horse into the frozen stream, breaking ice as far as he could go.

The ice seemed to grow thicker as it neared the steep bank on the opposite side of the river, and Taham turned back.

Sergeant Newgard said he would get undressed and try it on foot. He stripped down to his gray longjohns, and Henry Hughes tied a riata around the sergeant's big waist. The state policeman strode into the running water with his rifle and broke ice until he reached a point in the river where freezing water and chunks of ice swirled against his stomach and chest. His neck and face alarmingly darkened, his arms weakened, he staggered in the swirling water, and he screamed, "Pull me out, I can't make it, I'll drown."

A storm appeared to be blowing in from the northwest and the men agreed to give up and ride to Quinn River Crossing, the only bridge on the river, where the rest of the posse had gone.

Perry, who'd said nothing all the time the men were trying to ford, blurted out, "I didn't come out here to look at any goddamn river." He drove his horse into the water, pounding and breaking ice with the butt of his rifle until his horse was swimming. Nearing the other side his horse started to go under and Perry jumped from the saddle into the water and with reins in hand scrambled up the steep bank while pulling his lumbering horse behind him.

Mort and the others crossed one by one through the path of broken ice until only Sergeant Newgard and Henry Hughes remained on the west bank. The Swedish sergeant had so jaded his horse that when it entered the river and its legs went out from under it in deep water it could scarcely swim.

"Get off and give your horse a chance," Henry Hughes shouted. The big sergeant refused and clung to the saddle. His horse, exhausted and wild-eyed, began to go under.

"Let the stupid son of a bitch drown," Mort said.

Sergeant Newgard fell from the saddle, and Henry Hughes, throwing his riata out to the struggling horse, lassoed it around the neck, and pulled it back to the west bank while Sergeant Newgard clambered safely to the other side.

"There's no use taking this horse on," Henry Hughes shouted across the river. "It won't make it. I'll send mine across."

After tying a riata around his own horse's neck and sending it across the river for Newgard to ride, Henry Hughes mounted the sergeant's exhausted horse and began a seventy-mile ride, first back to Paiute Meadow for a fresh horse, then on to Quinn River Crossing to join the rest of the posse.

Mort and the three others stood at the river in the barren desert without brush for a fire. Mort took off his chaps, overalls, and socks and tried to wring out his clothes, but they were stiffening fast in the cold and he had to hurry to get his icy pants back on before they were completely frozen.

The afternoon was waning as the men rode east in hope of finding enough brush for a fire. They continued following the Indian trail and soon rode through blowing sleet and snow. It was getting dark when they spotted a tent on the desert. A small pile of hay lay near the tent but no one was around. Not knowing where they were, except that they were still on the Indian trail, the men gathered enough brush for a small fire and then all four climbed into the tent for the night, grateful for the windbreak.

In the morning they discovered that their tent was on the dirt road leading north to Quinn River Crossing, probably pitched there for an overnight stop by someone who'd then lost or abandoned it. The Indian trail, now about two weeks old, had turned south toward Rattlesnake Pass. The Indians, they thought, must have taken the low pass through the Jackson Mountains. They were far beyond the mountains by this time.

That night Mort and the others rejoined the rest of the posse at the Lay ranch on the western slope of the Jackson Mountains. Captain Donnelley and the sheriffs, thinking the Indians were hiding in the Jackson Mountains, had abandoned the pack train at the Miller and Lux ranch and had sent a message to Sheriff Lamb to meet them at the Lay ranch.

The next morning Mort learned that the posse would no longer wait for Lamb. They had to get on the trail if they were ever going to catch up with the renegades.

"What do you think Lamb's going to say about this?" Perry asked Mort.

"Who knows whether he's even coming out here," Mort said. "Captain Donnelley said they expected him last night if he was coming."

"That ain't what Sheriff Smith said. But he said Lamb would find us if he wanted to."

"I guess we can't just sit here while we know the Indians are getting away."

"I think they've done got away," said Perry.

The men rode hard across Jackson Mountains and dropped down to Lay's other ranch on the east side of the range, at the edge of Desert Valley. It was Ben Cambron, the older brother of the murdered stockman, who began taking charge. It was clear that the renegades were taking the low passes through mountain ranges and keeping in isolated country away from ranches.

The Indian camps grew closer and closer together, some only six miles apart. On deserts the trail had remained plain enough where the Indian horses had hard-packed the snow by stepping into each other's tracks. But on the edge of Desert Valley, east of the Jacksons, most of the snow had melted on the sandy wastes and the men lost the trail. The trailers, Henry Barr and Jim Taham, now in unfamiliar country, seemed spooked and ready to turn back. All afternoon Ben Cambron, his sandy mustache and pale eyes steady under his hat, urged the men on. Finding the trail more often than Taham or Barr, he picked up the renegade tracks and followed them into the sand dunes where he lost them again. After an hour's search, the men decided it was too late to go on. They'd lost the trail completely. Tired and discouraged, they returned to Lay's ranch in the late afternoon. There they found Sheriff Lamb, his brother Kize, and Skinny Pascal, waiting for them.

Mort watched as Sheriff Lamb approached Captain Donnelley. He was bigger than Mort had expected and he quickly let it be known that Humboldt County was his territory. He said he wanted to talk alone with Donnelley and the other sheriffs in the ranch shack. Donnelley and Lamb, along with Sheriff Ferrel and Sheriff Smith, went into the ranch quarters while Mort and some of the other men wondered what Donnelley might say about not waiting for Lamb as planned. "He can always say he got Lay's two ranches mixed up," Mort said.

Inside the shack Lamb helped himself to old coffee from the battered pot sitting on the wood stove. He sat at the kitchen table across from Donnelley. Sheriff Ferrel and Sheriff Smith sat at the end of the table.

"I suppose you're going to say I got your message mixed up," Lamb said.

"There does seem to have been a misunderstanding," Captain Donnelley said.

"There was no misunderstanding on my part. I got a message that we'd meet at the Lay ranch west of the Jacksons."

"There are two Lay ranches, Sheriff."

Sheriff Smith interrupted the captain. "We all agreed we were going to meet at Lay's other ranch."

"Yes," Captain Donnelley said. "That's true for our men, but that isn't the message I sent to Winnemucca. Why would I stay at that ranch if I discovered that the Indians were gone?"

"I want you to know," Sheriff Ferrel told Lamb, "that we weren't going on without you."

"But you did," Lamb said. "Next time, get your messages straight. Who's running the show here anyway?"

"We're working together," Captain Donnelley said, "but by law this posse is responsible to the Nevada State Police."

"I didn't ask who was responsible," Lamb said. "I asked who's in charge. 'Cuz from now on you're all in my county."

"This county is in my jurisdiction as well," Captain Donnelley said. "I ask you to cooperate with us, Sheriff."

"You cooperate with me, and we'll get along fine."

"I can tell you that the captain has cooperated with us," Sheriff Smith said. The short stout sheriff took off his driving cap and put it on the table. "It ain't necessary to argue about that. We got Indians to catch, and we want you to be with us when we catch 'em, Sheriff." The Modoc County sheriff turned to Captain Donnelley. "This territory may be yours according to law, Captain, but it's Sheriff Lamb who knows this country like the back of his hand. You've never even been out here before."

Captain Donnelley turned to Lamb. "I've been out here," he said. "Both Sheriff Lamb and I have been out here together."

"Not here," Lamb said, "but over north of Kelly Creek. That was a few years ago."

"What we mean," Sheriff Ferrel said to Captain Donnelley, "is that Elzie and I don't have no say over the boys any more. We're out of our counties. You see how they're listening to Ben Cambron. Sheriff Lamb here knows these boys. He's worked with them all his life. He can control 'em. This is his territory."

"It's my territory, too," Captain Donnelley said. "I just want that to be clear. And I don't think the sheriff has seen any of these boys before in his life."

"We mean buckaroos like them," Sheriff Smith said.

"Let's drop it," Lamb said. "We've got Indians to catch. While you boys were out chasing your shadows I was talking to the buckaroos on the ranch here and I know who these Indians are now. They're Shoshone, and they're probably from up on the Owyhee. I can't hardly believe they ended up all the way over in California. But if they get back into the Owyhee, we're going to play hell catching them. I need one of you to take a message out of here so we can block off the Owyhee."

Mort and the others were surprised to learn that the Indians they were trailing were probably Shoshone renegades from Duck Valley. The buckaroos working at the ranch had told Lamb that a group of Indians with women and children had stopped to trade at the ranch the previous spring and were later seen breaking colts near the Jacksons. Their description matched the one Ottie Van Norman gave of the Indians he'd seen in Little High Rock Canyon last November. Sheriff Lamb said they seemed to be the same Indians who were reported dead after killing a boy in Elko County last May. Those Indians were Shoshone, Lamb said, and if they were renegades from the Duck Valley Reservation they had to be cut off before they got back into the canyons and lava plateaus of the Owyhee River. "I didn't think those Shoshone would be out here in Paiute country," Lamb told the Eagleville boys, "but I guess I was wrong."

Lamb decided the men should split up until they either found the trail or regrouped at noon. Sheriff Smith and Ben Cambron would lead one group, Captain Donnelley another, and Lamb the third. Sheriff Ferrel left for Winnemucca to set up posses in the east.

Joe Reeder said he wanted to ride farther north and would take four or five of the Eagleville boys with him. Lamb pointed his finger at Reeder and said, "Joe, I think you want to come with me." Without waiting for Reeder to respond, Lamb swung his horse around and trotted away. After a moment, Reeder followed him.

All morning Mort rode without water through sand dunes. It was a bright cold day. Cloud shadows coasted hurriedly over the sand. He and Perry thought they found the trail close to where they lost it the previous afternoon, but some older buckaroos disregarded the kids' reports as leading them too far south. The search in the dunes continued without water, and toward noon, Mort waited with others for a courier from Lamb's group. Over a mile away two dots came into view.

"That's Kize Lamb on the sorrel," Ottie Van Norman said.

"The other's a gray," Joe Reeder said. "Looks like Skinny."

"That's right," Van said. "Skinny's on the gray."

"That's not Skinny," someone else said.

"Sure is," Van Norman said.

Until he began riding with the posse, Mort had never met anyone with better eyes than his, but some of the older men who had spent their lives riding for cattle and wild horses surprised him with their eyesight. Van Norman's sharp blue eyes seemed able to pick out things in the dark. But now Mort thought the men were stretching it. In the desert a man could ride into a flat and in less than a mile both man and horse would seem to vanish in the open space.

The men argued first about the color of the horses, then made bets over who was riding them. Mort saw only two spots, one darker than the other. He then agreed on the horses' colors, and as they came closer he saw that the first two men were right, the messengers were Lamb's brother and Skinny Pascal, on a sorrel and a gray. Mort wondered whether Van had set him up, had a hunch who the messengers would be and what horses they'd ride. He couldn't be sure.

The posse split again in the afternoon. Sheriff Lamb led one group and sent Skinny Pascal with the state police. Lamb and Captain Donnelley agreed for the groups to meet that night at a butte in the direction of the distant Bloody Run Hills.

Mort had never been so cold and thirsty at the same time. He didn't see how some of the smaller buckaroos just kept going and going. His horse stumbled in the sand, dropped its head, and tried to eat from patches of snow. Like the other men, Mort ate snow too, but he was still thirsty.

It was the first time he and Perry weren't riding together. When the groups had split, Captain Donnelley had asked Perry to go with him. Mort wanted to get away from the state police and to ride with Lamb. He felt the others were comparing him to Perry, and he was at the losing end of the comparison. Nobody had said anything, but Mort knew they thought Perry was all right. He couldn't figure it. He'd ridden all the way to Eagleville through a blizzard and the men acted like he was some kind of fool, while Perry took five minutes to cross a piss-ant stream and they all thought he was the cat's meow.

In the afternoon he felt drowsy. Nothing ahead but one sand dune after another, sparse brush and sand grass. Buttes in the distance seemed to waver and drift.

"What are you looking at, Mort?"

Sheriff Lamb reined in next to Mort and gazed toward the Slumbering Hills.

"I saw you staring out here for some time," Sheriff Lamb said, "and I thought you saw something."

"Nothing much," Mort said.

Lamb looked at Mort. "Are you eating snow?"

"Little bit," Mort said.

Lamb laughed. "Eat some more," he said.

Sheriff Lamb divided his half of the posse into smaller groups, but the men found no trail. At nightfall they began gathering at the butte where they were to meet Captain Donnelley's group. Some of the men lighted fires with sparse sagebrush and waited for the other men to show up. Mort felt a pain low in his stomach and realized he had not pissed all day. He wandered toward a clump of sage while he heard the Eagleville carpenter, George Holmes, telling

Joe Reeder, "I don't want to hear any more about the women you had, Joe." Mort remembered that George Holmes, now in his late forties, had supposedly once studied to be a priest in California before taking up ranch work and carpentry, but Mort had never thought to ask George if it were true.

"I want to hear about all the women you never got," George Holmes said.

Mort heard some of the men laughing as he unbuttoned his fly. For the past two weeks or so since leaving Eagleville his mind had been impervious to sex as even an idea, let alone a possibility. He looked down at his listless cock and tried to imagine what it might feel like to be with a naked woman. The idea seemed incomprehensibly alien to him, and he stared down as his brown piss stained the snow like rust.

When it grew darker and Captain Donnelley's party still did not show, Sheriff Lamb decided to lead the exhausted and dehydrated horses and men into Winnemucca for the night. After hitting a dirt road and following it in the dark some of the men began to grumble that the sheriff had picked the wrong road and they were lost. They reached a fork where an adjoining road came in. The sheriff stopped and pointed to the adjoining road. "That," he said, "is the road to Winnemucca."

Mort felt sure they were already headed in the right direction, but Van Norman said, "Keep still, kid, the sheriff ought to know his own district."

It seemed to Mort that they rode in a big circle before the lights of Winnemucca came into view. Mort felt they had ridden eleven miles around Winnemucca Mountain when a straight line would have taken them three miles into town, but none of the men complained and he wondered if without water these men were losing their minds.

It was after midnight when the sheriff unlocked the courthouse for the men to spend the night. Some of the boys went out for drinks, but Mort, content with coffee and a steak at the Elite Café, spread his bedroll on the court-room floor. He felt beat. He'd heard lots of stories about Lamb, but here they were in Winnemucca and they hadn't found the Indian trail. One thing he noticed was that Lamb always acted as if he knew what he was doing, even when they were wandering around in the dark. Mort wondered if that's what made the difference between a sheriff and just another vaquero.

When the boys returned from town, they said Perry was lost in the sand dunes. Captain Donnelley had called Lamb from Toll House on the old stage road through Paradise Valley to say his group had found where the Indians camped in Bloody Run Valley. They'd followed the trail east but apparently mistook the butte where they were supposed to meet Lamb. Donnelley had decided to take his men on to Toll House for the night. He'd sent young Perry to notify Lamb's group but apparently the boy got lost. Donnelley told Lamb to send the posse ahead to Golconda and he would meet them there the next day.

Mort wondered whether Donnelley intended to double-cross Lamb. Some of the boys heard in town that as much as fifteen thousand dollars was up for a reward. Now the state police were on the trail and Lamb was left sitting on his ass in Winnemucca. It seemed to Mort if he kept ending up in the wrong place he'd be out in the cold, too. Maybe he'd made a mistake not turning back with the Cedarville boys. He'd surely made a mistake not sticking with Donnelley. While he was trailing Lamb around in circles, Perry was out there looking for them and now he was lost. All the men had talked about how game Perry was when he drove his horse across Quinn River. Mort knew he was just as game as Perry, but to the other men he was still just the kid. If things kept going the way they were, that's all he'd ever be.

23

Perry had known it was coming when it started to get dark and no one from Lamb's group was in sight. Captain Donnelley turned to the men behind him and his eyes settled on the quiet kid. They'd been following the Indian trail since late afternoon, the same one Perry and Mort had found earlier. "You boys were right," Ben Cambron admitted to Perry, "we saw where you turned back." The trail headed east; Sheriff Lamb and his group were scouting the country to the west. There were two buttes in the distance, perhaps five miles apart. The farther one was not far from the Indian trail, and as they approached it, Donnelley asked Perry to ride over, wait for Sheriff Lamb, and tell him the rest of them were going on to Toll House for the night.

Perry was left alone. The other men turned off the trail and headed for Toll House. Perry knew that probably none of them, except Lamb and Skinny Pascal, had been in that part of the country before. Perry rode toward the butte but couldn't see anyone from Lamb's party. He was riding the young horse he had started out with but didn't know how much farther it could push that day. The posse had found no feed or water all afternoon. It was quickly getting dark. Still no sign of Lamb. A cold north wind started blowing sand and snow, and he decided to look out for himself.

Shoshone Mike

He rode back to the trail but it was so dark he could scarcely see the ground in front of him. He couldn't figure what had happened to Lamb and his posse. He looked back as he rode and saw small fires at different places behind him. He then became worried, wondering if he might have stumbled onto the Indians' camp. He kept his head turned, his eyes fixed on the strange fires, until he realized he'd paid no attention to where his horse was going. He could see no landmarks. All he could see were the diminishing fires that had shifted to his left.

He dismounted, lighted a match, and saw that his horse had stayed on the Indian trail, now headed north. He had missed the point where Donnelley's group had turned east toward Toll House. Wind snuffed out the match. Perry stood in the darkness and knew he was due for a night out.

The wind blew into his face. His horse could not go much farther, but he wanted to get someplace with a little shelter. His horse struggled over one dune after another, its hooves slipping and crushing small brush and sand grass. He finally came to a place where some posts stood askew in the dunes. He dismounted to see an old well, blown over and covered with sand. Three or four posts were still standing; a stack of old lumber and a large dry goods box lay buried in the sand. Perry knew this was his camp.

He unsaddled his horse, covered him with a saddle blanket, and tied him to a post. He dug the dry goods box out of the sand, turned it against the wind and huddled close, lying so he could watch his horse in case anyone approached. He would've given anything for a drink of water for his horse. He was shivering but didn't want to start a fire for fear of attracting unwanted attention. His fingertips and the edges of his hands were numb and stinging. Watching his horse, he lay there, dozing off and waking to think he heard whispers and footsteps in the dark behind him. A distant coyote howled above the wind.

When morning finally came, Perry saddled his horse and rode southeast until he picked up the trail. When he arrived at Toll House about ten o'clock, Captain Donnelley came out to the trough where Perry was watering his horse, took one look at him and said, "I guess there's no need to ask where you stayed last night." He told Perry that Lamb and part of the posse had gone into Winnemucca. He would call to tell Lamb that Perry was safe and the rest of the boys could meet them in Golconda. "You'll have a bed tonight," Donnelley said.

After feeding his horse, Perry went inside to lie down until it was time again to leave.

That night he lay in a featherbed. Captain Donnelley had left Sergeant Newgard at Toll House with Ben Cambron and Sheriff Smith to look for the Indian trail through Paradise Valley. Mort West and the other boys arrived from Winnemucca and along with Skinny Pascal they would try to intersect the Indian trail northeast of Golconda. Sheriff Lamb stayed in Winnemucca.

When the posse arrived in Golconda, they were short of stable room and there was almost a row when Ottie Van Norman moved Mort's horse out of a stall to make room for his own. Mort stepped into the stall and asked, "What are you thinking of doing, Van?" Van Norman licked his shaggy mustache and said, "I'm tying my horse in here, by God." Mort doubled his fist and jumped at Van. "Get that skate out of here," he said, "and do it quick." The cowboss nearly tripped over backward getting out of the stall, and Henry Hughes, who was watching Van return Mort's horse, laughed so hard he leaned against the stable wall and slid to the ground holding his stomach.

"What are you laughing at?" Van said. "The kid is weedy. His brain is wormy."

After the boys had a few drinks, it seemed they wiped the slate clean, although Mort still drank no booze. Some of the men in the posse said Mort's losing his entire family in a fire made him the way he was. They said he sure wasn't shortchanged when tempers were handed out, and he could get a look in his eye that scared everyone off. Word was that he'd fought in the ring a couple times in the bay area, under the name of George MacDonald, so his aunt in Oakland wouldn't find out he was fighting. He had big gnarled hands that looked like clubs when tightened into fists. Perry knew he wouldn't mess with Mort when he got that look.

Van Norman was more easy-going and usually able to take what came with a laugh. Perry noticed it was the same way with the sheriffs. Sheriff Ferrel joked about his pain on horseback and Sheriff Smith teased the men when they started ribbing each other. Lamb was harder to read but he seemed to enjoy riding through the dunes when everyone else was dying of thirst, and he wolfed down Ed Hogle's buckaroo beans as though they were actually good. Henry Hughes was that way, too, and if Perry were to lay odds on which of the buckaroos was most likely to become a sheriff he'd bet on Henry. It wasn't how big and strong a man was that mattered, it was how much he could take, day in and day out, year after year. That was something Mort didn't understand.

That night the boys talked about the reward. Some said it was ten thousand, others said fifteen, but their talk struck Perry as strange. It stayed in his mind that if those Indians had camped just twenty-five miles away in Wall Canyon, instead of Little High Rock Canyon, his own family might now be dead. Many of the other men, like Van and Mort, had no families out there. Van told Perry he'd run away from home when he was twelve because his stepfather always kicked the hell out of him. Perry's father also beat him and he carried scars from the buckle end of his belt, but he hadn't thought of running away. If something happened to his father he knew that his mother and twelve brothers and sisters had to depend on him. They all pulled together on the homestead in Wall Canyon, living off range cattle when they had to. It was strange. Miller and Lux buckaroos accepted that a homesteading family might have to borrow a steer or two; the buckaroos said they only wanted the homesteaders to leave the hides on the fence so they could keep count. But Perry's father never admitted taking cattle and always buried the hides. He claimed he only took winter strays that would have died anyway. Those Indians lived off other people's cattle, too. The difference was that nobody was going to let them get away with it.

Perry had a feeling they were no closer to catching the Indians than when they were looking for them in the sand dunes. For all he knew, Sheriff Ferrel or the Indian police from the reservation or one of the other posses coming from the east had already cut them off. Each day his place in the chase made less and less sense to him. He wondered what the buckaroos would say if they knew when he was a school kid he was sweet on a girl named June, the half-breed daughter of a Paiute woman. His mind seemed cluttered with shadows rather than thoughts. Last night he'd been alone, lost, and scared as hell in the sand dunes, while Mort West was tagging a county sheriff past one dark sand dune after another. Tonight they were both about to fall asleep on featherbeds. What difference did it make? They were still just workers, waiting for someone to tell them what to do.

24

On Friday morning, the day after he'd returned to Winnemucca from the desert, Lamb received word that a rancher had spotted the old tracks of the Indians five days earlier while he was out riding east of the Osgoods in Clover Valley. The rancher said he saw where the Indians had watered their horses. If the report was true, the renegades had already crossed out of Humboldt County.

It seemed to Lamb that Donnelley's posse now had little chance of catching the Indians. Donnelley was still in Golconda with one group of men, while Sheriff Smith and Ben Cambron were trying to pick up the trail in the Hot Springs Range. Lamb intended to stay out of the way of the posse until he got a clear lead on the Indians. All the latest reports indicated the renegades were at least a hundred miles northeast of Winnemucca.

Earlier that morning Frank Tranmer had told reporters at the county jail that he was satisfied he knew the Indians. The descriptions Lamb had brought back from the desert had convinced him that they were indeed the same Indians who'd killed his sixteen-year-old stepson, Frankie Dopp, at Cow Creek last May. Those Indians made their home around Twin Falls, Tranmer claimed, and belonged to the Shoshone tribe. Tranmer told reporters he'd known the leader of the Indians for at least twenty years. He was known in that country as Indian Mike and he was an old man.

It was late Friday afternoon when Deputy Muller handed the phone to Lamb and said, "Here's another one, Sheriff. Someone just spotted those Indians outside town in Long Canyon."

The call was from Constable Byrnes in Paradise Valley. A prospector had just seen some Indians and horses in a canyon about ten miles from Winnemucca. Three of the horses matched the descriptions of the bay, sorrel, and black Oregon horse belonging to the murdered stockmen.

"It's a funny time of year," Constable Byrnes said, "for local Indians to be in the canyon."

"You know how excitable people can get," Lamb said to the constable, "but if you go out there, don't go into that canyon alone."

Lamb called Toll House and left word for Sheriff Smith and Ben Cambron. He then sent Deputy Muller to find Donnelley and tell him the Indians might still be in Long Canyon, just outside of Golconda.

Lamb sat alone in his office. He checked through the day's reports and saw that there was no eyewitness spotting of the Indians except for the one in Long Canyon. All the other reports were several days old or secondhand rumors.

That morning it appeared likely that Sheriff Ferrel's men or the Tuscarora posse coming from the east had the best chance of capturing the Indians. Donnelley just seemed too far behind. The most recent camp the state police had found in Bloody Run Valley was at least twelve days old, plenty of time for the Indians to be deep in the box canyons of the Owyhee. Now the report from the prospector changed everything.

Donnelley would get Lamb's message that night. If the Indians were recently in Long Canyon, Donnelley would know by late morning. Lamb could then meet the posse at Willow Point and they could overtake the Indians in a day.

Shoshone Mike

As Lamb had told the newspapers, these Indians were not a marauding band of Modoc warriors out of the past. They were a Shoshone family. An old man, some women and children, a few bucks. Lamb didn't expect any trouble capturing them once they were overtaken.

Lamb turned out the lights. He would return in the morning to wait for Donnelley's call.

25

Perry woke to see a shadowy form approaching his bed. It was Sergeant Stone. Perry dressed and followed the police sergeant outside to where they met Captain Donnelley and Joe Reeder in the dark by a spring wagon. Donnelley, his voice hoarse with sleepiness and a cold, asked Perry to drive. The four men climbed into the wagon and Perry drove out of Golconda.

It was light as they approached the Stewart ranch, fifteen miles away. Donnelley sat in the back coughing into a white handkerchief, his lungs thick with fluid. Perry didn't know what Donnelley had in mind. The captain had simply said a report had come from Sheriff Lamb that the Indians had been spotted in Long Canyon but that Lamb couldn't guarantee the veracity of the report.

At the mouth of Long Canyon, Ben Cambron and Sheriff Smith were waiting. They'd been inside the canyon where they'd found the camp. The Indians had moved on, they said, but the camp was fresh.

Donnelley wanted to see the camp for himself.

"How are you going to track Indians through this country in a goddamn spring wagon?" Sheriff Smith asked Donnelley.

"We'll walk," Donnelley said.

The men on horseback rode into the canyon and the rest followed on foot. It struck Perry as absurd to have come all this way, to be so close to the Indians, and to be on foot. Joe Reeder was agitated and walked quickly ahead of the others, holding his rifle in both hands, glancing up at the rimrocks as he moved into the canyon.

At the camp Donnelley still seemed reluctant to believe it was the Indian camp until Ben Cambron showed him a scrap of hide, covered with unusual reddish hair, that he claimed was from his murdered brother's chaparejos.

Joe Reeder found a piece of cloth that Cambron identified as from one of the murdered men's coats. "These are the Indians," Ben Cambron said.

Perry and the police returned to the wagon while Ben Cambron and Sheriff Smith said they'd ride farther into the canyon to scout the trail for the next day. It was getting too late to do any more that afternoon. As they returned to the Stewart ranch, Perry wondered what Donnelley intended to do about the rest of the men in Golconda. Either he'd left them behind because he thought Lamb's report would turn out to be a false lead, or he was simply fed up with the whole bunch of them. Donnelley had seemed unresponsive when looking at the fresh ashes of the campfire and the leather scraps the men found in the camp. He sat in the back of the wagon, his cough worsening.

When Sheriff Smith and Ben Cambron returned to the ranch, they were excited. They said they found three dead horses farther up the canyon. The horses had been shot in the heads, obviously too poor to go on. The trail led out of the canyon toward the Osgood Mountains, and the Indians couldn't be more than a few hours away. They told Donnelley he'd better call Sheriff Lamb right away and tell him to send out the rest of the posse that night. The boys could leave their packs and gear in Golconda because all they would need were their horses and guns.

Perry saw Captain Donnelley talking to Sergeant Stone

and Joe Reeder. Donnelley told Perry to get the wagon ready for the rest of them. Outside, Joe Reeder saddled a horse and Perry saw him riding west toward the Little Humboldt River in the direction of the phone at Willow Point to call Golconda.

26

Mort took the call from Willow Point and told the other men in Golconda, "The sonofabitch state police tried to double-cross us but Ben and Elzie wouldn't let 'em."

"It looks like this is it," Ed Hogle said.

"Where's the Stewart ranch?" Henry Hughes asked.

"Somebody better try to find Skinny," George Holmes said, "or we ain't going to get out there."

Under a dark overcast sky the men rode out of town. Skinny Pascal, who'd been drinking with some of the men in Golconda, kicked his horse and galloped into the darkness. Mort and the other men spurred their horses to keep up, afraid to lose their guide in the night. Skinny drove his horse for about a mile until he pulled up, his horse winded, and rode quietly for another mile until with a kick and yell he took off again galloping into the night. Mort and the others dug after him, their horses lathered with sweat despite the cold, racing after Skinny, sure now the Paiute tracker was trying to lose them as they pounded through brush, over sand hills, down washouts, keeping their horses at a dead run through a country of badger holes until Ed Hogle's big buckskin plunged stiff-legged over a cutbank and tossed Ed from the saddle. Ed was being dragged, his foot caught in the stirrup, the horse's hooves kicking near his head as it ran wild-eyed through the brush. Mort and the other men closed in and squeezed the squealing buckskin between their own horses until they brought the runaway to a stop.

Mort dismounted and struck a match. Ed's face was scraped and bleeding, but he didn't seem to have been kicked. No bones were broken. All the horses were blowing hard in the darkness. The buckskin kept tossing its head and prancing backward, its hooves stamping the ground as it tried to pull away from Fruity who held the reins. Mort heard the sound of a boot kick into the buckskin's belly. The stamping of hooves stopped as the buckskin coughed and snorted to catch the breath that had been kicked from it.

Ed Hogle climbed back onto the buckskin without help. The men kicked their horses into a trot and resumed the ride to the Stewart ranch.

At the ranch the men found no feed for the horses. Mort rushed up to Sergeant Newgard who came out of the ranch shed where he apparently had been sleeping.

"What the hell is going on?" Mort yelled. "You knowed we were coming out. Where the hell's the feed?"

Newgard backed away. "Let's don't have no trouble," he said.

Mort walked side by side with Newgard toward the shed. "You big Swede son of a bitch, I will ride you through a hole in the fence."

Inside the shed the men saw there was only one bunk where Newgard had been sleeping. Captain Donnelley and the other men had gone up the Little Humboldt to find beds for the night.

"You're not going to take the only couch," Mort told Newgard.

"The hell I'm not."

"Not without a good fight, you ain't," Mort said. "You goddamn sons of bitches have been sleeping on featherbeds this whole trip. Tonight you're sleeping on the floor."

Newgard turned to face Mort, when Fruity, his fists

doubled, stepped in front of the police sergeant. "Look at me, Newgard. I'm the last living thing you're going to see."

Mort and the others began to laugh as they watched the 130-pound kid call down the 230-pound police sergeant. Newgard's lips sputtered as he glared down at Fruity. He lunged past the men and slammed the door behind him as he went into the cold.

The men spread their bedrolls on the floor and gave the bunk to Ed Hogle. Ed seemed to have had a lot of tough luck on the trail. He'd gotten his face burned when some saltbush exploded in the campfire and now he'd been thrown and dragged. Except for Ben Cambron, he was the one who knew the murdered stockman, Harry Cambron, better than anyone, but he was also the one having the hardest luck while chasing Harry's murderers.

It was not long before the weather drove Newgard back inside. Mort saw the dark imposing bulk of the sergeant, standing just inside the door, wrapped in his coat, glowering down at the men as they tried to sleep. Mort heard the ticking of snow against the cabin.

It was still dark when Donnelley and the other men arrived from upriver with fresh horses and a wagon of feed. The overcast sky was as dark as it had been at midnight. In the dark Mort heard only the sounds of cold creaking saddle leather and hooves against the frozen ground. A light snow was falling.

They rode northeast away from the Indians' abandoned camp and picked up the trail in Eden Valley where they were surprised to come upon another camp on the west side of the Osgood Mountains. The men climbed from their horses.

Ottie Van Norman hunkered down and examined the ground. "Their horses are played out," he said. "They can't be far."

Behind the mountains came the first cold light of morning. Several of the men surrounded the remains of the campfire where the burnt twigs and branches of sagebrush retained their shapes and looked like black snakes, all twisted together. Ben Cambron plunged his hand into the black shapes, breaking them into ashes, before he suddenly jerked his hand away.

Ed Hogle scraped some of the feathery ashes from the pit and held them up to Mort. It was as though a thread of ice ran through Mort's belly. The ashes were warm. In the center of the pit glowed live embers, still smoldering.

Mort looked down at Ed. His face was dark with bruises, the hair at his temples caked with dried blood. Ed grinned wildly up at Mort.

27

Eight miles from Winnemucca, Mike and his family might have seen lights as they passed through the sand dunes at night. They certainly saw some scattered ranch house lights as they crossed the Little Humboldt and moved toward the distinct black outline of the Hot Springs Range. Beyond those mountains they would move into more rugged, less populated country. They could then turn northeast toward Gollaher Mountain and their home at Rock Creek.

Henie later said they'd left Little High Rock Canyon and moved in short, unhurried stages to the west finger of the Black Rock Desert. They traveled at nights only when they approached ranches or towns. Snow was still deep in the passes of the Black Rock Range, and they drove their tired horses around the triangular black point and the steaming black pools that marked the tip of the range.

On the east side of the range they camped overlooking the main expanse of the desert. There they rested their horses. Henie's brothers shot range cattle for food. In the morning, they found the cattle flopped in the snow, their white eyelashes splattered with blood, frozen stiff to the ground. Henie helped her brothers and older sister cut meat from the frozen steers.

The days grew surprisingly warm while they camped on

the edge of the Black Rock Desert. Except for occasional range cattle, the country was empty of both animals and men. In late afternoon when the winter sunlight flooded the barren salt flats to the southeast, it looked as though the floor of the world had collapsed into an enormous white hole. At night Mike smoked his pipe and looked out over the white expanse they would soon cross.

Days passed, and they saw no one. It was clear they were not being pursued. They'd been on the trail for half a month and they'd seen nobody except a few animals and a snowy desert. They could take their time crossing the Black Rock Desert because no whites would go out there at this time of year. One night Mike's sons, Jake and Charlie, did an imitation of white men looking for Indians. They marched around lifting their knees high in the air and stomping the ground hard with their feet while swinging their rifles this way and that as they seemed to shoot everything in sight, the sky, the earth, each other. Mike and Nive laughed at their sons, and the children laughed, too.

His daughter Henie put a cloth around her head and pretended to be a white woman with a mincing walk. The little kids taunted her as she shook her finger at them and told them that they had to love Jesus who was the best gambler in the United States.

Mike was in a happier mood now. He told stories of when he was a young man and the Hukandeka were still raiding whites after the other Shoshone went to the reservation. He told about the time he and some young men were escaping after a raid for horses in the early morning just before light. They all sang their power songs and the sun didn't come up until they had escaped. "The sun waited below the horizon and the night stayed until we were gone."

He and his sons laughed about the time they were on the reservation and raided the wooden stakes. On the morning when part of the Indian land was opened to white homesteaders and miners, a gun went off and hundreds of whites ran and rode onto the reservation and pounded little wooden stakes into the ground to make their claims. That night all the whites were drunk and so were the Indians. Just before dawn the Indians went to raid the stakes. Mike threw a small stone up in the air, just as in the old days. They could see it rising in the darkness, and they knew it would soon be dawn. They mounted their horses and rode out into the reservation, challenging each other to swoop down from the racing horses and jerk the stakes from the ground. Many Indians were too drunk and fell from their horses and got kicked, but everyone had fun. They rode home under the fading stars, singing and laughing, prancing from a battlefield littered with fallen and broken stakes.

Afterward, when the agent and the Indian police came to their farms, Mike and the rest of the Shoshone admitted what they'd done. Even those who'd stayed home claimed to have raided the stakes. They knew there was no way the agent could put them all in jail.

"Why'd you do this?" the agent asked.

"We were all drunk," Mike told him, "and we thought it was a good idea."

"You people are in big trouble. That land doesn't belong to you any more."

"Maybe not," Mike said, "but we belong to it. You whites think everything is dead, and you can just do what you want and the land doesn't know."

The agent said there would be an investigation and those responsible would be tried. "If anything like this ever happens again," the agent had said, "I'll have you all shot or lynched or both."

Mike told his family, "Sometimes it was hard to talk to whites, but this agent was a good man. He left the reservation and did nothing to us."

Mike and his family talked about the other agent who had tried to make the children go to school. The Shoshone elders had told the agent that their children would go crazy and die if they went to the Fort Hall school. Twenty children did go and ten died of scarlet fever. Nive said that cutting the children's hair and burning it had caused the deaths. The agent wouldn't listen. He ordered the Indian police to force all the children to school, but the Indian police refused and when the agent tried to round up the children himself, no one would talk to him. In the tents and shacks, Mike and his family, like the other Shoshone, big, little, old, young, wrapped themselves in blankets and lay on the floor as if dead. The agent called for federal troops to drive the children to school, but the President of the United States intervened and said that sending a military force against the children was not a good idea.

A few years after Mike and his family had left the reservation, they heard that more and more children were going to school. Mike's uncle—his father's brother—Mosho Jim, came to their summer range from Fort Hall and said that hundreds of white people had come from Pocatello to watch the graduation that year. The graduating students in new blue school uniforms marched into the dining room in perfect order and said grace in unison. At the sound of a gong, the children seated themselves; at the second gong, they placed plates and coffee in position; and at the third, the meal began. After the supper, a group of eight girls and nine boys sang a song called "Hunters' Chorus." Susan Yupe recited "Visons of War," and the program ended with Jeanette Pocatello's recitation of "Olden Times."

Mike said he hoped his children and their children would never have to go to white schools. He didn't want them to die or become like whites. He hoped they would find a way to live as he had in the open range between Gollaher Mountain and Rock Creek.

Mike looked forward to returning to the Goose Creek Mountains for the harvest in the piñon pines. "Those trees there miss us," he said.

At night when the sky was clear, Henie could see the Road of Ghosts. In the north she saw the seven stars that once were Coyote's daughters and granddaughters. According to the old stories, they had flown up to the sky and become stars because Coyote was always trying to fuck them. When he saw them up in the sky, Coyote tried to jump up there again and again, but he always failed.

"That Coyote," Mike said, "he one time gave a girl a ride across the river and when they were out in the water he tried to get her pregnant. It was a good thing she had teeth in her vagina to bite his dick. Coyote howled, 'Oh, wow, this girl has bit my dick!'

"That was when Coyote and those other animals were people," Mike said, "long time back."

When they were alone together one night, Mike told Henie he thought it was better if she didn't get married. "It's not like before. All those men on reservations are like women now. That's how the white eyes have made them. You can see it for yourself. They all get married and they all die. I want you to live."

"Do you think we'll live?" Henie asked him. "Will we get home?"

Mike laughed. "Ask the raven, Henie, he don't know. Ask the lizard, she don't know. Maybe we will. Maybe we won't. I don't know."

A few nights later when Henie approached her father again as he was looking out over the desert, he turned suddenly toward her, and his eyes were old and angry. "Get away," he said. "We're all going to die. We can't help it. Our powers don't hear."

Afterward he came to her when she was lying down. She lay wrapped in a wool coat taken from one of the men murdered in the canyon. His hand touched her shoulder. His fingers smelled of smoke from his pipe. "I didn't mean to make you sad," he told her. "I wasn't talking just about us but about all our people. We're vanishing. I don't know why this is happening. I don't think we are useless."

Almost two weeks passed while Mike and his family camped on the edge of the Black Rock Desert. The days again turned as cold as the nights. The sky grew sullen. Mike said they had to leave. Henie helped her mother pack blackening beef onto the horses. The family again moved eastward, straight across the flat desert and the frozen Quinn River to the Jackson Mountains.

Far south of King Lear Peak they struggled through Rattlesnake Pass. Henie took turns with her older sister carrying the baby. Her mother's feet were wrapped in rags. It made Henie's heart hurt to see her mother stumble in the snow. Mike helped Nive over the pass. The horses were too weak to ride and they all walked, except the small children.

One of the stockmen's horses ran away and now there were only seven. In the morning the horses stood stiff, the hair on their backs matted with ice, hip bones and ribs jutting against sagging skins, bellies swollen, eyes dark and large under frozen lashes. Henie worked with her mother to cut the stockmen's overalls and shirts into clothes for the children. Henie's little brother, Cleve, wore one of the stockmen's caps.

Most of the other living creatures seemed gone from the frozen earth, except for the ravens who squatted in dark rocks and watched them pass, saying nothing. In the sand dunes even the ravens and magpies seemed to be gone. Some animals lay in rock burrows or underground, out of the wind and ice; others like wild horses or pronghorns, or even sagehens, had wandered elsewhere in large bands for the winter. Only Mike and his family plodded across the desert. Buried in burrows below the frostline, sagebrush chipmunks chewed on stored seeds and fruit until warm weather would bring them out for the spring larvae of moths and butterflies. Coiled in dark rock shelters, rattlesnakes slept. The sagebrush lizard, full of ticks and snails, slept with her pale-blue belly and throat flattened against dry rock in a narrow crevice, safe from hawks and badgers until spring. Sage thrashers and sage sparrows had flown away, the interiors of their abandoned nests lined with shredded bark like the floors of old Shoshone winter huts along Rock Creek and the Snake River.

Mike and his family struggled through blowing sand and sleet. Their horses ate frozen grass and stripped leaves from occasional bushes of winter fat. The branches of shadscale were bare. The children ate remains of meat packed at the camp. Mike's sons watched for jackrabbits to bound out of the night. In the moonlight the apparition of a white owl rushed up from the dunes and flew into the darkness. The children uncovered mounds and sent ants bristling over the cold ground like fiery sparks, hurrying in and out of their burrows to form long living streams through dead sand. The children gathered ants, and the women roasted, winnowed, and stored them in a sack to eat.

Everything became turned around. They traveled and hunted at night and slept in the days. They passed Winnemucca and made their way toward Paradise Valley and the Little Humboldt. They were now all on foot, their horses barely able to walk. The starving horses ate incessantly, but dry winter grass gave them little strength. Frozen brush and grass waterlogged and bloated them. Blood streaked their cracked hooves. The family reached the Hot Springs Range and made their camp in Long Canyon. There in a side canyon they shot three of the dying horses that couldn't go on.

They stayed in Long Canyon, ten miles from Winnemucca, for over ten days. Mike and Nive, their three grown sons, Henie and her older sister, the two adolescent boys, and the three smaller children—Hattie, Cleve, and the baby—all kept out of sight in the protected camp during the day. Hogozap, Wonig, and Nogoviz hunted at night like coyotes.

One morning they saw a prospector looking at them from the rim of the canyon. "We have to leave now," Mike said, "even though it's daylight. We can't stay here."

They left Long Canyon and crossed the Osgoods the following night and made their morning camp at the base of the mountains under a gray sky. A light snow was falling. They were now on the east side of the Osgood Range. Their camp overlooked the wide expanse of sagebrush and greasewood of Clover Valley. Patchy snow covered the valley. Muddy-edged drifts in washes and hollows waited for the spring melt. At the far end of the valley stood a stand of bare cottonwoods and the buildings of a ranch. To the northeast lay Gollaher Mountain and the country of Rock Creek Canyon. In a few days they would approach the last stretch of their return home. The days would grow warmer. Grass would be making the streambeds green. They would hear the loud mating thumps of the sagehens. Everything was supposed to be that way. The sage thrasher would appear, back home, poised in the sagebrush, its eye pale yellow, its short tail jerking up and down in the spring sun.

28

Father Enright turned around from the altar and announced that next Wednesday would be Ash Wednesday, the beginning of Lent. Ashes would be distributed at the eight-o'clock mass to mark the time of penitence and fasting, and to remind us that we were dust and into dust we would return.

He asked the congregation to stand for the reading of the Holy Gospel. The Gospel for Quinquagesima Sunday, the last Sunday before Lent, was from St. Luke. The Epistle for Quinquagesima Sunday was from St. Paul's first letter to the Corinthians, chapter thirteen.

The Gospel told how the apostles did not understand Jesus when he told them they were going to Jerusalem and everything written by the prophets concerning the son of man would be accomplished. He would be delivered to the Gentiles, mocked, stripped, scourged, and killed, but on the third day he would rise again. The apostles could not comprehend what he was saying.

As they approached Jerusalem, a blind man sat on the road begging. The blind man heard the crowd going by and asked what was happening. They said, "Jesus of Nazareth is passing by."

The man cried out, "Jesus, Son of David, have pity on me."

The people in the crowd tried to make him shut up but he screamed all the louder, "Jesus, Son of David, have pity on me."

Jesus stopped. He ordered the blind beggar to be brought to him. When the man came up, Jesus asked him, "What do you want me to do for you?"

The blind man said, "Lord, I want to see again," and Jesus said, "See again, your faith has made you whole."

Instantly the man could see and he followed Jesus, glorifying God, and all the people gave praise to God for what they had seen.

There was rustling and stirring in the pews as the people, mostly women and children, sat down and awaited Father Enright's sermon. Dim winter light filled the cold church. The red sacristy candle glowed, surrounded by the shiny doll faces of the saints and the bloody doll face of Christ on the cross. In the shadowy light Father Enright saw fog emerge from his lips as he spoke.

He said he liked to think of what the blind man saw, of what we see when we experience the kingdom of God in our hearts and become children of light, children of day.

St. Paul helps us understand the Gospel, Father Enright said. He helps us see what was hidden from the apostles themselves, what they could not understand.

We are fortunate to have our church named for St. Paul, Father Enright said, this man of the cities. As the bishop of Rome said after Paul's death, "He taught righteousness to all the world," and he can teach righteousness to us as well.

Repay no one evil for evil, Paul tells us, *never avenge yourselves.* Leave it to the wrath of God, for it is written, "Vengeance is mine," saith the Lord, "I will repay." No, if your enemy is hungry, feed him; if he is thirsty, give him drink. Bless those who persecute you, bless and do not curse them. Do not overcome evil by evil, but overcome evil with good. Stop judging one another and love one another with brotherly affection. Let us do things for peace and build up a common life. It is not the hearers of the law who are righteous, but the doers of the law. You cannot condemn others for breaking the law and break the law yourself. Love your enemies, and pray for them.

How can we do such things? we ask. It is childish to believe that we can love our enemies and not repay those who hurt us. But the Gospel says: Yes, it is childish. Whoever does not receive the kingdom of God like a child will not enter it. You may know every hidden truth, you may have faith strong enough to move mountains, but if you have no charity, no love, you are nothing.

These words from St. Paul tell us what the blind man saw and what those who praised God were made to see when Jesus turned from the crowd and saw the blind man crying out. The people who were with Jesus scolded the man and wanted him to shut up, to become unseen, for he was nothing but a beggar, an outcast. But Jesus heard his cries and saw his need and let him see.

The people with Jesus wanted to be like the people in the parable of the good Samaritan. They did not know this outcast was to be loved. They did not see they were to show him charity.

I want justice, you say, not charity. But there is no difference. To love our neighbor is to treat him with justice, to love our enemy is to treat him with justice.

That is the whole law. He who loves his neighbor has satisfied every claim of the law, St. Paul says. All the commandments are summed up in the command to love your neighbor as yourself. Love does no wrong to a neighbor, therefore love is the fulfilling of the law.

Who is my neighbor? you ask, and the Gospel tells us in the parable of the good Samaritan. There was a man on his way to Jericho who was robbed, stripped, knocked unconscious, and left for dead on the side of the road. One minute this man was a person on his way to Jericho, the next he was a bloody lump in the dirt. A thing.

A priest came down the road, but when he saw the body, he passed by on the other side. So, too, did another clergyman, a Levite, who passed by. But a Samaritan who was making his journey saw the naked man and the Gospel tells us when he saw him he pitied him. He bound up the stranger's wounds, pouring oil and wine on them. He took the man to an inn and paid for his care. The Samaritan's response was simple: compassion moved him, he respected this man as a person. The priest and the Levite passed the body as though it were nothing more than the carcass of a jackrabbit or badger or mole in the dirt.

I saw some boys by a woodshed, Father Enright said, who had uncovered a swarm of dark moles under a wood-pile, and they began hitting the moles with sticks, killing them, smashing their heads and their bodies. The boys seemed to act as if it were their right to kill those moles. Why were the boys unable to let the moles be? How could I tell them that they were not better than the moles, they were only stronger? To the boys the moles were just things for them to kill.

The man on the road to Jericho was just a thing to the Levite and the priest as they passed by. They did not see what the Samaritan saw, for the Samaritan was moved by love. Love, says St. Augustine, means: I want you to be. The Samaritan said: I want you to be.

Paul tells us in today's Epistle that love does not insist on its own way, but in the Gospel the people insist on their own way with the blind man. They want him to shut up and do what they want, but Jesus asks the man, "What do *you* want?" "I want to see," the man says. Jesus, who loves the man, says, "See again."

Now the Gospel asks a hard question. Which of the three—the priest, the Levite, or the Samaritan—is neighbor to the man who fell among the robbers? For us the answer is easy. For the Jews in the time of Jesus the answer was horrifying. They despised Samaritans as an inferior race. They did not consider Samaritans to be religiously and racially pure like themselves. Samaritans were outcasts in their own land, and no Jew would expect to be treated decently in a Samaritan village. The reason the lawyer in the Gospel cannot answer the question directly is because he cannot even bring himself to say the word *Samaritan*. The idea that a Samaritan could be good was incredible.

Now we must see the full revelation of the parable. To love our neighbors does not mean simply to do good deeds for them. It does not even mean that we simply must do good deeds for our enemies. If that were the only point of the story it would be more sensible for the Levite or the priest to be the good neighbor to an injured Samaritan. The shocking revelation of the parable is that the despised outcast, the hated enemy, the monstrous Samaritan, is the good neighbor, not us. He is a human being capable of goodness and compassion and we must love him. He is our neighbor.

Imagine the pain of those who were forced to accept such a truth. Now there was no order in the world as they had known it. Now they had to become like children again in a new world where nothing was certain. In a world where one could love a Samaritan, miracles were possible. Righteousness and justice were possible, too.

For Jesus proclaimed that salvation was for everyone, not just a few. It is for those who are most despised and feared, those who are considered most offensive to God, those who are outcasts in their own community. It is for those who are not like you. It is for the Samaritans, enemies you hate, who are not like you. It is for the whores and the swineherds who are outcast, despised, and not like you. It is even for the tax collectors, representing the godless Romans governing your land, who are not like you. It is for the desert Indians, the diggers, the dirt eaters, who are not like you. The evil we do is to insist on the rightness of our own way. I say it simply with Paul: Respect every other human being. Only then do you enter your house justified. Only then are you children of light, children of day.

29

Behind the mountains came the ghost light of morning. The men rode across the scurf of fresh snow toward the north end of the Osgoods. By late morning the snow stopped falling, the wind picked up. In the mountains dull clouds cut off the peaks and rolled through the passes like smoke.

Hills and rimrocks rose up on the sides of the pass and the men halted. Captain Donnelley refused Mort's offer to scout ahead. "We're apt to get shot up in there," Mort said.

Donnelley replied they would keep together so they could help each other. He told Sergeant Newgard to take the lead. Skinny Pascal would order the Indians to surrender, and the men were not to shoot if they did.

Joe Reeder laughed. "Let 'em have their way. The Injuns are as like to shoot a sonofabitch state policeman as anyone else."

The buckaroos insisted on stringing out as they rode through the pass. Ben Cambron took the lead with Mort close behind him. It was almost noon but the cloudy sky remained dull with the light of early morning. Mort looked back to see that Donnelley had fallen far to the rear of the line.

Watching the rocks above him, Mort kept his rifle ready,

expecting at any moment to feel a bullet. When he looked back again he saw that Perry had pushed his horse into a trot and was riding up to the front of the line. They rounded a low rimrock on the east side of the pass when Van Norman said, "There they are."

The hills fell away into a broad snowy plain. Mort looked down in the direction Van was pointing. His eyes followed two faint draws through the brush and snow, then he saw the horses. Half a mile away three or four hobbled horses grazed in a bunch. As he watched, he saw them hop.

In the wind it was hard to hear what the men were saying. Skinny Pascal was pointing toward the southern draw. Mort shifted his gaze and squinted against the wind, following the draw rod by rod until he saw a faint bluish haze rising against the snow. The smoke rose from a campfire at the base of the hills, near the edge of the valley, almost in open country.

The men were ordered to separate and they galloped in two groups around a butte where they dropped into a protected hollow, a hundred yards from where they'd started. Sergeant Newgard said that if they weren't going to stay separated, they should spread out into a line. He said that if they could get within speaking distance, Skinny Pascal was to order them to surrender. It was hard to hear Newgard above the wind. Word passed from man to man, "Spread out, spread out." Someone shouted above the wind, "Let's go." They spurred their horses and the men came up out of the hollow riding over the hill, side by side, in a crescent line.

They started at a trot toward the camp. Mort rode at the north end of the line. He could see sagebrush banked in a circle around the camp. Saddles and blankets were thrown against the sagebrush as a windbreak. A dog barked, and Mort saw a young squaw running and shouting toward the main camp from where she must have been guarding the horses. She was screaming.

People scrambled everywhere in the camp; three or

four grabbed rifles and ran out toward the men, some ran back into the dry wash of Rabbit Creek. The men kept riding toward them.

Mort heard someone shout, "There, over there." Cracks of gunfire popped in the wind. He saw some men circling around the far side of the wash. No one was ahead of Mort except Ben Cambron who kicked his horse into a gallop. There were more shots, and men were jumping from their horses. As he jumped from his horse, Mort lost his balance and fell to the ground. Back on his feet, he turned and Cambron's runaway horse almost knocked him over again. Other horses crashed through the brush. Mort ground-tied his horse and rose to see Ed Hogle and Sergeant Stone behind sagebrush. Bullets whined in the air. Mort stood and fired in the direction of the camp.

The young squaw ran back out to the horses and was trying to drive three of them toward camp. Bullets spit up snow around her. Someone shouted, "Shoot the horses." Sergeant Stone fired and the squaw fell over a bush. Ed Hogle's lips curled back from his teeth like a horse's. "You shot the squaw." He was laughing. Sergeant Stone said, "Oh God." He held his rifle in his hands and looked aghast. The girl's head rose from the brush. Mort yelled, "She's up," but as she got to her feet the horse she was leading lurched against her and she fell under the wounded horse as it toppled to the ground. Bullets hit the other horses. One lay with its neck thrashing wildly up and down while another stood seemingly indifferent, stupefied, as blood poured from its belly. The girl was up again and running toward the camp as the last of the horses threw its head toward the sky and slumped to the ground.

Mort ran toward the camp until he heard men shouting for him to get down. Two hundred yards ahead a black head appeared in the brush. There was a volley of shots and the black head dropped behind sagebrush. "I got him that time," someone shouted. The head popped up again and a rifle cracked. A running form collapsed into the brush. The men fired at the spot where the form disappeared, only to be answered by a shot several yards to the left of where they were shooting.

Mort realized that the Indians were overshooting him. He looked back and saw that his own weary horse and other ground-tied horses were still all right. Behind them Joe Reeder rode toward the Osgoods trying to round up the runaway horses.

On the far side of the camp Mort saw Skinny Pascal rise from the brush. He stood in front of his horse, aiming his rifle at the camp. There was an exchange of shots, and Mort caught a glimpse of a white-haired Indian firing from behind a sagebrush embankment near the camp. Skinny was running back to his horse. The horse bolted in the direction of the Osgoods with only the toe of Skinny's boot showing over the cantle as he hung over the side of the horse and rode at a gallop away from the fighting. Mort saw the stationary head of the horse, a half mile away in the hollow where the Paiute tracker had retreated.

Henry Hughes ran up to Mort, his face slick with sweat. "I think they got the old man," he said.

"Then there's a dead man shooting at us," Mort said.

Between them and the camp a dog was barking. A tricolored collie bounded between the lines of fire. Back and forth the barking dog ran beneath bullets as if in play.

"I see where he is now," Henry said.

Mort thought he saw movement near a spot of green in the gray bank of sagebrush. Both men fired.

"You shoot," Henry yelled. "When he pops up, I'll get him."

Mort fired and saw the head of the man rise instantly. Henry's army Winchester exploded next to his ear and seemed to slam the head back into the brush.

Mort heard Henry laughing before he realized he was laughing, too. "That settles him," Henry said. A bullet cracked back from the brush. Both men looked at each other. "We're too far away," Mort said.

Mort saw that the main body of men had formed a line and was advancing slowly on foot toward the center of the camp. He and Henry stood far to the outskirts of the advancing line. They ran forward to join the men when someone hollered, "They're getting away."

Six or seven flitting forms streaked through the brush as they made a break from the camp and ran down the dry wash of Rabbit Creek, their dark heads bobbing above the tops of sagebrush as they ran down the creekbed into the valley. Those in the camp fired repeatedly while the others made their escape down the gulch.

Mort reached Ben Cambron and told him the Indians were escaping. Ben's pale eyes glanced helplessly in the direction of his runaway horse. He ran to Ed Hogle who knelt in the snow loading his rifle. He ran back to Mort and said, "I can't get any of these galoots started. Will you go?"

"My horse won't make it," Mort said.

"Ed says take his."

Mort and Henry Hughes ran back to the ground-tied horses. Mort mounted Ed Hogle's horse and circled around the Indian camp to where he picked up the outline of Rabbit Creek running into the valley. The country ahead was a rolling brush-covered plain of rises and hollows, gulleys and knolls. He and Henry followed the crooked wash along the bank and saw Joe Reeder and Sergeant Newgard riding down the other side. Behind them the sounds from the camp became distant irregular cracks and whines. Half a mile down the men closed in and dismounted. Joe Reeder fired from the opposite bank of the ravine. Four or five Indians broke cover, running toward Mort and Henry before they dropped into a side wash. They were about a hundred yards away, hidden behind the high brush along the bank. Reeder and Newgard were on the other side of the wash. To the east there was a rise that would bring the Indians into the open if they tried to break in that direction. Mort then saw Van Norman and George Holmes riding into view from the west. The Indians were blocked on all four sides.

Gunfire burst from the cutbank. Van Norman's horse reared and Van slid backward out of the saddle. George Holmes started to dismount when he seemed to change his mind and, flinging himself head first from the saddle, found himself caught trying to get off both sides at once. For a moment he lay sprawled and kicking across the saddle until the horse bolted and piled him off on his head. George shouted, "Van, are you dead?" There was no sound or movement from Van Norman. Then Mort heard a long loud "Naw!" and Mort, relieved, couldn't help laughing at George's outraged cry, "You son of a bitch, let's get out of here." Henry was laughing too at the sight of the men scrambling into the brush on their elbows and knees, rear ends raised like straddle bugs.

A shot cracked from the opposite side of the ravine, and Mort yelled to Henry, "We better get out of here before we shoot each other."

He ran around behind the hillock on the eastern side of the ravine and took off his coat and chaps. Lying on his stomach he worked his way up the knoll with his elbows and toes. He could hear the Indians down in the wash. When he peered over the top of the rise he saw an old woman, a hundred yards away, who looked to be pounding a drum as young boys and some of the children wailed and chanted. Their faces looked black, smeared with mud.

Mort made a run toward the side of the cutbank and saw Joe Reeder. He dropped down and watched Reeder coming through the brush toward a young squaw who shuffled toward him waving a spear with a steel blade at the tip and eagle feathers dangling from the end. Reeder was talking to her. She looked sixteen or seventeen. Her long black hair swung against her face as she weaved and danced forward, jabbing the spear at Reeder, then ran back toward the ravine. She moved back and forth with quick shuffling steps. Reeder kept walking toward her, moving closer to the ravine.

Mort thought he saw someone crawling toward Reeder

in the dry creek below him. He rose up, fired, and the crawling form sagged against the bank. Mort fired again as soon as his sights lined on the swath of black hair. He saw snow fly above the buck's head. Another shot and snow again flew above the dark hair. An arrow flew past Mort. He dropped behind a bush, sure he hadn't overshot the buck twice.

An arrow fell from the sky and landed fifteen feet away, another ten. Mort rolled over the ground and caught sight of the low sky moving above the tips of the sagebrush. The earth seemed to be tilting. Rising high into the air a thirty-inch arrow shrank to the size of a sewing needle before it arched and came whizzing down. Mort rolled from arrow to arrow, jerking them out of the ground, breaking others off at the shaft. He felt enraged. He bit into the arrows, leaving indentations of his teeth on the shafts. He wanted to mark the arrows that were trying to kill him.

When he looked up, the young girl was coming toward him through the brush. Her spear raised, she was running. Mort got up and the upper half of a man rose thirty feet away aiming a rifle at him. Mort fired quickly in the direction of the man and he heard the blast of the man's gun blending with his own. He felt as though he had been punched. He started to run forward, wild with rage, intending to get at the man who shot him. He ran about ten feet when he realized he was not hit. He scraped his face on sagebrush as he fell to his stomach. "You goddamn fool," he said, "you dumb shit." His heart pounded the ground like a fist. He fired toward the rise where the man had been and waited for a head to show. The young girl with the spear had disappeared into the wash.

A horse crashed through the brush behind him and Sergeant Newgard shouted, "What are you shooting at?"

"There's a buck on that rise," Mort said. "Get below and see if we can't crossfire him."

Newgard looked indignantly at Mort, as if astonished by his orders. He threw his head back and wheeled away.

"You goddamn Swede son of a bitch," Mort shouted.

Henry Hughes was out of breath when he reached Mort. He'd seen the man shoot at Mort. "I think he's over there," Mort said. The two men separated and worked around to get the Indian in their crossfire, but when Mort reached the end of the gully, he yelled to Henry, "He's gone."

Both men sat down in the hollow with their rifles on their knees. A bullet whined through the brush. Near the ravine a woman crawled behind a stand of greasewood.

"I'm going to make her jump," Henry said.

"If you shoot, do a good job," Mort said.

"Watch her jump."

Dirt flew within inches of the woman. Her body was like a log. Mort stared ahead and the woman stared back. For a moment she lay still, staring at the two men, then deliberately shoved herself back out of sight.

As the two men moved toward the cutbank, Joe Reeder joined them, and the young girl with the spear danced out in front of them. "I'm going to shoot that little devil," Joe said.

Henry yelled at Joe, and Mort grabbed the muzzle of Joe's rifle. Joe turned on Mort, swearing, his eyes crazy. Mort held the rifle and suddenly twisted it out of Joe's hands. An astounded look of helplessness crossed the bigger man's face as he gazed hesitantly into Mort's eyes. His lips went slack. "Let me have my rifle," he said. His voice was like a child's.

"Promise you won't shoot the little squaw," Mort said.

"I won't shoot her," Joe said.

Mort returned the rifle and Reeder turned away.

"He'll shoot her," Henry said. He was grinning.

Van Norman rode up and said that Newgard wanted them to take back their old positions on the other side of the ravine.

"You can tell that son of a bitch to go plumb straight to hell," Mort said.

"Tell him yourself," Van said.

Newgard rode up behind Van, and seeing the expressions on the men's faces, he said, "What do you boys think we should do?"

"You can go to hell for me," Henry said.

"Take Van with you," Mort said.

"Forget these assholes," Van Norman told the police sergeant, and the two men rode back up the ravine.

Mort was furious at the stupidity of his position and the opaque stillness of the ravine. He was enraged at Henry, too, for the way he was grinning. "We should've stayed up with the others," he said. "There's nothing but women and kids down here."

"They can still kill you," Henry said.

"Where's Donnelley?" Mort asked.

"Who the hell knows?" Henry said.

The two men separated and Mort found himself alone watching Henry's hat drop into a hollow to the south of the cutbank.

At the upper end of Rabbit Creek the shooting had stopped. Sergeant Stone suggested that a couple of men circle around to where the Indians had last been seen. The other men would keep them covered.

Perry rode in a wide loop around the camp and halted. He looked toward the camp and scanned the brush around it. He thought he saw something move but there were no shots. He sat on his horse and waited. He could hear the fighting going on in the valley below.

It was getting late, and Perry knew that if any Indians were still alive, they probably were out of ammunition. There was nothing to do but charge.

Perry kicked his horse and rode at a full gallop down through the camp. He wheeled around and galloped back into the center of the camp, dismounted, and quickly tossed blankets and gear in all directions. He found no bodies nor

anyone hiding in the camp. He remounted and rode in a
circle back to where the Indians were last seen, closer to his
own men. He dismounted again. The bodies of two dead
men lay in the brush. Perry heard distant sounds of gunfire
from the fight in the lower wash. A few feet away, the old
man lay in the snow near a light green stand of greasewood.
Perry saw where the old man had crawled and dragged himself through the snow from where he had last been shot.
Part of his neck was shot away and blood soaked through
his clothes from wounds in his stomach and chest. He was
still alive, looking at Perry as he came toward him. His old
rifle lay cocked in the bush beside him. He tried to raise his
head but seemed unable to move toward the rifle as Perry
reached down to see if he might have a weapon in his
clothes. Perry pulled a pocket knife and bundle of dollar
bills from his pocket. The old man groaned. Perry's hand
came away smeared with blood.

Other men hurried through the brush. Ben Cambron
was running, breathing hard, as he came up and pointed
his rifle at the old man's face. "You'll kill white men, will
you?" he shouted. "What kind of damn Indian are you?" He
shoved the rifle into the old man's mouth and pried up his
lips from red toothless gums before some of the other men
pulled him back. Ben swore and jerked himself free. "You'll
kill white men," he shouted. "What's your damn name?"
The old man turned his head from side to side. Flat black
eyes moved and glared from one man to another. "Me
Shoshone, me Shoshone," he said. Other men pointed their
rifles at him. Perry turned away.

Perry mounted his horse and rode away from the shots
behind him toward the fight in the lower wash. He rode
down the draw to where he saw Van Norman and Sergeant
Newgard. Ed Hogle and Joe Reeder rode up behind them.
The rest of the men remained at the upper end of the wash.

Mort and Henry Hughes joined the men in the lower
wash. Sergeant Newgard ordered them to spread out in a
military line. They would advance into the wash where the

last of the Indians were hiding. Mort objected, saying the Indians were probably down to their last two or three shots. "If we rush 'em quick," he said, "they're apt to get excited and miss. If we walk in they'll have dead aim."

The police sergeant said, "We'll walk in slow. We can shoot better." Van Norman agreed. The men spread out and walked toward the wash. Fifty yards away a black head appeared. The young squaw with the spear broke from the brush and ran toward the men. An arrow flew past Perry and struck George Holmes in the chest. The arrow hung at an angle from the lapel of George's coat and he looked at it curiously. He was wearing two coats and a vest, and a quizzical smile came to his face as he pulled the arrow from his coat.

Twenty yards ahead Mort saw a woman with a bow. He walked toward her, pointing his rifle and yelling for her to put down the bow. The woman yelled back at him in her own language. She motioned at him with her fists and yelled the same words over and over at him. She started to step toward Mort when farther to the left he saw a boy rising from the brush just as two shots knocked pieces of his skull into the air. The young girl with the spear ran down the side of the wash toward the boy. An arrow flew past Mort. He looked back toward the woman with the bow in front of him. A black spot appeared on her forehead, her hair bounced all over her head, and she dropped to the ground like a sack of rocks.

Joe Reeder ran after the girl with the spear. She turned and dodged and ran back toward Reeder, jabbing at him with the spear. George Holmes joined Reeder, and the two men ran and swerved through the brush as though chasing a rabbit. Ed Hogle ran quickly ahead of Mort into the wash. Henry Hughes yelled, "Get back, Ed." A shot cracked from the wash. Ed Hogle dropped his rifle, turned and walked back toward Mort and Henry. Ed was holding his arm tightly across his chest. Blood rolled through his fingers. He spoke as if in disbelief, "My God, Mort, I'm shot." He staggered past the men and dropped face down into the snow.

Mort thought Ed was holding his arm until he turned him off his face and saw the wound in the side of his chest. His lips moved, but he couldn't speak. His eyelids were half closed, the pupils smoky.

"He'd dead," Mort said.

The men rushed into the ravine, Mort and Henry in the center. Others spread to the sides. A man jumped up from the brush and started to run down the wash. He staggered under the first shots hitting his back. A barrage of bullets seemed to lift him off his feet and slam him face-down. The man's back looked as though it had been jabbed with pitchforks. Mort picked up the pistol lying loosely in the man's fingers. The man's eyes followed Mort's hand. It was Harry Cambron's thirty-eight automatic. Mort kicked the man over onto his back and his dark eyes went rigid and dull as dirt.

Farther down the wash bullets struck the old woman who slumped across the drum she was beating. The young squaw dropped her spear and screamed. Running down the wash, she fell to the ground and threw her arms around her mother.

Two children grabbed gravel from the creek bank and threw it into the faces of the approaching men. Some of the men pointed their rifles at the young squaw, but Sergeant Newgard stepped in front of them and yelled not to shoot. They needed her for questioning. The young girl sounded as though she were crying but there were no tears. As she wailed for her dead mother, she had her arms around a crying baby.

Joe Reeder grabbed one of the children, who was also crying, when a boy, about seven or eight, struck at him with a steel-pointed arrow. Before Reeder could grab the boy he ran down the wash. Joe chased him, trying to run through the brush while still wearing his heavy chaps. The small boy was leaving him behind and Joe yelled for help.

Two men rode out on horses and finally caught up with the boy a half mile from where the last of the Indians had fallen. The boy stabbed at the horse's withers with the arrow. Joe Reeder ran up and slapped the boy across the face, but the kid still scratched and bit as he was lifted into the saddle. A buckaroo mounted behind the boy and repeatedly slammed the kid's head against the saddle horn. When the men rode back to where the young squaw still wailed, the little boy's face was covered with blood.

Mort grew aware of the sound of his own feet as he walked back to the knoll where he had left his coat and chaps. The diminishing afternoon light gave the snow across the valley a blue sheen. He saw a horseman in the distance riding toward the Kelly Creek ranch on the east side of the valley. It would be close to dark by the time he got back with a buckboard. Mort looked at his watch. It was just after three.

Mort put on his coat and gathered some of the arrows that had been shot at him. He looked at the carefully made tip of one and saw that his hand was shaking. He expected to hear a shot or a scream, but there was only the uneasy silence, the distant voices of men, and the high-pitched mourning of the squaw and children. He had the lingering sense of being jarred from something unfinished. Something was eluding him. One moment he was running through the cracks and whines of gunfire, the next he stood in abrupt silence. He could not make the connection.

He returned to the wash where the men searched through the brush. No one seemed able to stand still. Mort found a bow and empty quiver in the snow. Henry Hughes called him over to the edge of the cutbank. Ed Hogle lay on his back, his eyes staring at the sky. Henry held the thirty-eight automatic pistol. The buck had killed Ed with the last cartridge in Harry Cambron's own pistol. The only thing Mort could think was that something unfair had happened.

The buck had waited in the brush with one remaining shot and it turned out to be the last shot the Indians had. Ed was killed when the battle was virtually over.

Farther up the wash, Henry said, "I thought you had one in here."

"I thought I did too," Mort said, "I guess he played possum on me." Mort described how the snow flew past the buck's head as he lay against the creekbank.

"Come here," Henry said. The bodies of two dead boys, about twelve and fourteen, lay in the snow. From the way they had fallen, or were dragged, they looked to be holding each other. One was shot in the breast. Mort looked closer. The boy was also shot in the eye and about an inch and a half away in the temple.

Mort and Henry rode to the upper end of the wash, where the men were searching through the Indian camp. The state policemen had piled blankets, skins, saddles, and weapons in the center of the camp. Sergeant Newgard stood guard. He told Mort and Henry to put everything they found into a pile. "This belongs to the state police," he said.

Fruity stepped forward, his face flushed under his boy's cap. "Who in hell gave it to the state police?" he said. He grabbed what looked like an otter skin from the pile.

"Put it back," Sergeant Newgard said.

Mort and Fruity rushed together at the police sergent and sent the big man clumsily sprawling over the pile of Indian loot. Men jumped forward and grabbed bridles, spurs, rattles, and other rawhide work. Newgard lumbered to his feet and yelled for the men to get back.

"Look at these," Fruity said. He showed Mort a ninety-foot braided riata and a pair of silver-mounted spurs. "They were sure crafty," Fruity said.

Van Norman was laughing. He said it was just like a bunch of dumb vaqueros to leave the valuable stuff and get dazzled by a bridle or a pair of spurs. The men continued to grab things they could use, leaving a feathered headdress, skins, drum, and spears for the state police. One of the men found Harry Cambron's gold pocketwatch on one of the dead Indians near the camp. He gave it to Ben Cambron.

In the dusk a team and wagon arrived from the Kelly Creek ranch, six miles away. The men loaded the dead buckaroo and three Indian children into the wagon, but the young squaw refused to leave the body of her mother. She scratched and kicked whoever touched her. "Get in the wagon," Ben Cambron shouted. The girl didn't move.

Mort laughed. "She don't talk United States, Ben."

Ben was angry. "Can you make her get in the wagon?"

Mort walked over to the girl and while telling her to get into the wagon he put his left hand on her shoulder. Whirling around, the girl grabbed Mort's hand and brought it to her mouth and he hit her on the jaw with his fist. He took the girl by both shoulders and shook her until her neck went limp. He motioned to the wagon and she climbed into it.

At the Kelly Creek ranch the men carried Ed Hogle's body into one of the rooms of the ranch house. There was a large buckaroo room with a stone fireplace. They put blankets down on the floor by the fire for the squaw and children. Captain Donnelley asked a Shoshone buckaroo at the ranch to try to talk to the squaw. One of the ranch hands took in a tin plate of food and some milk for the younger chidren. When the Shoshone buckaroo came into the room, the Indian girl threw the plate of food at him and yelled at him. She pulled at her hair and made a hacking motion with her fingers. The Indian buckaroo turned to Captain Donnelley and shook his head. The girl apparently thought he had been in the fight against her family.

There was no telephone at the ranch, and the office in Golconda was closed for the night. Donnelley sent one of the men ahead to the North ranch to make a call first thing in the morning. There was nothing more to be done, no way to get news to the outside about the battle, Ed Hogle's

death, or the capture of the young Indians. Far into the
night the Indian girl and the children with blankets over
their heads rocked and wailed for the dead.

It was almost noon the next day before the coroner from
Golconda arrived at the ranch. When the coroner told the
men they had to bury the Indians, the men became furious.
They threatened to scalp the bodies first. Ben Cambron said
he would cut a razor strop out of the old man's back. The
constable said they were under orders to get a hole dug and
get the Indians buried. Mort proposed to know exactly how
the constable and coroner intended them to dig a hole in
ground that was frozen solid. The constable said he didn't
care how they did it.

Some of the men were about to return to the ranch
when they sighted other horsemen coming across Clover
Valley. "It's Lamb," Mort said.

Sheriff Lamb and two other men rode up the wash.
Lamb stopped by the wreckage of the Indian camp and dismounted. His brother Kize and Deputy Muller were with
him. The sheriff then circled the camp and rode back
toward Rabbit Creek. Dead people and dead horses lay scattered in every direction. He reined up, turning toward the
men grinning at him. His body seemed to rise in the saddle
and his face glowered as he shouted at them. His voice
boomed. "What in hell has been going on around here?"

The men quit grinning. Some of them rode forward and
Mort watched them talking to Lamb, who said nothing. He
sat slumped in the saddle. When Mort approached he heard
someone saying the coroner and constable expected them
to bury the Indians. Lamb told the coroner and constable to
return to Golconda and send out some men with dynamite
to blast a grave. "These boys have done enough already," he
said.

Lamb wheeled his horse around, and Skinny Pascal

joined the sheriff and two other men when they headed back toward Golconda.

In the afternooon Mort tied a rope around the neck of the man who had killed Ed Hogle. He mounted his horse and dragged the boy to where other horsemen were dragging bodies and tossing them into a pile. The coroner had been worried that the men coming from Golconda wouldn't find all the bodies. The four dead Indian men, two women, and two young boys lay in a mound, the bodies heaped on top of each other. "They ought to be easy enough to find now," Henry Hughes said.

The next morning they hitched teams to two wagons. Captain Donnelley sat with the coroner and constable in the spring wagon carrying Ed Hogle's body. The tricolored collie, tied to the back of the wagon, trailed behind. Ben Cambron asked Mort to get the squaw into the other wagon. Mort led the squaw and three children to where Sergeant Stone and Joe Reeder waited. Under the young girl's filth and rags Mort saw dark eyes, smooth round cheeks, and a pretty mouth. But coming through the brush with her eyes crazy and her hair flying, she had been a wildcat. Some of the boys said Donnelley and the Shoshone buckaroo had finally got her to talk and she had confessed to the killings.

The wagons set out from Kelly Creek and the rest of the men mounted their horses for the fifteen-mile ride to Golconda. Frank Perry said nothing as he led Ed's riderless horse. Fruity broke the silence to complain about the coroner. Mort said Lamb seemed so dejected because he could feel the reward money being plucked right out of his pocket.

Seven miles outside Golconda the road turned and ran parallel to the railroad tracks. When Mort saw the steel rails and smelled the creosote-soaked ties, it hit him that the whole thing was finished. Over twenty days had passed since leaving Eagleville and now they were done with it. He felt sore, tired, and empty. He had expected something different. He plodded along in silence, staring at the dark rails, until someone said, "Hey." Mort looked up. Coming from town were saddle horses and wagons. An energetic footman pumping a handcar down the Southern Pacific tracks joined the growing parade as it met the posse and turned toward town where crowds of people behind windows and in second-story balconies waved handkerchiefs and cheered as the men rode into Golconda.

IV
INQUEST

30

POSSE BRINGS IN INDIAN PRISONERS, THE BODY OF COMRADE AND TROPHIES

Bringing with them their dead and the four prisoners captured in Sunday's bloody battle, which resulted in the practical extermination of Shoshone Mike's band of renegades and murderers, the victorious posse of seventeen men arrived in Golconda shortly after 3 o'clock yesterday afternoon after traveling since early morning from the Kelly Creek ranch, six miles from the scene of the fight.

Golconda was crowded with throngs of the curious, its own population largely augmented with people from Winnemucca and neighboring places.

The four prisoners were first to arrive. The Indian girl, her baby sister in arms, another girl and boy, the one about six and the other eight years of age, were placed in Golconda's little boxlike jail, where the girl shrank into a corner, covering her face with a blanket to evade the gaze of the curious crowd. Indian women were permitted to enter the jail to care for the little prisoners, and of one woman the girl asked for a pair of scissors in order that she might cut off her long jet-black hair, saying that she must do this to carry out the tribal custom of mourning for her dead. The request was refused, for fear that the girl might

[255]

try to kill herself and possibly her brother and sister as well.

SHOSHONE MIKE'S BAND

The last stand and the final extermination of Shoshone Mike and his band of Indians as was told by members of the posse was a reminder of early-day experiences of the pioneers of this Western country, when battles with the redskins were a common occurrence.

The effects found by the posse in the camp of the Indians showed conclusively that the band had kept aloof from civilization and had returned to the wild state characteristic of the Indians with whom the whites fought in the State's earliest days. There were bows and arrows, war spears and tomahawks, two Indian war drums whose staccato sound had encouraged the Shoshone bucks to fanatical desperation, and a war bonnet of feathers, probably the headdress of old Shoshone Mike.

One of the most interesting relics of the battle is an ingenious vise, made by the Indians from two large bull horns. The curved horns are bolted together at the small ends, the larger ends being the jaws of the vise, with saw-like teeth, the natural spring holding them tightly together. It is a genuine curiosity, as even the Indians around Winnemucca had never seen anything like it. It is one of the many articles made by Shoshone Mike's band indicating their extremely primitive nature. They were real savages, unmixed of blood, who had carried into these days of civilization all the savagery of the days before the white man's coming.

By their murderous act committed in Little High Rock Canyon, these Indians had threatened the lives, the property, and the peace of the entire State. As long as they were free to move about, no man in all that wide country might feel safe to leave his ranch or to follow his occupation.

CREDIT FOR THE POSSE

Captain Donnelley and his men began at the beginning and remained to the end. They did not speculate. They did not falter. Without haste and without rest they followed the trail. When the grinding monotony of the pursuit changed to the fierce activity of warfare, they were equal to that emergency and throughout it all they comported themselves with credit and honor to the best traditions of the race.

SHERIFF LAMB
UNFAIRLY TREATED

Sheriff Lamb returned to Golconda from the battlefield, he having reached the Kelly Creek ranch Monday about noon. To him is due much of the credit for the victorious result of the chase after the Indians, he having given the posse the information which resulted in the trail being picked up Sunday morning. That Sheriff Lamb was not in at the finish was due to a misleading telephone message sent to him that the trail was not the right one, when it was known by the entire posse that the facts were exactly contrary. Had Sheriff Lamb been treated decently he would have joined the posse at Willow Point Saturday night and would have been with them the next day. In fairness to the posse in general, it should be stated that the misleading message to Sheriff Lamb was by one of the members of the State Police. This unfairness toward Sheriff Lamb is censured most strongly by Sheriff Smith and the Eagleville boys, who were extremely anxious to have Humboldt County's intrepid and fearless Sheriff with them at the finish.

"SKINNY" PASCAL
A REAL HERO

"Skinny" Pascal, the noted Paiute trailer, who lives in Winnemucca, is looked upon locally as one of the real heroes of the battle Sunday, and it is probable that his unerring aim laid the leader, Shoshone Mike, low early in the fight, else the posse's loss would have been far greater.

HOW HOGLE MET DEATH

Ed Hogle, his body bullet ridden, plunged from his horse and fell inert and lifeless upon the desert sands.

He did not die for glory nor for gain. He was a humble range rider and prospector and pursued those peaceful avocations without thought of the public or its opinion.

Ed was not a hero in his own opinion. He simply did his duty and earned his pay, saving it against the time when he could send for that California girl and install her as mistress of his heart and home.

But Ed had a man friend, a stockman who had aided him on several occasions and who stood ready to assist him whenever he might find it necessary to ask for help.

Cambron and Hogle may not have been Damon and Pythias in the intimacy of their association, but they were good, true friends. And when news came that Cambron had been assassinated by merciless savages whom he had done no wrong, a lump came into Hogle's throat and he saw red.

He it was who galloped first in Captain Donnelley's avenging posse and who did not seek the shelter of brush or rocks, but who rode down upon the murderous redskins and avenged with his rifle the death of his friend, before he toppled from his saddle.

This was not an everyday occurrence; it was a chapter in the world's story of heroism and devotion.

31

When Jean arrived in Golconda for the inquest, a Paiute boy by the name of Young Sue was taking photographs. Raised in Winnemucca and trained by a woman there to finish his own prints, Young Sue was considered one of Winnemucca's best amateur photographers. He took a picture of the Indian children as they were loaded onto the train by Sheriff Ferrel and Skinny Pascal for the trip to Reno. Jean got only a glimpse of the Indians. The older Indian girl and little boy kept their faces partially covered with the blankets draped over their shoulders. He was surprised to see that after months on the run through the worst of winters, the little children were plump. He expected to see scrawny, ratty savages. The little boy's pants, too long for him, bunched up around his shoes, torn in front, revealing tiny dark toes. The boy wore a dark brimmed cap much like Jean's own. The little girl wore a single strand of threaded beads around her plump neck.

When Young Sue took pictures of the Eagleville boys and the state police, Jean's uncle, Peter Itzaina from Gerlach, posed with the men as though he were one of the Indian fighters. The men in the posse casually dangled their rifles from the crooks of their arms or held them by their sides, resting the butts on the ground. Jean's uncle held his unfired thirty-thirty with both hands in a ready position in front of him, looking as though he were scanning the brush for an Indian to shoot. Young Sue snapped the picture and the men headed for the bar.

Jean sat through the long testimony of the inquest. During the second day of hearings, the jury concluded that Ed Hogle came to his death as the result of a wound received in the battle with the Indians, and the young squaw who was captured was instrumental in causing Hogle's death. The state police testified that the squaw, who brandished a long pole with the blade of a butcher knife attached to the end, acted as a decoy and drew men into the line of fire from bucks hidden in the brush. She was charged with complicity in Hogle's death but would not stand trial because no one could testify that he'd actually seen her shoot an arrow or a rifle during the battle.

After the inquest into Ed Hogle's death, the coroner proposed to investigate the deaths of the eight Indians individually, but the men's protests at the impracticality of his plan led him to rule that one inquest for the entire group would suffice. The posse complained that Justice Buckley and the jury were trying to turn the proceedings into a murder trial. "Yeah," Mort said, "but they're making us into the murderers." Two of the troublesome jurors delayed matters further by insisting on visiting the scene of the battle. "They're treating us like we're the renegades!" Joe Reeder said.

The members of the posse testified that at no time during the battle did any of the Indians intimate by voice or gesture the slightest desire to surrender. They said that one small boy, eight years old, led them on a mile-long chase through the brush. When the kid was captured and put on a horse, he was so wild, they said, he tried to butt out his brains against the horn of the saddle. A six-year-old, when overtaken, threw rocks at the posse and fought desperately before being captured. The women and children fought right alongside the men. No one willingly gave up. Even after Shoshone Mike and a buck were wounded shortly after the battle began, they refused to surrender. They lay in the brush and continued to fight.

Captain Donnelley, Sergeant Stone, and Sergeant New-gard were the first to be excused from further testimony. They testified that the police had tried to capture all the squaws and kids, but those in the thick of the fight had been shot accidentally. On Friday afternoon Sheriff Smith and Ben Cambron were released, but the other men were still held on subpoena. Before Frank Perry was excused from further testimony, he was told he would have to make good the twenty-six dollars he'd found on Shoshone Mike. George Holmes spoke up and asked, "Why?" The coroner replied that it was against the law to search a dead man, and George Holmes replied, "Hell, he wasn't dead."

Six days after the battle, on Saturday evening, the jury finally concluded that the gunshot wounds inflicted by Captain Donnelley's posse were unavoidable and that Captain Donnelley and the posse were justified in their actions.

At the train station for the trip to Winnemucca Jean joined the other men who were complaining to reporters about their treatment by Golconda officials. They maintained that everyone else in Golconda had treated them royally, but they were angry about their detention. What took four days should have taken only half a day. They'd gotten a rotten deal.

When the train pulled into Golconda, the brakeman and conductor tried to stop the men from boarding the train with their weapons and ammunition. The kid Fruity put his hand over the conductor's face and pushed him back. "We're deputy sheriffs," Fruity said. "If a sheriff hasn't a right to a gun, who has?"

The men shoved the brakeman and conductor aside and stomped into the Pullman where passengers turned their heads in alarm. The laughing men found seats and soon were showing curious passengers some of the relics they'd hidden from the coroner. Mort West unwrapped his bedroll to reveal a quiver, five arrows, a bow, a feathered gauntlet, and a rattle.

In Winnemucca, Jean stayed with his uncle and again met the men the next morning when the sheriff gave them a tour of the prisoners' cage and let them talk to Tranmer and Urie, who'd been in the gunfight with Shoshone Mike's band in Idaho. The last time Jean had seen Tranmer was just before the shovel had slammed down and broken his nose. Tranmer now wore blue overalls and a blue workshirt and it looked as though someone had cut his hair with a bowl over his head. He'd also shaved off his mustache.

"I knowed that old Indian Mike for twenty years," Tranmer said from behind the bars of the cage, "and he was nothing but a renegade who'd steal acorns from a blind sow if he had half a chance."

Nimrod Urie was in the next cell but he wouldn't talk. The kid just lay on his bunk with his back to the men.

"Sheriff Lamb's been trying to blame me for starting this whole dad-blamed Indian mess," Tranmer said, "but I didn't start nothing. I always get nailed for everything. Some even tried to blame me for killing my own stepson like I was some kind of savage. It's a wonder I don't get blamed for killing them black Bascos, too."

Jean felt his face grow hot, but he knew there was nothing he could do. He would never get back at Tranmer for breaking his nose, and he turned away in disgust.

Later that afternoon, when he boarded the Western Pacific for Gerlach with the Eagleville boys, he saw the sheriff and his wife coming up the station landing, Lamb in his dark coat and tie, Nellie in a big hat and fur collar. Lamb shook hands with Jean and wished him good luck. Nellie kissed him good-bye.

"If you ever come back to Winnemucca," Nellie said, "you always have a place to stay."

"No offense," Jean said, "but I'm not coming back."

People at the station were congratulating the posse for rounding up the renegades. As Jean stepped toward the caboose, a woman grabbed his arm and said, "There's only one thing you boys didn't do that you should've. Nits breed lice. You should've killed them all."

As the train began to pull through Winnemucca, telephone wires whipped past the caboose window, the wires twisting and turning against a lambent blue sky, flying up out of sight and slicing into view again. The caboose rocked and swayed as the train began to pick up speed at the edge of town.

Jean looked up to see Ottie Van Norman's blue eyes gazing at him. Van Norman sat down and put his hand on Jean's knee. "I knowed your father," he said. "He was a fine feller. I'm sorry this happened." Jean nodded. The cowboss was the only member of the posse to speak to him about his father.

In a couple of days he'd be home. He felt no relief. For some reason he'd needed to stay in Golconda to the end, to see the inquest through. His uncle, Peter Itzaina, had returned to Gerlach before the hearings were over. His Uncle Paul had never left Winnemucca. He said he could read about it in the newspapers. "They say if Sheriff Lamb had been out there," his Uncle Paul said, "this thing never would've happened."

"He wouldn't have made any difference," Jean told his uncle. "Once those boys started over that hill, once they fired the first shot, nobody could've stopped it, not even Lamb."

"He would've tried, though," Jean's uncle said.

Now that he'd stayed for the inquest, Jean came to see the whole thing as a charade. He'd been stunned when he'd seen those little Indian kids climbing into the train. How could anyone be angry at them? Everything had turned out as his mother had said: there were no heroes; the whole thing was stupid, mishandled; the truth was that the Indians were just camped out there and thought his father and the others were coming to get them. Federal troops should have rounded them up and shipped them back to the reservation and been done with it. Why were sons of bitches like Tranmer and Urie left to live and not these Indians?

As the train veered northwest out of Winnemucca, the Sonoma Range came into view behind him. Jean gazed at the gently pleated mountains stretching quietly across the sagebrush plain. Under the blue sky, the dark violet range looked unreal, motionless and silent, as if nothing at all had changed since the day he'd first stepped off the train as a boy from the country. Now that the Indians were dead and the inquest finished, he felt things closing around his father like water around a stone dropped into a lake. The only thing different from when he'd left home was that nine more people were dead: five men counting Ed Hogle, two women, and two children. Altogether, fifteen people had died as a result of Shoshone Mike's clash with Tranmer. If he'd been there with the posse to shoot old Shoshone Mike in the head, what difference would it have made? His father would still be dead.

It distressed him to realize that if his father hadn't been killed, he might've never returned to Eagleville. Now he had a family to take care of. Someday he'd probably be doing what his father never had a chance to do. He'd take over the bands and build them up and buy land. He'd be finishing what his father had started. It made him sad to realize that his father's loss would be his gain.

The train wailed its departure from Winnemucca, answered in the distance by hoots of a freight on the Southern Pacific tracks, a long line of boxcars and flatcars shooting through town away from Jean. On the receding freight Jean saw two flatcars loaded with new automobiles, on their way to Reno and California.

32

When Mort climbed onto the roof of the caboose, he found some of the Eagleville boys in the cupola with their rifles. One of them had fired a shot into the air as a farewell to Winnemucca.

As the train picked up speed outside town, the caboose rocked and swayed. It was a bright, clear afternoon, but the sun was dropping fast. The desert in the distance looked red. Joe Reeder spotted a jackrabbit running parallel to the train and fired. The boys cheered as the jackrabbit tumbled in the dust.

As the train chugged past Jungo and the Antelope Hills, the boys hollered and whooped when they saw something to shoot at—a running jackrabbit, a loping antelope, a dust cloud raised by a distant herd of wild horses. Anything alive and moving drew shots from the exuberant lads as the caboose rattled across the desert.

Mort grew bored and climbed back down the ladder into the caboose. He pulled from his pocket a postcard he'd gotten in Winnemucca from a cousin in California. She congratulated him for his part in tracking down the Indians. "Your grandfather, father, and all your uncles from the Civil War days would be proud," she wrote.

All his life Mort had heard about how his relatives had

ridden into battle with the cavalry in Tennessee. Now he'd been in his own battle.

He tore out a piece of lined paper from his notebook.

"Dear Cousin," he wrote. "Yours received. Came just after we got to Winnemucca from our Injun Fight. We have had Parties and Receptions of all kinds in Golconda and everyone there called us Heroes and slobbered over us until we had to hide out. People there sure treated us fine. I had the fun of plugging one of the sons of gun. I sent two holes through him about a inch apart. He's one of the good Indians."

Mort looked out the window. It was starting to get dark. Occasional gunfire and shouts still broke through the monotonous rumble of the train as the boys continued to amuse themselves on the roof of the caboose. He remembered after the battle looking down at the two Indian boys lying in the snow, arm in arm, shot through their heads. It was strange how some of the posse were reacting to the battle. When he'd tried to talk to Perry about it, he got up and walked away. "I don't want to hear any more horseshit about this deal," Perry had said. Mort knew that Perry just wanted to get home to his family. He'd probably also been thinking about his Indian girlfriend. Whatever it was, Perry acted like he'd gone through some sort of hell. Mort knew that in later years they'd all remember that day as the height of their lives.

He continued to write to his cousin. "I was with Ed Hogle when a Indian Buck shot him through the chest. I can still see Ed's dying Eys looking up at me. I will never forget them."

Mort looked out the window. The gray landscape passed like shadows. He thought about the way Ed Hogle had died, shot with the last bullet in his friend's pistol. It seemed so unfair. He saw Ed lying in the patchy snow staring up at him with his dead eyes. He couldn't get those eyes out of his mind. It was like the image of his father's face behind the small window of the burning hall before the building had collapsed. All these years the memory of that night had preyed on his mind.

He bent over his notebook paper.

"From that night in Silver Lake, Oregon," he wrote, "when Les Duncan and I as small Lads fought through a roaring wall of fire, leaving behind us forty-three who would never again see the light of day, among them all I had in the world, my Father, Mother, Brother, and Sister, I have known that Life is Tragic.

"But memories are more tragic for they bring back: Ghosts."

33

One night during the inquest Father Enright came to the jail to talk to Lamb. A splotch of gray candle grease stuck to the sleeve of the priest's cassock. He kept removing his glasses and running his fingers over his eyes and through his hair. His distressed voice was tight as though the room held insufficient air for him. "What's going to happen to the children?" he asked.

His thin face appeared gaunt, ridged from lack of sleep, his puffy eyes colorless.

"I don't think you have to worry," Lamb said. "They've been through enough already."

"They're putting them on trial."

"It's just an inquest," Lamb said. "It's routine. I think they'll be taken care of."

Lamb saw that the priest was crying, but there were no tears. Grief pressed his voice into a thin reed. His neck and face became mottled. "They never had a chance," he said. "None of them had a chance. People wanted them dead. They didn't want justice. They wanted those people dead. Why are we all so afraid?"

Lamb stood up and walked to the dark window, as though he felt a need to show the priest he had no answer.

It was as if they stood at the dead end of their meeting; they could stand there all night or move on.

"We talk about bringing the kingdom of heaven into this world," the priest said, "but it's not possible. The violent bear it away."

"Bear what away?" Lamb asked. He returned to the priest and put his hand on his arm. "I don't think I can be any more help to you. You have to remember those Indians massacred innocent people. They had wives, families, friends. People felt threatened."

"That's what we said," Father Enright replied. "We said they were savages. We said they were going to destroy our homes, our families, our laws, everything that made us people. Then we went and did that to them. We did to them exactly what we said they were going to do to us. What does that make us?"

34

High dust clouds streaked the horizon as the last bands of sheep crossed the desert toward the shearing corrals. At the makeshift pens near the Western Pacific freight house at the edge of town, Nellie Lamb climbed from an automobile with three men in business suits to watch the shearers at work. In the open-air shed over thirty men stood amid dust and bawling sheep as they clipped away mounds of wool to be packed into long burlap sacks. Slowed by a cool rainy spring, the men now made up for lost time. Nellie watched Skinny Pascal hug a sheep against his knees, shears flashing, cascades of fleece spilling over his hands, until a ewe, bleating for her lamb, stood naked and nicked, shorn of her coat.

Skinny shouted his number to the counter who sat perched above the din of bleating sheep. Stretched through the brush outside the corrals bands of other sheep waited to be shorn. In the distance a high pale blur of dust against the metallic sky marked the coming of another thousand or more along the road from Sulphur.

It was late Friday afternoon. Nellie was returning from where the Indian battle had been fought several weeks earlier in Clover Valley. She'd gone out to the valley with the landowner, Henry Pratt, and two bankers to look at 55,000 acres Mr. Pratt was planning to sell to an Eastern corporation. The land in Clover Valley was to be subdivided into farms and colonized. Nellie wanted to see it before it went on the market.

Lamb was still in Reno. Lawyers for Frank Tranmer had gotten a change of venue to Washoe County for his trial, and Lamb had delivered him to the jail there. Since the trial was to start on Monday, Nellie didn't expect him home for at least another week.

That morning she'd looked out over the land in Clover Valley and imagined what it might be like to have a ranch there. It was a clear spring morning. Snow water ran down the mountainsides and into washes where willows showed red along the banks. The valley bloomed with clusters of pink sand flowers. Green patches of native hay made her think of her father's ranch when she was a young girl.

The Eastern investors planned to establish a water project that would conserve and distribute water over Clover Valley in a system of reservoirs and canals. Nellie had heard that a number of farmers from the Eastern states were ready to occupy the land once the project was completed. It would be the biggest land sale in the history of Humboldt County.

"We'll just have to see what happens," Nellie told Henry Pratt.

"A person would have a tough time without water," Henry Pratt said. "It's all right for cattle now, but it would be hard country for a dry farmer."

On the way home the men pointed out where Rabbit Creek cut through Clover Valley toward Kelly Creek. The spring sky looked so wide and quiet over the dull expanse of sagebrush that it was hard to imagine men running through the brush killing wild Indians. In the noon glare the faded blue humps of the Osgood Range looked somnolent against the pale sky. The rolling plain and brush stretched motionless and empty. Nearly all the stockmen had already driven their cattle out of the valley into the

Santa Rosa Mountains for summer grazing. Behind the mountains, dark columns of smoke furled into the windless sky from where dry farmers were clearing land in Paradise Valley. Over the Indians' grave, someone had erected a post and a wooden sign: SHOSHONE MIKE AND HIS BAND OF MARAUDERS.

"I hope we've seen the last of it," Henry Pratt said.

"Graham thinks we have," Nellie said, "but he has to be careful. People are scared. They think there's going to be more Indian uprisings on the reservations over this deal. There are a lot of Indians left in this country."

"Thank God they're not like these renegades. They say that young squaw confessed to seventeen murders besides those stockmen."

"Graham says that's all rumor," Nellie said.

"No, I read it in the newspaper. The state police got her confession. They don't know what to do with her because they're afraid she'll run off any reservation they put her on. She wants revenge."

"Then the same thing will happen to her as the rest of these renegades," Nellie said. "I hear when they found that old Indian out here—old Shoshone Mike, his body looked like a sieve."

"He got what was coming to him," Henry Pratt said.

Later in the afternoon, Nellie felt her thoughts drift as she stood next to Henry Pratt watching the shearers at work on the sheep. It was a relief to have the Indian mess over with, to feel relaxed, to watch the men at work. Engulfed in the dust and heat of late afternoon, the oily smells, and the bleating of sheep, she found her eyes fixed on Skinny Pascal's hands, shiny and soft from greasy wool, holding the throat of a ram as his long slender fingers worked the shears back and forth. Skinny was about the same age as Graham, though he had a younger face and no mustache. Oiled with raw lanolin, his hands looked smooth as cream. It was said that no woman had softer hands than a sheepshearer.

Some sheepmen claimed Mexicans, and some local Indians like Skinny who joined them, were the best shearers, although machines were beginning to make most shearers equal. From where Nellie looked through the wool and dust floating in the late afternoon light, the men looked much the same, bent over the sheep, moving at a similar pace. It was difficult to tell an Indian from a Mexican. Their leather aprons were black with oil, the wooden floor of the shed slick. A tall Mexican with a thin mustache took a break and smoked a cigarette near the canvas siding of the shearing shed. Nellie heard him called *capitán*. His hand glistened in the late afternoon light.

Nellie remembered that the softest hands she ever touched on a man were those of the Englishman in San Francisco. When he took off his lemon-colored gloves and shook hands with her, his skin felt silky. She found herself dreamily wondering how Pascal's hands, glistening and brown in the thick wool, might feel against her own skin. She imagined those fingers touching her, running under her breasts, moving over her stomach and down the bare skin of her legs. At one point Pascal looked up, recognized her, and smiled. She smiled back and felt a physical sensation, as if a breeze had passed over her heart. It seemed strange to her how her mind could so suddenly run to impossible thoughts. It was as if life unexpectedly became vaporous a few moments after it seemed most solid, as when she'd ridden in the car with Henry Pratt and the bankers talking of land sales and mortgage rates. Now, as she watched Skinny Pascal, the talk and concerns of the morning seemed unreal.

She could imagine herself stepping across the borders of her own life into a side of experience known to strangers. She remembered the surprise of freedom on a billowy bright day in San Francisco when she'd walked through the streets looking at the men, seeing them look at her, feeling herself open and warm in a way that made her sense her nakedness under her clothes. It was as if she'd gone over the wall into a new country, a new life, as she walked down the streets open to all who looked at her. The Englishman she had met at her sister's was actually a man she'd met before, on the night train between Reno and San Francisco. He had been kind to her on the train, offered her a pillow and blanket for the ride, and brought her a cup of tea from the dining car. They had ridden side by side through the night, and it was she who had invited him to her sister's for dinner and a card game.

One afternoon they went together to the Greek theater at the Berkeley campus across the bay. They rode the ferry back and forth. After dinner she went up to his hotel room while he got a coat to wear against the evening fog, and it was there he asked her to join him when he sailed from San Francisco. Nellie remembered him standing by his hotel window, smoking a cigarette. She had realized how easy it would be to go with this man, almost as easy as not to go with him, or to spend the night with him, or simply to sit and talk for a while and then go home.

His question did not surprise her; they'd become friends. She knew how things happened in other people's lives, how fragile life was. She could understand how a man like Justice Fitts could live with one woman, follow another to Reno, and find his life in shreds. Others could judge so quickly only because they did not understand themselves. The Englishman was kind to her, showed such feeling for her. She so often found herself taking care of others, like Justice Fitts or the Erramouspe boy. Graham seldom needed such care. Now here was a man willing to love and care for her rather than the other way around. She was touched. Maybe something might have happened if she could have stayed with him without leaving Graham. She found herself wanting this man, but she wanted Graham, too. She could imagine herself with two men, if life allowed it, one to love and one to love her.

After the Englishman sailed alone from San Franciso, Nellie confided in one of her new friends after a Christian

Science meeting, and the woman told Nellie, "It might be animal magnetism, but it couldn't be love." Nellie was shaken by the woman's certainty. She came to realize after further thinking that the Englishman who cared for her, or seemed to care for her, really needed her so much more than she needed or cared for him that even the temptation of sleeping with him seemed ridiculous. She read in the section on marriage in *Science and Health* that "infidelity to the marriage covenant is the scourge of all the races." The possibility of her thoughts stunned Nellie. She thought of Kent and Ray, and her situation seemed preposterous.

When she returned to Winnemucca it was as if she'd crossed a border from a freakish dream back into real life. There they were—the real, solid faces of Kent, Ray, and Graham. There were chickens to kill and cook, school clothes to buy, meetings to attend, card parties, Eagles' socials, her house and friends. After the dreadful nightmare of the Indian chase was over, things began to look up. In California she'd felt progress swirling all around her; in Winnemucca, she became part of it. Everything began to happen at once. Friends asked if she'd serve as a vice president of the local branch of the Nevada Suffrage Society. Plans had to be made now, Nellie was told, because it wouldn't be easy to win the popular vote in Humboldt County. Both state senators and both congressmen from Humboldt had failed to vote for the amendment in the last legislature.

A new burst of progress came with the spring, and Winnemucca entered a streak of luck. Everywhere Nellie looked, things were changing. The new gambling law went into effect, and slot machines, roulette wheels, craps and faro tables moved out of sight. The new school law passed, and Lamb made the rounds to serve notices to all the occupants and house owners in the red light colony, telling them they had thirty days to relocate outside town. Support grew in the senate for Winnemucca to become the state capital. The sheriff's office got a new paint job, and the state police finally installed the Bertillon system. Cement sidewalks lined almost all the main streets. The town looked new except for all the box elder trees beginning to die along the streets. The leaves mysteriously dried up, the twigs and branches became sticky with some kind of small insect. Spraying seemed to do little good.

Nellie marked her kitchen calendar with things to do with the boys. The 101 Ranch Real Wild West Show came and went. As usual, local Indians had begun gathering at the fairground days in advance, and on the Saturday morning when the show pulled into town, practically the entire Indian population of Humboldt County seemed on hand to greet it. Several shaggy buffalo with clouds of flies buzzing around their heads rode through town on a float. It was the first time the boys had seen live buffalo. Ray was disappointed, Kent indifferent.

As Nellie rode through Winnemucca with Henry Pratt, she noticed posters in shop windows announcing that the magician from Tonopah was coming to the Nixon Opera House. She remembered that every time the magician from Tonopah came to town Graham was away. The last time she'd gone to see his performance she went with Justice Fitts. She wondered what Graham might be doing while waiting in Reno for the Tranmer trial. It was even easier for a man than a woman to become involved with someone. A man didn't have to go to the cribs for a sporting girl. In Reno they were everywhere.

It was still late afternoon when the automobile stopped in front of Nellie's house and Henry Pratt escorted her to the front gate. She told him she'd enjoyed being with him. He'd been a real gentleman.

When she reached the front door, her skin burned with the heat and dust of the afternoon. She looked forward to a long bath in the empty house. She'd arranged for the boys to stay with friends after school since she didn't know when she would return.

The coolness of the dark living room brought immediate relief as she stepped through the door until she was startled to see the form of a man rise from a chair and say, "Throw up your hands." The man grinning at her was Lamb. "Graham!" she said. "You're home."

"Just got here," he said. "I didn't want to waste two days in Reno. I can go back Sunday."

"I can't believe it."

"I thought we'd eat at the hotel," Graham said.

He pointed to the chair where stacks of coiled roping lariats looked greased in the dim light. "I bought the boys those ropes."

"Let me get changed," she said.

After her bath and with a new ruby pin on her blouse, Nellie walked with Graham to the Lafayette Hotel. Graham wore the tie she'd given him on his birthday and ate fresh oysters and fried spring mallard. Nellie ordered broiled salmon in anchovy butter.

On the way home in the last light of day Nellie pointed to a poster announcing the performance of the magician from Tonopah.

"The show's tomorrow night," she said. "Do you think you finally want to see this guy?"

"I don't see why not," Graham said.

Nellie took his arm as they crossed Bridge Street. "Well, I'll be damned," she said. "Maybe our luck's changing."

They passed the lot where digging had begun for the foundation of the new federal building. People nodded and waved as they passed. The elms and poplars along the streets looked golden in the dusk, but it made Nellie sad to see all the box elders dying.

As they passed St. Paul's Church, Nellie said, "Father Enright never really got over what happened to those Indians. The last time I saw him, he kept saying, 'It should've never happened.'"

"He's right," Lamb said. "It shouldn't have."

Nellie looked at Graham from the corner of her eye. She didn't want to get into it again about the massacre and the

Indians. It still struck her as bizarre that on the morning of the battle she was at a Christian Science service while Graham was in his office. Neither knew the fight was on. She knew he was still mad at Captain Donnelley, but she was just as glad that the state police hadn't told Graham they were on a hot trail. He would've been right in the thick of it. What happened to Ed Hogle might've happened to him. There was something almost fated about the way things had worked out.

"I just think those boys did the best they could with those Indians," she said. "They captured that squaw and those kids. I can feel sorry for those kids, but it's hard to feel sorry for the rest of that bunch after what they did to Jean's father. I don't see how it would've been better to round them up just so they could be tried and lynched. Would that be better?"

"We thought that way about Tranmer and Urie," Lamb said, "so why not the Indians? Why couldn't they be caught and tried, just like anybody else?"

Nellie felt uncomfortable. She didn't like comparing the Indians to Tranmer and Urie. She felt unfairly pressured, as when Father Enright had tried to trick her into comparing those renegades with civilized people. "If they don't behave like everyone else," she said, "why should they be treated like everyone else?"

"What about Tranmer? He killed two people in cold blood just to get their money. You can't get much more savage than that."

"I don't remember Tranmer cutting up the faces of those people. Those Indians weren't like him. They were out of the dark ages. Those boys had a job to do and they did it."

"I guess a lot of people feel the same way," Lamb said, "or else it would've never happened."

Nellie felt the argument drawing them apart, as if they were falling back into their old ways. "Sometimes I don't know where you get your ideas, Graham." She pulled his arm and tried to laugh. "Come on, the boys'll wonder where we are. Let's get home."

Winnemucca looked peaceful in the evening light. It seemed to Nellie much longer than a couple of months since she'd walked through the streets, socked with snow and ice, feeling sad for Jean Erramouspe's father and the other men murdered in the desert. She didn't blame the Indian children for what had happened, they had no choice in the matter, but she felt threatened by what they stood for. Killing people was terrible, but a fearful world was worse. If decent people started getting sentimental about a barbaric past, she knew that her sons would never know what it meant to live in a civilized and peaceful world. It was to have evenings like this one, she realized, that Graham and the state police had to go after those savages. It was on evenings like these that she remembered as a young girl riding happily with her father and mother across their ranch. It was incredible how much had changed in such a short time. Her own boys were now the same age as she when she had ridden with her father and mother. She now had to think about her own children and their future.

35

After Lamb delivered Nimrod Urie to the Nevada State Penitentiary in Carson City, he went to find Superintendent Donnelley of the Nevada State Police. It was his second visit to the state capital within a week. Nimrod Urie had been convicted in Winnemucca of first-degree murder even though his confession had been thrown out of court. The defense maintained that Lamb had used improper methods to get the confession, and the judge agreed. Urie was still sentenced to die, but his case was under appeal, and Lamb suspected that after the appeal, Urie's sentence would be commuted and he'd be out on parole before long.

Tranmer's trial was going on in Reno and Lamb knew he'd be doing a lot of traveling back and forth in the next few weeks. The change of venue from Winnemucca to Reno had helped Tranmer. He was likely to be convicted, but appeals and stays of execution would keep him out of the death cage for years.

When Lamb reached the state police headquarters, he found Donnelley at his desk getting ready to leave for the state legislature to make an appeal on behalf of the Eagleville boys. It seemed the state had reneged on its reward. Both the state of Nevada and the state of California claimed that no reward had been formally offered. Only the

Cambron cattle company and the citizens of Surprise Valley kicked in any money at all, but it was tied up in litigation. Superintendent Donnelley looked up from the papers he'd gathered together on his desk.

"Of course, none of my officers will collect a cent," Donnelley told Lamb. "We were just doing our job. But even so, it looks like the most those boys will ever get is a little over a hundred dollars apiece, if that. I think the state owes them something more after what they went through."

"Those boys were brave," Lamb said, "there's no doubt about it. They really didn't know what they were up against, and they stuck it out."

"That's why I want to get something for them."

"I know they'd like some money, but most of them weren't out there for just the money. It was too cold for that."

"They didn't even know about the money until we got to Winnemucca," Donnelley said. "Those boys were driven. They wanted to get those Indians."

"That's why you should've been at the front of that line when they caught up with them."

"I wanted those Indians, too," Donnelley said. "And I got them."

"But you were the law out there. Those boys wanted vengeance. It was your job to keep them in line."

"I don't really appreciate being preached to, Sheriff, especially since you weren't out there. Things are different when you come through a blizzard against a bunch of savages with rifles ready to kill you."

"I wasn't out there because you didn't want me out there."

"Let's be reasonable, Sheriff. Even if you were out there, the outcome would've been the same. Those Indians would've never given up without a fight."

"I know that," Lamb said, "but they might've been taken. Shoshone Mike was wounded and helpless at the end of the fight. He was still alive."

"He was as good as dead. Let's face it. There's no place for such Indians any more."

"That's where you're wrong. Those Indians got along fine with people up north before this thing started."

"There might've been a day when you and those Indians could've got along, Sheriff, but your day's over. You can't reverse the sweep of history. You said yourself those Indians were out of the past. Nothing could've saved them."

"You could've tried."

"It was only a matter of time. If we hadn't wiped them out, somebody else would've. It was inevitable."

"Nothing's inevitable," Lamb said, "especially that."

A week later, Lamb walked with Superintendent Asbury of the Carson Indian Training School toward the red brick jail where the young squaw and three children had been kept since their return to Reno.

No decision had been made about what to do with Snake and the three little snakelets, as people called them. Because of the young squaw's avowed desire for revenge, one plan was to split them up and ship them out to reservations in different states, but the squaw became hysterical when she learned she was to be separated from the children.

An application was made to the Bureau of Indian Affairs to secure the children for a vaudeville engagement. Another application came from a moving picture concern preparing to go over the route of the chase from the scene of the Little High Rock massacre to where the Indians were wiped out. At Rabbit Creek the company intended to stage a reproduction of the battle with real Indians filling in and using the squaw and children in the reproduction, in order to give the picture some variety and special interest.

The four children were moved back to the jail after Henie ran away from the Carson Indian Training School.

She and another Shoshone girl named Ida Best escaped one night without a trace. The papers reported how she had frequently lamented that she herself had not been able to kill all the white men in the avenging posse.

"There was a lot of fuss because some of the papers said Shoshone Mike had killed nineteen people besides those stockmen. They said the squaw would get some other reservation Indians and go on another rampage."

"Shoshone Mike must've hid all those murdered people pretty good," Lamb said, "since none of the bodies ever turned up."

A week after running away, the young squaw mysteriously reappeared at the school. "She wouldn't say where she'd gone or why she'd returned," Superintendent Asbury told Lamb, "but it was obviously the other kids that brought her back. We think she and Ida Best headed back up to Idaho, but she wouldn't say. We think she just couldn't stay away from the kids. They're all the family she has. That's why I was surprised she left at all. You should've seen her when she thought they were all going to get split up."

Superintendent Asbury told Lamb that when he first visited the Indian children in the Reno jail he found them so ragged and dirty, so like hunted creatures, he felt he had to do something until some disposition was made of the case. "Those children are not criminals," he told Lamb. "Some of the people in town here have made them clothes and sent things like cookies and candy. Others think some of the ladies are slobbering over them too much." He chuckled. "The newspaper reported that the squaw was still alive despite the fact that she was forced to take her first bath a few days ago."

Superintendent Asbury had appealed to the Department of the Interior to have the children permanently transferred to his school, but a request had come from their relatives in Idaho to have them returned to Fort Hall. "I think they will decide to send them back up there to their relatives, but I'm sorry about that. They would get a good education at the training school. I don't think she'd run away again."

Lamb and Superintendent Asbury entered the dark jail where a Shoshone woman, Mary Austin, a former pupil at the Carson Indian Training School, was with the children. The superintendent had sent her ahead with candy to pave the way for their interview.

"Well, I'll be damned," Lamb said.

The four children, their faces freshly scrubbed, sat on a wooden bench against the far wall talking to the Shoshone woman. The young squaw called Snake sat resplendent in a late model black hat, a new dress with creampuff sleeves, and red ribbons galore. She held a hem-stitched handkerchief and sat with her ankles crossed. The little girl was similarly dressed while the boy wore a sailor jersey, shined shoes, and a checked driving cap. The baby looked like a doll stuffed into layers of taffeta, her small face peeking out beneath a white bonnet tied tightly around her plump chin.

The young squaw turned dark languid eyes toward Lamb. Her smooth round cheeks were scrubbed and shiny in the noon light.

"I'd like those people who talk about Snake wanting revenge to see her now," Lamb said.

The young girl's thin lips tightened and her eyes closed down into hard slits. A staccato of harsh guttural words spit from her lips.

The Shoshone interpreter smiled at Lamb. A straight fringe of dark bangs cut straight across the top of her wide, friendly face. "She say her name not Snake," the woman told Lamb. "Her name Henie. Her brother is Cleve, and her sister Hattie. The baby no have name yet."

"Henie's learning English real quick," Asbury told Lamb. "She'll be a good pupil."

"I'll be careful what I say," Lamb said.

He took a chair between Asbury and Mary Austin, facing the young girl. He kept his eyes on Henie as he spoke to the interpreter. The girl's face remained impassive as she politely answered his questions. At times she looked toward Superintendent Asbury, as if for help, and he would tell Lamb things the girl had already revealed in previous interviews.

The girl told Lamb that prior to leaving Gollaher Mountain, her family had never killed anybody, and they had never stolen any cattle or horses. They shot the white boy in retaliation for the murder of her brother. They then took some horses from the white men who had attacked them.

"Ask her about the buried horses near Gollaher Mountain," Lamb said.

Translating the girl's reply, Mary Austin said, "She say she know nothing about buried horses. Why would they want to kill and bury horses? They need horses to leave the country."

For nearly an hour, the girl told Lamb about her family, the flight across the desert, and the return toward Gollaher Mountain. They wanted to go home, Henie said. They just wanted to be left alone, to live as they had.

An automobile honked outside, and Superintendent Asbury crossed the room. The horn sounded again, and the little boy, Cleveland, ran toward Asbury and peered around his legs as the superintendent opened the door. "It's Charlie," the superintendent announced.

Outside, Sheriff Charlie Ferrel sat in a big open-top Austin, ready to take the four Indian children for a ride. The little girl, Hattie, led her tiny sister toward the door. Cleve had already run outside.

"One more question," Lamb said to the interpreter. "It's been reported that you're revengeful, Henie. People say you'd take advantage of any opportunity to kill white people if you're released."

Mary Austin translated Lamb's words. Henie shook her head and replied to the Shoshone woman. "I have no desire to kill any person," she said. "I don't like to see dead people."

Henie turned hard, dark eyes toward Lamb. Shadows fell across her face, and for a moment he saw again Shoshone Mike's rigid face lying frozen beside the green greasewood northeast of Winnemucca.

Lamb followed the children outside and watched Henie climb into the front seat of the car next to Sheriff Ferrel. Her sisters, brother, and Mary Austin were in the back.

"You want to go for a ride, Graham?" the red-haired sheriff shouted above the roar of the engine. "There's room up here."

"I have to head back to Winnemucca," Lamb hollered.

"How about you?" the sheriff shouted to Superintendent Asbury.

"Next time," the superintendent yelled.

Sheriff Ferrel saluted and pulled a pair of driving goggles down from his cap over his eyes. He gunned the engine a couple of times and ground the transmission into gear. The car lurched forward. Henie reached up and straightened her hat. She folded her hands into her large, creampuff sleeves, and looked straight ahead.

Lamb and the Indian superintendent watched black smoke trail from the automobile as it roared down the street.

"Those kids are lucky," Superintendent Asbury said. "Their past may be dead, but they're survivors."

"The future, too," Lamb said. "Their future's dead, too."

"What do you mean, Sheriff?"

Lamb nodded in the direction of the disappearing children. "Well, now they're just like us, aren't they?"

Afterword

The central events of the preceding story occurred not far from Battle Mountain, Nevada, where my grandparents lived after moving to the United States from the Basque province of Vizcaya. This novel, then, is a rendition of a story—or a series of stories—surviving in the minds and words of people I have met.

For dramatic purposes, the fictional chronology of this novel varies at times from the actual chronology of certain historical events. For the record: Sheriff Lamb arrested Frank Tranmer and Nimrod Urie on January 7, 1911, the day after the murders in Imlay. Captain Donnelley arrived at the Ely-McGill strike with a posse of over ninety men on October 18, 1912. Ishi began living at the University of California Museum of Anthropology on September 4, 1911.

At the time of his death, Peter Erramouspe had two young children, John and Albert. John Laxague also had two young sons, George and Pete, and another, John, who was born shortly after his father's murder. Bertrand Indiano and Harry Cambron were unmarried.

The four Shoshone children who survived the massacre at Rabbit Creek were taken to Fort Hall on November 17, 1911, and enrolled as members of the Mosho family. Hattie Mosho died of spinal meningitis the following spring. Henie

Louise Mosho died of tuberculosis on July 26, 1912, and Cleveland Mosho died of the same disease six months later. The baby, Josephine Mosho, declared tubercular and ordered from the reservation, was taken into the home of Superintendent Evan W. Estep where she recovered and grew up as Mary Josephine Estep.

I have conducted interviews with people in Nevada, Utah, Idaho, Washington, and California. Other information for this story comes from newspapers—the *Humboldt Star, Humboldt Silver State, Reno Evening Gazette,* and *Nevada State Journal;* unpublished letters and journals; municipal, county, and state documents; census records and superintendent reports from the Stewart Indian School in Carson City, Nevada; the Duck Valley Indian Reservation in Owyhee, Nevada; and the Fort Hall Agency in Fort Hall, Idaho; and federal reports and correspondence from the Office of the Attorney General and the Bureau of Indian Affairs. For help in obtaining information I am indebted to many courteous and efficient librarians, consultants, and curators who assisted me while I did research in the files of the Nevada State Archives and the Nevada State Museum in Carson City, the Nevada Historical Society and the University of Nevada Library in Reno, the North Central Nevada Historical Society, the Humboldt Museum, and the Humboldt County Library in Winnemucca, the Northeastern Nevada Historical Society in Elko, the State University of Idaho Library in Pocatello, the Twin Falls Public Library and the Twin Falls County Museum in Twin Falls, Idaho, the Modoc County Museum in Alturas, California, the regional branch of the National Archives and Federal Records Center in Seattle, Washington, and the Legislative and Natural Resources Branch of the National Archives in Washington, D.C.

For interviews or other special assistance, I am especially grateful to George Laxague, John Laxague, Janie Laxague, Ann Odgers, and Sid Harris of Cedarville, California; Mary Erramouspe Cook, Davy Groves, Charlie Nolan, and Frankie Cambron Stevens of Eagleville, California; Leona Cambron, Ernest Groves, and Irene Groves of Alturas, California; Lee Berk and Robert H. Amesbury of Susanville, California; Charlotte Crockett and Hattie Weighall Pound of Kimberly, Idaho; Birch Brown of Magic Valley, Idaho; Hud Brown of Twin Falls, Idaho; Brigham D. Madsen of Salt Lake City, Utah; Thomas C. Wilson of Reno, Nevada; Donald R. Tuohy of Carson City, Nevada; June Perry, Phillip Van Norman, and Nora Van Norman of Yerington, Nevada; Hazel Deputy of Fallon, Nevada; Father Harold F. Vieages of Lovelock, Nevada; Warren "Snowy" Monroe and Kenneth Scott of Elko, Nevada; Fred C. "Fritz" Buckingham of Paradise Valley, Nevada; Gene Christison, Jody Christison, Fred Barnes, and Dorothy Barnes of Golconda, Nevada; Blanche Foster, Pansilee Larson, Pete Pedroli, Lee Case, Earl Pitt, Grace Duvivier, Don Rose, and also Jack Murdock, Noreen Murdock, and Sheri Allen of Winnemucca, Nevada.

I am indebted to Kay West Guaglianone and Lorraine Pierce for permission to use the unpublished journal of their father and cousin, Mortimer David West, and to Grace Perry Kendrick for the use of the journal of her father, Frank Perry. To Jim Goodwin and Greta Lamb I am grateful for the use of family albums, photographs, and letters of Sheriff Selah Graham Lamb and Nellie Lamb.

For details of early reservation life and history I am indebted to the pioneering studies of Robert H. Lowie and Julian H. Steward, the Southwestern studies of Ruth M. Underhill and Angie Debo, and the Great Basin research of Brigham D. Madsen, Wick R. Miller, Robert F. Murphy, Yolanda Murphy, and Omer C. Stewart. I have relied on verbatim reports and autobiographical accounts by Hoavadunuki, Chona, Sam Newland, Geronimo, and many anonymous Native American storytellers. Without their narratives my rendition of the stories, dreams, and reflections of Shoshone Mike and Henie would not have been possible.

Shoshone Mike

To Sven Liljeblad, linguist, anthropologist, and model scholar, who has devoted over forty-five years of service and scholarship to the Shoshonean peoples of the Great Basin, I am grateful for the generous attention and care he has shown toward my research since the time of our meeting in 1980.

To the Shoshone-Bannock people of Fort Hall and especially Eli Mosho, Duane Thompson, Daniel Warjack, and Bel Boyer, I am deeply thankful for support and cooperation.

For other advice and encouragement, I wish to thank friends and relatives who heard and read this story during various stages of composition, with special thanks to Bill Heath, Zeese Papanikolas, and Jack Vernon, who read and wrote commentary on more than one draft of the manuscript.

My deepest debt is to Holly St. John Bergon, who began as sole reader of the manuscript's first draft and ended as final reader of the last revisions.

I also deeply appreciate the kindness and assistance of Ottie Daniel Van Norman and Mary Josephine Estep, last survivors of the massacre at Rabbit Creek, who are here joined through their stories as they were not on February 26, 1911.